THE COLORS OF ALL THE CATTLE

THE COLORS OF ALL
THE CATTLE

Alexander McCall Smith

Alfred A. Knopf Canada

PUBLISHED BY ALFRED A. KNOPF CANADA

Copyright © 2018 Alexander McCall Smith

www.penguinrandomhouse.ca

Knopf Canada and colophon are registered trademarks.

Library and Archives Canada Cataloguing in Publication

McCall Smith, Alexander, 1948–, author
The colors of all the cattle / Alexander McCall Smith.

(No. 1 Ladies' Detective Agency ; 19)

Issued in print and electronic formats.
ISBN 978-0-7352-7634-5
eBook ISBN 978-0-7352-7635-2

I. Title. II. Series: McCall Smith, Alexander, 1948– . No. 1 Ladies'
Detective Agency series ; 19.

PR6063.C326C62 2018   823'.914   C2018-901809-7
                                               C2018-901810-0

Jacket illustration by Iain McIntosh
Printed and bound in the United States of America

2 4 6 8 9 7 5 3 1

Penguin
Random House
KNOPF CANADA

This book is for Karen Myhill-Jones.

THE COLORS OF ALL THE CATTLE

CHAPTER ONE

PICKED UP BY THE WIND
AND BLOWN AWAY

Mr. J.L.B. MATEKONI, owner of Tlokweng Road Speedy Motors, and one of the finest mechanics in Botswana, if not the finest, was proud of his wife, Precious Ramotswe, progenitor and owner of the No. 1 Ladies' Detective Agency. Many men are proud of their wives in one way or another, although not all of them are as vocal in their pride as their wives might like them to be. This is a failing of men, and must be added to the list of men's failings, although all of us have failings and weaknesses—men and women alike—and it is not always helpful to point them out.

But of Mr. J.L.B. Matekoni's pride in Mma Ramotswe there could be little doubt. Sometimes, for instance, he would just gaze at her in silence and think, *There is no other lady quite like Mma Ramotswe in all Botswana.* That thought alone filled him with pride, just as much as it was a comfort to him. To think that of all the women in the country she should have come into his life—that was a humbling realisation, and reminded him of just how great a role chance plays in our human existence. It could so easily have been otherwise: she might have decided not to go out on that fateful day on which they had met. She might have gone elsewhere, encountered somebody else altogether, and married that somebody else. And yet she had not. They had met, and after a great deal of anxious hesitation he had eventually plucked up enough courage to ask her to be his wife. And she—oh, heaven-sent good fortune—had agreed.

As to his pride, there were so many reasons for this. Mma Ramotswe was a fine-looking woman, a woman of traditional build, a woman of sound and sensible views, a woman who embodied all that was praiseworthy in the national character. Yet she was also human. She was reluctant to condemn other people for not being quite as good as they might be. She was not one to expect unattainable standards. She understood that many of us would like to be better in our personal lives but somehow could not seem to achieve it. She recognised that sometimes the best we could do was simply to muddle through, getting some things right but also getting many things wrong. She knew all that, and was never too quick to blame or offer reproach.

She was kind; she was forgiving. She did not think that people should be punished too severely for their actions, as long as they acknowledged that what they had done was wrong. *If you punish somebody harshly,* she said, *then you are simply inflicting more pain on the world. You are also punishing not only that person, but his family and the people who love him. You are punishing yourself, really, because we are all brothers and sisters in this world, whether we know it or not; we are all citizens of the same village.*

He liked her ability to exercise forgiveness, but there were other qualities that explained the pride he felt in her. One of these was the fact that she was a good cook—not necessarily one of the very best cooks in the country, but certainly somewhere in the top ten per cent. Being a good cook, he thought, was not something that could necessarily be taught. You could watch other cooks, you could study recipes and experiment with new ways of doing things, but that did not necessarily mean that you would become a good cook. Being a good cook was not dissimilar to being a good mechanic—you had to have a *feeling* for what you were doing, and that was something that you either had or did not. He thought of his two apprentices, Charlie and Fanwell. Fanwell had a feeling for engines—he sympathised with them; it was as if he knew what it felt like to be in need of an oil change or to be labouring under the disadvantage of ill-fitting piston rings. Charlie, for all his bluster and his bragging, never really had that. An engine could be telling him something as plainly and as unambiguously as it could, but he would fail to pick up the unmissable signs of distress. And then, when the inevitable mechanical failure occurred, rather than trying to understand what signs had been overlooked, he would *bully* the engine. There was no other word for it: he would bully it by removing bolts and nuts brutally; he would rip out a fuel hose, an engine's crucial aorta, rather than coaxing it gently off its nozzle; he was not even averse to applying a hammer blow here and there in the hope of shifting some mechanical log-jam within the engine block.

Fanwell was much more gentle. At a very early stage in his training he had grasped the need to listen to what a vehicle was saying. He understood that at heart engines wanted to oblige us; it was their destiny to fire properly and to run sweetly for as long as their owner wished. Engines knew that, and, if only you treated them correctly, they would do your bidding. But hit an engine, or subject it to any of the other cruelties that thoughtless owners could devise, and the engine would become as stubborn as a mule.

It was the same, Mr. J.L.B. Matekoni thought, with cooking. If you were gentle, if you blended ingredients together gently, folding them in with all the delicate care of a mother tucking a child into bed, then they would co-operate. If you took the trouble to understand what temperature cooking oil liked, then it would seal the beef perfectly or soften the onions to just the right consistency. If you tasted a soup regularly, adding salt and pepper pinch by pinch rather than all at once, then the result would be perfectly seasoned rather than too salty or too hot. This was an art, he was convinced, and it was one to which Mma Ramotswe seemed to have been born.

Of course, instruction was required. Children might be endowed at birth with the instincts of a good cook, but this inherent talent still had to be nurtured through tuition. Usually it was the mother who did this teaching, and usually it was the daughter who learned, but these days, much to Mma Ramotswe's delight, boys were at long last being encouraged to cook. Puso, their foster son, had already learned at school how to make a number of dishes, and even if his efforts so far had not proved universally edible, at least some were. He was proud of his ability and beamed with pleasure when Mma Ramotswe told him how much she appreciated his custard with jam or his only slightly burned sausages served with soggy fried potatoes. Of course, there were certain traditionally minded people, some of them curmudgeons by instinct, who thought it wrong that boys should be taught to cook, but these people were out of touch with the modern world and their opinions no longer needed to be given much weight. And this came rather close to home—at first, Mr. J.L.B. Matekoni himself had been doubtful as to the appropriateness of teaching boys to cook, but he had soon been set right on that by Mma Ramotswe.

"Do men eat?" she asked him one day.

He looked up, surprised. "Of course men eat, Mma. Everybody must eat."

She nodded. "I agree with you, Rra. Men like to eat—some men like it a lot."

"In particular," said Mr. J.L.B. Matekoni, "they like to eat meat. Men are very keen on eating meat."

"That is true, Rra. Men seem to need meat. And if you need to eat, then I would have thought you need to be able to cook—even if you are a man."

They exchanged glances. He was not sure where this conversation was going, but he detected in it an element of gentle reproach.

"Mind you," he ventured, "there are some men who do not eat meat. They're called vegetables."

Mma Ramotswe laughed. "Vegetarians, Rra."

He looked puzzled. "Yes, vegetarians. That's what they're called."

"You said they were vegetables."

"Did I? Then I was wrong, Mma. I meant to say vegetar . . ." He stumbled on the word.

"Vegetarians."

"Yes, that. There is a vegetarian here in Gaborone who drives an old Land Rover. He lives out near the Sanitas Garden. They say that he has never eaten meat in his life—even when he was a boy."

Mma Ramotswe smiled. "I think that man is a Hindu. They are like that as a matter of belief. They think that cows are sacred."

Mr. J.L.B. Matekoni could go some way towards sympathising with that—cows were special, there was no doubt about that—but he was not sure whether he would go so far as to consider them sacred.

"He is a very gentle person, that man," he went on. "But his Land Rover is very old and I think it's losing heart. You can always tell when a vehicle loses heart."

"He should get a new one."

Mr. J.L.B. Matekoni smiled. "I told him that. I said that there were some very smart new Land Rovers. But he just shook his head and said that his Land Rover was an old friend and he would not desert it. That is an attitude that I can understand, Mma."

Mma Ramotswe knew what he meant. She felt that same thing about her tiny white van. She had resisted his attempts to change it for a more modern version—well-intentioned attempts, yes, but nonetheless misplaced.

"This man with the Land Rover," Mr. J.L.B. Matekoni continued, "he is very weak, I think. Not weak in his mind, but in his body, Mma. He looks as if the wind could blow him over if it ever tried. You know that look? There are some people who seem to be at real risk from the wind."

"He is getting on a bit," said Mma Ramotswe. "He is almost as old as his Land Rover—maybe even older."

"It's not age," said Mr. J.L.B. Matekoni. "I think it might be lack of meat, Mma. If he ate some good Botswana beef, then he would be stronger. If you eat Botswana beef, then you will never be blown away by the wind."

For a moment they were both silent. Mma Ramotswe was remembering something. A long time ago she had been told a story—it was one of those stories you heard as a child—this one about two children who had been picked up by the wind and blown out into the Kalahari. They had wandered about in that dry land for days and had just been about to succumb to thirst when they had been met by a band of San people. These hunters had taken them in and shown them where their water was hidden. They had empty ostrich shells buried under the sand and these were filled with precious water. They had saved the lives of those two children and had kept them with them for years, looking after them because they had no idea where the wind had picked them up and where they might return them to. Eventually the children had grown and, because they were not San people, who are short, they had towered over their rescuers. What had happened then? She could not remember. She thought that it had been decided to send them back to their Batswana roots because you cannot take tall people on the hunt—the animals will see you and will run away. Some day she would have to find out what happened.

She looked at Mr. J.L.B. Matekoni. This view—that men *had* to eat meat—was an old-fashioned one, but she doubted whether she would ever be able to get her husband to see that. Some beliefs were very deeply ingrained, and, although you could expect men to make some adaptations, they were not always capable of making themselves entirely modern. Another thing was certain too: she would never succeed in converting him to vegetarianism, even had she wished to do so. That would take centuries, and none of us had centuries; which was fortunate, in a way, at least for men, because most men, if they lived for centuries, would be centuries out of date at the end of their time, and that would be insupportable, she thought, for their wives, and possibly for others too. If Mr. J.L.B. Matekoni had, as he undoubtedly did have, this high opinion of Mma Ramotswe, and if, as was certainly the case, he thought that there was no respect in which she could possibly be improved, she did not share this view of herself. She did not contemplate herself very much, of course, and would probably not have given more than a passing thought to how she was doing in life, had her old friend and colleague at the No. 1 Ladies' Detective Agency, Grace Makutsi, not happened to raise the matter one morning during their second tea break.

"I have been reading something, Mma," said Mma Makutsi, as she took a sip of tea. "It's an article in this magazine."

From her chair on the other side of the room, Mma Ramotswe glanced at the magazine lying on Mma Makutsi's desk. It was, as she had thought, the same magazine from which Mma Makutsi regularly extracted various ideas and theories. Some of these were interesting enough, and some, she imagined, were also quite true; others, though, were more dubious, their function being, Mma Ramotswe suspected, purely that of filling up the space between the magazine's glossy advertisements.

Mma Ramotswe raised her cup of red bush tea to her lips. "And what did it say, Mma?" she asked.

Mma Makutsi reached for the magazine. Flipping through the

pages, she came to the article, and began to read it out loud. *"Does your life have any point?"* she began.

Mma Ramotswe looked surprised. "Why do you ask me that, Mma? That is a very strange question to ask somebody you have known for many years."

Mma Makutsi smiled at the misunderstanding. "No, Mma! That is not me speaking—that is what the article says. That is the title." She jabbed with a forefinger at the open page. "You see? That is a general question to the readers. It is not me saying to you—not personally—does your life have any point. I would not say that to you, Mma—not in any circumstances."

Mma Ramotswe laughed. "That is a big relief, Mma," she said. "It would be very alarming for us if our friends suddenly asked us a question like that. Just imagine—you would be going along quite nicely and then a friend would ask you whether your life had any point, and you would become highly confused as a result. It would be very unsettling, Mma."

Mma Makutsi reassured her that this was precisely why she would never ask Mma Ramotswe if her life had any point. But then she went on to say that, even if the article's title was a bit abrupt, what it said was worthwhile and thought-provoking. "You see, Mma," she continued, "the person who wrote this article says right at the beginning that she was somebody whose life did not have much point, but then she changed and now she feels her life has a point after all. That is what she says."

"And is she happier now?" asked Mma Ramotswe. "Because that's the most important thing, isn't it, Mma—to be happy?"

"She is much happier, Mma," replied Mma Makutsi. "Look, this is a photograph of her, and you will see that she is smiling. She has a very big smile now." She held up the magazine so that Mma Ramotswe could see the picture of the author of "Does your life have any point?"

"She is certainly smiling," said Mma Ramotswe. "Although we need to be careful about smiles, Mma. There are some people who smile on the outside when they are not smiling on the inside."

Mma Makutsi was well aware of that particular issue. "Oh, I know about people like that, Mma," she said. "But you can always tell—or, at least, I can always tell. I'm not sure if ordinary people can tell, though . . ." The reference to *ordinary people* was one that cropped up occasionally in Mma Makutsi's conversation. Ordinary people, clearly a large category of persons, were either those who had not attended the Botswana Secretarial College—Mma Makutsi's alma mater—or those who had no experience of being a private detective. Both of these backgrounds seemed to endow one with qualities of understanding and percipience well beyond that enjoyed by even the most worldly-wise members of the general population.

"But that is not the point," Mma Makutsi continued. "It is very clear to me that this lady's smile is both an inside and an outside smile. That is because she is definitely happy inside, and she is happy inside because she has examined her life and has now found a point to it."

Mma Ramotswe drained her teacup. "That is very good," she said. "And what was that point, may I ask?"

Mma Makutsi looked down at the magazine. "The point she found was to help other people find out if their lives had a point. That is her point, you see."

It took Mma Ramotswe a few moments to work this out. "Am I right in thinking, Mma," she asked, "that once she started to help other people to find a point in their lives, then she thought: This is my own point—to help people find a point? Is that what happened, Mma?"

"Exactly," said Mma Makutsi.

Mma Ramotswe was silent for a moment. This, she thought, was definitely one of those "filler articles." But she was still intrigued by the question. Did her own life have a point and, if it did, what would that be? "So what else does it say, Mma?"

Mma Makutsi looked at the magazine once again. "It says that many people do not have a point. She says that most people, in fact, are pointless."

"And?" prompted Mma Ramotswe.

"She says that you can be pointless for many years—just living your life without ever really doing anything—and then one day some-body asks you what your point is, and the truth comes to you that your life has no point."

"That must be a very sad moment," said Mma Ramotswe.

"Very sad," agreed Mma Makutsi. "But it is not the end of the world, because, when you realise that you have no point, then you will want to find one. And, once that happens, then you will feel much more . . ." She looked down at the article. "You will feel much more fulfilled, Mma."

"I am sure it will be better," said Mma Ramotswe. "It is better to be fulfilled than to be unfulfilled, I think."

Mma Makutsi nodded enthusiastically. "Oh, yes, that is certainly true. But there is more to this article than that, Mma. It is three pages long, and there is a questionnaire at the end. It asks you questions, and they help you find out if your life has a point."

Mma Ramotswe was not surprised by the addition of a question-naire. It seemed to her that many of the articles that Mma Makutsi read in that magazine of hers involved a questionnaire of some sort. And now Mma Makutsi read out one of these questions and waited expectantly while Mma Ramotswe considered her answers.

"Think of the last six months," Mma Makutsi began. "Then make a list of the things you have achieved. What can you put on this list? Ten things? Five things? One thing? Or nothing?" She paused, watching as Mma Ramotswe refreshed her cup of red bush tea. "That's the ques-tion, Mma. What have you achieved in the last six months?"

Mma Ramotswe looked thoughtful. Then her expression of thoughtfulness turned, almost imperceptibly, to one of regret. Now that she thought about it, she had achieved nothing very much in the last six months. She had done her job, of course, and she had helped various people with the problems in their lives—but that was just her job, nothing more. At home, she had cleaned out the kitchen cupboards, but that was hardly an achievement—anybody could clean out their kitchen cupboards—and indeed many people cleaned out their cupboards on a much more regular basis than she did. They were *achievers,* perhaps, and could answer the question with much greater credit. She had, of course, spent a lot of time with the children—with Puso and Motholeli—and had helped them with their various projects. She had helped Motholeli to make a quilt, and that had been sold at a school fund-raising event for a respectable sum. That was an achievement. And then she had guided Puso through the transfer of his collection of stamps to a new stamp album—that was an achievement too. But she had her doubts as to whether Mma Makutsi's magazine would think much of that sort of thing. And this meant, she concluded, that she would almost certainly fail the test behind the questionnaire. Her life, it seemed, was pointless—at least in the eyes of Mma Makutsi's magazine, and possibly the eyes of the world at large. *Mma Ramotswe, Private Detective . . . and Pointless Person.* It was a bitter pill to swallow.

But then she laughed. "Such nonsense, Mma," she exclaimed. "That magazine of yours is full of nonsense."

Mma Makutsi looked wounded. "You should not say such things, Mma. Just because the truth hurts, you should not say such things."

Mma Ramotswe was quick to apologise. Mma Makutsi was sensitive, and she did not want to upset her over such a minor matter as this. To put Mma Makutsi into one of her moods over something as unimportant as a magazine article . . . that was something that would certainly qualify as a pointless act. "I'm very sorry, Mma," she said. "I did not mean to say that. I spoke as I did because I felt that the article was touching on some very important truths."

Mma Makutsi was suitably pacified. "Well, there you are, Mma," she said. "Sometimes all that it takes to make us re-evaluate our lives is a simple question—a very simple question, Mma."

It was time for the tea break to end. The cups were washed, and the teapots—Mma Makutsi's ordinary teapot and the special one that Mma Ramotswe kept for her red bush tea—were both put away in the cupboard. Work resumed, but a seed had been planted, and the subject would crop up again a few days later when Mma Ramotswe travelled along that bumpy and dusty road to the Orphan Farm presided over by her friend and confidante, the redoubtable Mma Sylvia Potokwane, stout defender of children, and a woman whose life most clearly and unambiguously had a clear point to it.

CHAPTER TWO

A SILENT BOY, AND TEA

TWO TINY EGGS, pale brown but speckled with pink; impossibly fragile, they seemed, for a landscape such as this, with its hard out-crops of rock and its baked red soil; a single touch, a puff of wind, might be enough to break them. And a third egg had already broken in the pocket of the boy's khaki shirt, making a wet patch that soaked through the fabric, a stain of guilt.

The boy—no more than six, thought Mma Ramotswe—was stand-ing in front of Mma Potokwane, not far from the acacia tree under which Mma Ramotswe invariably parked her car when she came to visit her friend. Nobody spoke at first, and the sound of the cooling of the van's engine, that *click click* of heated machinery returning to normal, was all they heard. Then Mma Potokwane, turning to greet her visitor, said, "You see these eggs, Mma? You see these eggs taken from some poor bird? A guinea fowl, I think."

She held the two eggs in her outstretched palm. Mma Ramotswe looked at them, then at the boy, who did not meet her eye. It was obvious to her what had happened; the child had stolen the eggs from a nest and had been found out.

Mma Potokwane was rarely severe with the children, but she was clearly struggling not to show too much displeasure. "This is Mpilo," she explained, and then, to the boy himself, "Mpilo, this auntie is Mma Ramotswe. You must greet her."

The boy's eyes remained fixed on the ground in front of him. She saw his fists clenched tight; she saw that at the back of his neck there were two small scars. How did he get those? Boys were always falling over and bruising their knees—it was nothing unusual for a boy's knees to be covered with cuts—but at the back of his neck?

He said nothing. Embarrassed, Mma Ramotswe smiled and issued the first greeting herself. This brought no reaction.

"One day he will learn," muttered Mma Potokwane apologetically. "One day."

The boy glanced up, a quick, furtive glance before he resumed his staring at the ground.

"Mpilo has taken eggs from a bird's nest," said Mma Potokwane. "And we must put them back now." She paused. "Because these do not belong to us, do they, Mpilo?"

She looked at Mma Ramotswe, as if for confirmation of the decision.

"The bird will need them," said Mma Ramotswe gently. "They will become the bird's children, you see."

The boy looked up again. There was a flicker of something, thought Mma Ramotswe, but she was not sure if it was understanding.

"So now you must show us where you found them," pressed Mma Potokwane. Her tone had softened, the note of disapproval replaced by gentle cajoling. "You understand, Mpilo? You know what I'm saying to you?"

There was an almost imperceptible nod from the boy, but it was enough.

"Right," said Mma Potokwane. "Mma Ramotswe will help us. You show us where these came from and we will all put them back."

He pointed, and they followed, walking behind him on one of

those almost invisible tracks that wound their way through the scrub bush behind Mma Potokwane's office. These tracks are everywhere in the African bush, used by animals for the most part, known only to the creatures that had reason to go that way, petering out inexplicably, joining other tracks, forming a network of secret passages. The boy wore no shoes, but, like all children who lived on the edge of the bush, his feet would be hardened to the rough texture of the ground. Now he made his way effortlessly past the stunted vegetation of the late summer, avoiding the restraining grasp of the thorn bushes that would delay the unwary, walking almost too fast for the two traditionally built women behind him.

Somewhere ahead of them they could hear cattle bells, and could smell, too, the sweet dung of the herd. This smell of cattle, so redolent of the Botswana countryside, always made Mma Ramotswe think of her father, the late Obed Ramotswe, who in the last years of his life had lived for his cattle—*my other children,* he had called them; *not as important to me as you are, Precious, but still my children.* He had been understanding when as a young girl she had been badly behaved; he had always been patient, had never raised a hand to her. But children had to learn, and this boy had to be taught not to steal the eggs of birds. If children did not learn this lesson, then there would be no birds, and the air would be silent. Mma Potokwane had to teach him.

They did not have far to go. Suddenly the boy stopped in his tracks and pointed to a spot off to his right—a small cluster of rocks between which tufts of grass protruded. Grazing cattle, perhaps deterred by the rocks, had left the spot alone, and the grass had grown high, bent here and there by the wind or the movement of birds.

"So that is the nest," said Mma Potokwane.

The boy nodded, but did not say anything.

"Put them back where you found them, Mpilo." She had been cradling the eggs gently in her hand and passed them back to him now. He took them, making a cup with both hands.

"On you go."

He picked his way between the rocks and then bent down. Standing up again, he pointed down at the ground to show that he had
complied.

"Now we can go back," said Mma Potokwane. "And you can have
a piece of cake from your housemother. I will tell her that you have
been a good boy. I will explain to her about your shirt."

The boy looked up sharply, and for a moment there was a flicker
of expression that had not been there before.

"HAS HE ALWAYS BEEN LIKE THAT?" asked Mma Ramotswe as she
watched her friend pour her a cup of red bush tea.

Mma Potokwane sighed. Her sighs were always deep ones—not
short sighs of the sort that most people sigh, but long-drawn-out sighs,
like the sound of air escaping from an inflated tyre. It was remarkable,
thought Mma Ramotswe, that anybody could have so much air in their
lungs, but the matron had a large chest, and there must be room for
it somewhere in there.

"More or less," said Mma Potokwane at the end of the sigh. "We
got a little bit out of him when he first turned up here. The social
work people from Selibi Pikwe passed him on to us. We get quite a
few children from up there, you know. The mine sends them. They're
good about it—they always give us some money to start things off."

Selibi Pikwe was a mining town halfway up the country's eastern border. Like all mining towns, it had a floating population; men
came and went for the work, and women followed them. Some of the
women came from over the border, earning their living in the way that
women trapped in poverty sometimes felt they had to do. In some
cases they looked out for their children as best they could, while in
others the young ones were passed on or simply abandoned.

"What did he tell you?" asked Mma Ramotswe.

"Not very much. We got his name from them—the social work people had got that wrong, but who can blame them? They're under pressure these days. Then he said he had a sister, but I think she's late. He cried when he told us that. He gave us a name and then started to cry. We didn't get much more out of him." She shrugged. "We often have to start afresh, you know, Mma. We're used to it. There are some children who are just struck dumb because of what has happened to them."

Mma Ramotswe asked if the boy spoke Setswana, and was told that he did. "At least I think he does," said Mma Potokwane. "He seems to understand well enough, but, as you've seen, he doesn't really speak any longer. We have a battle to stop the other children making fun of him; you know what children are like."

"The back of his neck . . ."

Mma Potokwane nodded. "Yes. Those scars. And he has some on his right leg. Very strange. The nurse did get something out of him when she asked him about that. He just said: lightning. That's all—lightning."

Mma Ramotswe raised an eyebrow. "He says he was struck by lightning?"

Mma Potokwane laughed. "So it would seem. And yet, you know, Mma, you can't really put too much store in what a six- or seven-year-old says. They're very inventive."

"Like some adults," Mma Ramotswe observed. It was not a sarcastic remark—Mma Ramotswe never showed sarcasm; it was more rueful than anything else. Her profession, after all, brought her into contact with people who were sometimes less than truthful, and she knew only too well how people could embellish reality, or make it up entirely.

Mma Potokwane agreed. "Indeed. There are some very inventive adults, Mma. When you listen to them, you have to divide everything they say by two, and then take away ten. As you have to do with some politicians."

"Politicians . . . ," mused Mma Ramotswe. "Yes, maybe you are right, Mma. But not all of them speak like that, of course. There are some very good politicians—honest ones." She thought of Botswana's good fortune in its early leaders—that great man Seretse Khama had been one such; and there had been others, men in his mould who had made Botswana the country that it was.

Mma Potokwane knew of Mma Ramotswe's opinions, but had a more jaundiced view. "Some are honest," she said quite forcefully. "You are a very kind person, Mma, but you must remember that there are many politicians who say, *We'll make everything much better. Vote for us and there'll be hundreds of new jobs . . .*"

"There may be jobs, of course . . ."

"One new job," interjected Mma Potokwane. "One new job for a politician."

"Ah," said Mma Ramotswe. She did not have strong views on politics. She did not like the confrontational nature of much political discussion; why could people not argue politely, she wondered, taking into account the views of others and accepting that people might differ with one another in perfectly good faith?

Mma Potokwane, having pronounced on politicians, wanted now to move to more interesting subjects.

"And how is Mma Makutsi doing?" she asked. "What is her news, Mma?"

Mma Potokwane and Mma Makutsi enjoyed an uneasy relationship. There had been a time when the two had clashed, their incompatible temperaments making it impossible for them to agree about very much. That had all changed, though, with the passage of time, and they were now on good enough terms, even if they remained slightly wary of one another.

"She is on good form," said Mma Ramotswe. "She is always talking about something new."

Mma Potokwane smiled. "She reads those magazines, doesn't she? She gets a lot of ideas from them."

"Yes," said Mma Ramotswe. "Only the other day she was telling me about an article about having a point to your life. There is some lady who thinks that most of us don't have much point to our lives."

Mma Potokwane looked thoughtful. "Maybe, Mma. Maybe that's right. There are many people who don't seem to know where they're going."

Mma Ramotswe studied her teacup. "I sometimes wonder if I'm such a person," she said.

Mma Potokwane was quick to dismiss this. "You, Mma? No, you are certainly not one of those people. You know exactly where you're going."

Mma Ramotswe demurred. "I'm not so sure, Mma." And then she added, "Where am I going, Mma? Do *you* know?"

It was a little while before Mma Potokwane answered, and then it was with a question of her own. "Do *I* know where you're going, Mma?"

"Yes. Where *am* I going, Mma?"

"You are going in exactly the same direction you've always been going," said Mma Potokwane. Her tone was firm—like that of one who knows not only where another is going, but also where she herself is going. But it seemed to her that Mma Ramotswe needed persuading, and so she continued, "What else do you need in life, Mma? You have a fine husband—which is one of the most important things that anybody can have."

She waited for Mma Ramotswe to acknowledge her good fortune in this respect. Mma Potokwane's admiration for Mr. J.L.B. Matekoni knew no bounds, stemming from the days when, unpaid and without complaint, he had kept the Orphan Farm's ancient, wheezing water pump going. That pump had been replaced and the focus of his effort had shifted to the equally demanding minibus that Mma Potokwane used to transport children. Only a mechanic of his patience and ability could have kept that vehicle on the road, and Mma Potokwane had understood that. Such a man, she had always thought, would make an ideal husband for some fortunate woman, and her pleasure had been profound when she had discovered that he and Mma Ramotswe were to get married.

"And then," Mma Potokwane continued, "you have a successful business. You have the two children. You have your Zebra Drive home. You have so much, Mma." She looked at her friend with a touch of reproach. "You have nothing further to achieve, Mma. Nothing."

Mma Ramotswe was very much aware of what she had, and of how grateful she should be. "I know that, Mma," she reassured her friend. "I know that I have much to be grateful for—and I am. I was not denying any of that."

"Well, then?" challenged Mma Potokwane. "What is this nonsense that Mma Makutsi has been putting in your head?"

"Nothing, Mma. Nothing. It's just that . . . well, I wondered whether I needed a bit of an extra challenge, that's all."

"Nonsense," said Mma Potokwane with renewed firmness. "Nonsense."

And that was where the conversation might have ended, were it not for a parting shot from Mma Potokwane on the subject of magazines.

"These magazines," she said, "are full of nothing, Mma. I see them, you know. Some of the housemothers buy them and I see them. They are full of things that don't matter, Mma. Full of such things. And they make the people who read them think, *My life is not much because I don't have the things in this magazine. I'm not as pretty as the ladies in this magazine. I don't make food that tastes as good as the pictures of food in this magazine.* All that is nonsense, Mma. Nonsense."

And then came the final advice. "You tell Mma Makutsi that, Mma Ramotswe. You tell her."

Mma Ramotswe smiled. "I shall think about it, Mma. If the subject comes up again, I shall think about it."

That satisfied Mma Potokwane, who cut them both a further slice of fruit cake and served a third and, she thought, final cup of tea. As they ate their cake and drank their tea, a possibility had occurred to Mma Potokwane that might be, she felt, just the thing for a friend who was looking for a project to give more point to her life—not that she needed that, of course.

"There's one other thing," she said, putting down her teacup. "One other thing I must tell you about before you go, Mma."

"Oh, yes, Mma?"

Mma Potokwane lowered her voice. This was not necessary, as they were alone in her office and there was nobody to hear, but it underlined the sensitivity of the news she was about to impart. "Have you heard about that new hotel?" she asked.

Mma Ramotswe nodded. "The one in the papers?"

"Yes, that one, Mma."

Mma Ramotswe frowned. "I'm surprised that they aren't listening to all those people—the ones who do not want it. There are many people opposed, aren't there, Mma?"

Mma Potokwane's voice rose with her indignation. "There certainly are, Mma. And I'm one of them." She paused. A fourth cup of tea was unusual, but there were circumstances in which it was justified, and these were such. As she poured the tea, she explained her opposition. "The Big Fun Hotel indeed, Mma! Right next to the cemetery, where all the late people are—including, might I say, my own late mother. The Big Fun Hotel!"

"It is very tactless," said Mma Ramotswe. "We all know what sort of hotel that will be."

"We do, Mma," agreed Mma Potokwane. "And yet they say that

the council is going to give permission for it to go ahead. Can you believe it?"

Mma Ramotswe wondered whether public opposition would change the council's mind about planning permission, but this, Mma Potokwane told her, was unlikely. She had a friend on the council—one of those members who was vigorously opposed to the scheme—who had told her that the deal was as good as done. A public outcry was all very well, this friend said, but there was a much more powerful force working in favour of the application, and that was money.

"It's always like that," said Mma Ramotswe. "We were talking about politicians earlier, Mma—this is the sort of thing that some of them do—the bad politicians, that is. They let people build disrespectful hotels next to cemeteries—that sort of thing."

"Exactly, Mma," said Mma Potokwane, leaning forward as she spoke. "But let me tell you something. There's going to be a vacancy on the council. One of the members is not well and is going to resign his seat." She looked intently at Mma Ramotswe. "And that means that there will be an election for that seat, and a new member."

"I suppose so," said Mma Ramotswe.

Mma Potokwane lowered her voice again—almost to a whisper. "And that also means, Mma, that some good person—some person who might just be a woman this time—could stand for that seat."

It took a few moments for Mma Ramotswe to respond. Then, eyes wide with surprise, she said, "You, Mma?"

Mma Potokwane smiled. "No, Mma. You."

CHAPTER THREE

I AM NOT THE RIGHT PERSON

THAT EVENING, Mma Ramotswe did not reveal to Mr. J.L.B. Matekoni what Mma Potokwane had suggested earlier that day. The main reason for her silence on the matter was the sheer unlikelihood of what Mma Potokwane had proposed. What she had said was simply impossible, and that meant that there was no real need for it to go any further. But there was more to her reluctance than that: in the back of her mind was her knowledge that Mr. J.L.B. Matekoni always took a great interest in what Mma Potokwane said, and this led to a concern that he might actually agree with the matron on this particular matter, and she would therefore find herself under pressure on two fronts. That was a good reason, she thought, not to reveal the details of the extraordinary, and somewhat unsettling, conversation that had taken place in Mma Potokwane's office.

And so, over dinner that night, when Mr. J.L.B. Matekoni asked her how her afternoon had gone, she simply reported that she and her friend had enjoyed a natter over tea and cake and that nothing very significant had been said. She told him, though, of the little boy and the guinea fowl eggs, and he smiled and confessed that as a boy at his grandfather's cattle post he had thought nothing of robbing birds' nests and eating the eggs raw with the other herd boys.

"It was different in those days," he said. "There seemed to be more than enough for everybody—for the birds, for the animals, for people. We didn't dream that the world would run out of such things."

Mma Ramotswe agreed. "Even land," she said. "There was more than enough land for everybody back in those days."

Mr. J.L.B. Matekoni thought it right that children should be taught to look after birds and wildlife. "We can't go back to those days," he said. "It's far too late." He shook his head sadly. "That little boy—lightning, you say?"

"That's what he told Mma Potokwane, but she wasn't at all sure. He hardly speaks."

"There was a man from Lobatse who was struck by lightning a few years ago," said Mr. J.L.B. Matekoni. "They found nothing apart from his shoes. That's what they say, Mma—I'm just reporting it." He paused. "He is late, of course."

"I'm not surprised," said Mma Ramotswe.

After dinner they retired early to bed, and Mma Ramotswe, who had not had a good night's sleep the previous evening, soon drifted off. As sleep claimed her, she found herself thinking of what Mma Potokwane had said. She had protested, of course, when her friend had suggested that she should stand for the vacant council seat; she had pointed out that she had no experience of politics, even at a local level, and, quite apart from that, she had no affiliation with any political party. Mma Potokwane had summarily dismissed both of these objections.

"Everybody has to start somewhere," she pointed out. "If people said they could not do anything because they had no experience, then how would anybody get started?" and to that argument was added a telling point: "When you started the No. 1 Ladies' Detective Agency,

Mma, I don't think you had had much experience as a private detective. In fact, you had had none, if my memory serves me correctly."

Mma Ramotswe could not deny that. She and Mma Makutsi had begun the business without the slightest idea as to what to do, and it was only after she had stumbled upon a copy of Clovis Andersen's seminal tract, *The Principles of Private Detection,* that she had begun to understand the rudiments of her new profession.

As for political affiliation, Mma Potokwane had similarly refuted Mma Ramotswe's objection in the most insouciant manner. "Nobody bothers about political parties these days, Mma. You can be an *independent candidate.* That is a very well-known way of fighting an election these days. Being independent is very fashionable—everybody likes to vote for an independent candidate."

It was difficult to argue with Mma Potokwane once she had espoused a cause, and Mma Ramotswe had barely tried. Eventually, as her old friend had seen her out to her van, she had conceded that she would think about the possibility of standing as a candidate. "I am not the right person for that sort of thing, Mma," she said. "But at least I shall think about what you have said today." Her words were carefully chosen. She would *think* about it, and thinking about doing something was very far from agreeing to do it. In fact, thinking about something was often a prelude to deciding that you could not possibly do it; and that, she felt, was the inevitable outcome here.

"That's very good," Mma Potokwane had said. "It is very important that you think about strategy, Mma. You need to think about things like what you will say to the newspapers. You need to think about how you will raise money for your campaign."

Mma Ramotswe had stopped her there. "Money, Mma? Do you have to pay some sort of deposit to stand for the council?"

Mma Ramotswe found this amusing. "Oh, no, Mma—nothing like that. But advertisements cost money, you know, and you will need advertisements. I'm sure, though, that there will be people who will want to help you with that. Your supporters will pay."

Mma Ramotswe was silent. "My supporters? Do I have any supporters?" She made a mental list of those who could possibly be called her supporters. There was Mma Makutsi, of course; she would be a supporter, and would almost certainly vote for her. Then there was Mr. J.L.B. Matekoni, whose support would be rock-solid, and who of course would also vote for her, although she now remembered that he had forgotten to vote in the last parliamentary election because he had been busy fixing the suspension on a troublesome car and had only emerged from underneath it just after the polling booths had closed. But he would certainly be vocal in his support, and would probably try to get various people in the motor trade to vote for her as well. Why would they do so, though? Would it be just because she was married to a prominent and much-respected mechanic, or would she have to say something complimentary about cars—and mechanics—in order to get their votes? That was one of the things that worried her about politics: you had to cultivate people, and in Mma Ramotswe's view, the cultivation of others could very quickly deteriorate into the worst sort of flattery.

Her train of thought almost led to her missing Mma Potokwane's reply. "You have many supporters, Mma Ramotswe. If they had a meeting, they would need a very big hall, you know. You have hundreds of supporters—you just don't know it yet, but they are there, Mma."

Mma Ramotswe did not know what to say, other than to bid her friend goodbye and make her way back from Tlokweng with a series of confused thoughts in her mind—thoughts of unknown supporters, thoughts of expensive advertisements, thoughts of journalists with awkward questions. No, she would not do this. Mma Potokwane was one of her oldest friends, and her dearest friend too, but there were limits to what you had to do for your friends. If they came up with strange ideas about what you should do, then you should listen to them—and she had listened to Mma Potokwane—but they should not presume on your friendship as far as making you do things that you had no desire to do. Friends did not have that right, whatever other claims they could make on you.

Those thoughts, present in her mind as she drifted off to sleep that night, were still there the next morning when she got the children ready for school and in due course drove into work at the No. 1 Ladies' Detective Agency. Now, however, she was adamant that she would telephone Mma Potokwane that morning—if not first thing, then certainly before the mid-morning tea break—and tell her that she had deliberated long and hard over her suggestion but she would definitely not be standing for election to the council. She would say all that before Mma Potokwane had the chance to do much more than pick up the phone: it would be what Clovis Andersen in his *Principles of Private Detection* called a *pre-emptive call. Don't let the other side start raising objections,* he wrote. *Say your piece immediately. In this way it is you, rather than the other person, who sets the agenda.*

She was the first at work, with Mma Makutsi arriving ten minutes later.

"I have booked somebody in," said Mma Makutsi as she came into the office. "Somebody phoned yesterday when you were at Mma Potokwane's place. It was a man, Mma, and he wanted an appointment with somebody he called 'that detective lady.' I corrected him on that, Mma. I pointed out that there were two detective ladies."

It was the sort of small triumph that Mma Makutsi enjoyed. There were far too many people, she felt, who failed to understand just how things were in this world. There were people who were ignorant, it seemed, of the most elementary facts—people who barely knew that

Gaborone was the capital of Botswana or who claimed never to have heard of the Botswana Secretarial College . . .

"Who is this man?" asked Mma Ramotswe. "What is his name, Mma?"

Mma Makutsi consulted the diary that lay open on her desk. "He is a Mr. Marang, Mma. That is the name he gave. Marang." She looked again at the page. "He did not say what it was about."

Mma Ramotswe looked up at the ceiling. Marang? The name was a reasonably common one in Botswana, but there was something about it that was chiming with her somewhere deep inside. There had been a Marang somewhere in her life, but she could not work out where, or when. It was a vague memory—one of those memories that never quite come to the fore, but that are somewhere deep in our mind, like the memories of early childhood. Early childhood? Marang? Marang?

She closed her eyes and allowed her mind to wander, hoping that it would come up with an image, a recollection, a face. And what she saw was Mochudi, the place where she had been born, with its dominating hill on which the old school building perched, looking down over the village itself and its surrounding countryside. From below, drifting up on the wind, came the sound of cattle bells, that sound of the landscape of her childhood, that landscape that was always lovelier than any other because it belonged to you, as of right, your real home in the world, your place. And in her mind's eye she saw from that hill, far below, the roof of the hospital, which in those days was of red-painted and corrugated iron. And then she knew.

YET MMA RAMOTSWE barely recognised him when he came into the office later that morning, leaning for support on a woman of about her own age. He moved slowly, with a curious gait, taking each step gingerly, as if feeling for a floor that was moving unpredictably beneath him. He was wearing dark glasses, which would have made recognition difficult, even without the damage that had clearly been done to the face. Something had rendered this lopsided, the mouth pulled down sharply on one side and twisted on the other into a set grimace. The imbalance was reflected in the jaw, which sagged badly and was covered in scar tissue.

The woman looked about her anxiously, first at Mma Ramotswe and then at Mma Makutsi. "This is the right place, is it, Mma?" she said to Mma Ramotswe. "This is the No. 1 Ladies' Detective Agency?"

It was the man who answered. "Yes, this is the place, Constance, because I can see who this lady is. This is Precious Ramotswe, I think."

Mma Ramotswe had had the time to recover from her shock. Rising from her chair, she crossed the room to stand before the visitors. She reached out and took his hand, at the same time dropping a knee in an old-fashioned curtsy. That was ancient habit—something she had not done for many years, not since childhood, perhaps, when it had been the way to greet a much-respected elder. Now it came back, instinctively, naturally—an echo of a Botswana that had not quite disappeared in a world of modern informality.

They voiced the traditional greeting, and then, when he took off the dark glasses, the man smiled. The smile came through the distorted face, a light from somewhere within.

"Dr. Marang," she said. "It is so many years—so many, Rra."

His voice was thickened, but the articulation was clear enough.

"You were just a girl, I think. Not very old at all."

She nodded. "That's right, Rra."

He turned to the woman beside him. "You won't remember my daughter, Constance. She lived with her grandmother much of the time and so wasn't in Mochudi a great deal."

Mma Ramotswe shook hands with Constance. She had no recollection of meeting her.

Behind her, Mma Makutsi cleared her throat politely. There was a further introduction, after which Dr. Marang said, "You are the secretary, Mma?"

It was politely meant, and Mma Makutsi understood that. She also understood that these were not circumstances in which a sharp correction would be justified. She tried to smile, as if what had been said was a matter of little importance. "Actually, I am joint managing director," she said. "There are two of us."

Mma Ramotswe drew in her breath. *Joint managing director* was a new title—a step further than the directorship that Mma Makutsi had claimed last time her status had needed to be explained to anybody. But if Mma Makutsi sensed the importance of this moment and the courtesy that should be shown to their visitors, so too did Mma Ramotswe; any discussion of roles in the agency was private business, not to be aired in front of others, and particularly not in front of this distinguished and much-loved doctor.

Mma Ramotswe invited Dr. Marang and Constance to sit down. The client's chair was already in place; Mma Makutsi quickly fetched for Constance the spare chair that was kept behind the filing cabinet. Tea was offered, and accepted, and then, with Dr. Marang settled, Mma Ramotswe began the interview.

"It is very good to see you, Rra," she said, adding quickly, "and you too, Mma. I did not know at first that it would be you."

Dr. Marang nodded sagely. "And I did not think—even just a few months ago—that I would be sitting in the offices of a private detective. We cannot tell what is going to happen in our lives, can we?"

"We cannot, Rra," agreed Mma Ramotswe.

Dr. Marang looked thoughtful. "Nor, I think, would your late father have imagined that his daughter would end up in a No. 1 Ladies' Detective Agency."

Mma Ramotswe laughed. "He certainly would not, Rra. He always thought I should run a hardware store if I went into business. Hardware stores are very sensible."

Dr. Marang seemed to appreciate the humour of the situation. "I'm sure he would have been happy. He was always very proud of you, you know."

Mma Ramotswe swallowed. It was hard, sometimes, when people spoke of her father; they always said good things—nobody to her knowledge had ever spoken ill of Obed Ramotswe—but it was still hard, even after all these years.

It was as if Dr. Marang had read her mind. "You must still miss him," he said. "Even now."

"Yes," she said. "I do." She could have said so much more. She could have said what she said to those who had lost somebody: *Late people are still with us.* And they were. They were with us in the things that they had said, which we remembered long after they had gone; they were with us in the love that they had shown us, and which we could still draw about us, like a comforting blanket on a cold night; and, if the late people had had children, they were with us in the look in the eye of those children, in the way they held their heads, in the way they laughed, or in the way they walked, or did any of the other things that were passed on, deep inside, within families.

She did not say any of this, although she was thinking it. She answered, instead, what he had said about pride. "I am the one who was proud," she said quietly. "I am the one, Rra."

"I can see that, Mma," said Dr. Marang. "But let me tell you what I have come to see you about. You are a busy lady, I think, and we should not take up too much of your time. Let me start."

The kettle that Mma Makutsi had switched on was now boiling, and she busied herself making tea. Dr. Marang had difficulty holding his, and was helped by his daughter, who dabbed carefully at his mouth with a handkerchief after he had taken a sip.

"I'm afraid I'm rather slow," said Dr. Marang between sips. "Perhaps Constance can tell you what you need to know." He turned to his daughter. "You tell the ladies, Constance."

Constance spoke softly, in a strangely high-pitched voice, rather like the voice one would expect a bird to have.

"My father has been retired for some years," she began.

"Fourteen years," supplied Dr. Marang.

Constance resumed, "Yes, fourteen years. He left Mochudi years before that—he went to Lobatse, to the hospital down there. You probably know that, Mma Ramotswe."

"I knew you had gone away," Mma Ramotswe said. "You left before my father became late, I think. But I wasn't sure where you had gone."

"It was Lobatse," said Dr. Marang, "as Constance just said. But, when I finished working there, I came back to Mochudi. I had a small plot of land where we grew vegetables. We kept goats—some very good ones. And I ran a small clinic—just two days a week—for minor conditions. It was a retirement job, really—nothing more than that. But it kept my hand in."

"My father is not a lazy man," said Constance. "He does not like to be doing nothing."

"If you do nothing, you die," said Dr. Marang.

Mma Makutsi had been silent until then, but now she had an observation to make. "Doing nothing is a big mistake," she pronounced. "Do nothing and you'll find yourself doing nothing in the graveyard."

Constance looked slightly confused. Dr. Marang, though, turned in his seat and nodded his agreement. "You are absolutely right, Mma. That is what I always said to people who were thinking of retiring. I said: Don't do nothing. Keep yourself busy." He paused, and then urged Constance to continue.

"So my father was living just outside Mochudi and then one day . . ." Constance looked down at her hands, her voice faltering.

"Then one day he was crossing the road that passes our house and a car appeared from nowhere and knocked him over."

Mma Ramotswe winced. "Oh, Mma . . ."

"It was going too fast and it didn't stop," Constance continued. "It was what the police called a *hit-and-run*. My father had two badly broken legs and a fractured hip. And there was damage to his face, to his head. You can see that, Mma Ramotswe."

Dr. Marang intervened. "I already had a condition," he said. "I had something called Bell's palsy, Mma. It made my face slip rather badly. But then this accident involved further injuries, and the result is as you see. I would not get a job in the films as a result . . ."

"Oh, Rra . . ."

He laughed. "That doesn't matter at my stage in life. But the other injuries were very debilitating. It was a long time before I was able to walk again."

"And he still cannot walk far by himself," chipped in Constance. "He needs me—or somebody else—to help him."

"I am very sorry to hear all this," said Mma Ramotswe. "Did they catch the driver?"

"That is why we are here," said Constance. "The police could not find out who was driving the car. They made some enquiries, but they have more serious things to deal with and so they have moved on. They are not doing anything more."

Dr. Marang said that he did not blame the police. "They have too much on their plate," he said. "They cannot devote too much time to finding out who was driving that car."

"They should," said Constance indignantly.

Dr. Marang laid a hand on her arm. "Hush, Constance. We cannot blame them. It is not their fault. If the government took on more policemen, there would be the resources for this sort of thing, but even the government can't do everything it needs to do."

"We want you to find out who that person was," said Constance, her voice raised. "We want a private investigation."

Her demand made, Constance sat back in her chair. As she did so, she fixed Mma Ramotswe with a challenging stare. Her father, though, was more cautious. "That is," he said, "if this is the sort of thing you do. I don't know."

"They are private detectives, Daddy," snapped Constance. "This is what they do."

From behind them came Mma Makutsi's voice. "Yes, we do that sort of thing. We help people with all their problems, you see—no matter what the problem is."

Mma Ramotswe inclined her head in Mma Makutsi's direction. "What Mma Makutsi says is right. We do not turn people away . . . although this sounds like a very difficult matter, I think . . ."

"Not difficult," said Mma Makutsi. "We can make enquiries."

Mma Ramotswe was concerned about raising expectations. In different circumstances she would have reminded Mma Makutsi of what Clovis Andersen had to say on that. *Do not promise the client anything that you cannot deliver,* he wrote. *A disappointed client will not thank you for promising a result you cannot achieve. Be realistic.*

"As Mma Makutsi points out," said Mma Ramotswe evenly, "we can make enquiries. But I must stress that there are many cases when, however much we enquire, we cannot get to the bottom of things."

"Not many cases," retorted Mma Makutsi.

Mma Ramotswe shot her a glance. "But some, Mma. Some."

Constance had something more to say. "We need to be able to claim against the insurance of that driver," she said. "We have had to pay for a nurse. That costs money."

Mma Ramotswe said that she understood that.

"We can, of course, pay your fees," said Dr. Marang. "I am not a poor man. I have a good pension."

Mma Ramotswe shook her head. There was an immediate decision to make, and it was clear to her what that should be. "There will be no fees in this case, Rra. That is what my father would have wanted—and it is what I want too."

Dr. Marang was insistent. "No, I must pay."

"No, Rra. There will be no fee." She paused. "But, as I said, it may be that we can find out very little. Did you see the driver?"

Dr. Marang shook his head. "No, all I saw was his car. And all I remember about it was that it was blue. That is the only information I have."

"Not even the model?" asked Mma Ramotswe.

This was met with a shrug. "How can anyone tell modern cars apart these days, Mma? They are all the same. It was just a blue car."

Behind them, Mma Makutsi scribbled a note on a pad of paper.

"We shall do our best," said Mma Ramotswe. It was true—they would do what they could, but there was something in her tone of voice that was doubtful. This was not the sort of enquiry they were used to, and she had no idea how they might proceed. How many blue cars were there in the country? Not as many as there were white—by far the favourite car colour in Botswana—but how could one establish which of these many thousands of blue cars had been on that road at that particular time? As she thought about this, Mma Ramotswe realised the magnitude of the task she had taken on. It seemed impossible, and she was not surprised that the police had been unable to do very much. They were also doing their best, but if they could do nothing with all their resources—hundreds and hundreds of police officers throughout the country—how could a tiny firm like the No. 1 Ladies' Detective Agency, with its two full-time ladies, its young man Charlie who was half junior, untrained detective and half unqualified mechanic and its part-time assistant-detective-cum-chemistry-teacher Mr. Polopetsi—how could such a small concern as that solve an issue concerning which the police had drawn a blank? Of course she had to help Dr. Marang—it was inconceivable that she could turn down an approach from a man like that, a doctor who had been widely appreciated by people in Mochudi, a kind and honourable man who had known her father, a man of the generation that had built Botswana and made it the fine country that it is. She could never turn such a person away; never. She would have to do something. But right at that moment she had no idea at all as to what that could possibly be. Would Mma Makutsi have any idea? she wondered. Her *joint managing director* had been quick to say that it would not be difficult, but had she thought about it before she reached that conclusion? Mma Ramotswe thought not.

Dr. Marang looked at his watch. "I have another appointment in town," he said. "And we have taken up far too much of your time, Mma Ramotswe."

"You have not, Rra," she reassured him. It was typical of people of her father's generation, she reflected, that they should be apologetic about making demands on people. They had always made their time available to others, had been uncomplaining about what was expected of them, but never thought of their own entitlement. It was so different now, when everybody was so keen on what they could get out of others; when everybody felt no compunction in making shrill demands for more of everything: their rights, their due, their legitimate expectation. Of course people had rights, of course they were entitled to something, but what about giving back? Who spoke about that, and, if they did address the subject, who was there to listen to such voices? What about thinking of what you could do for others rather than what others could do for you? Who would say anything about that?

Perhaps the answer to that was closer than Mma Ramotswe expected. "Our time is yours," Mma Makutsi contributed from the back of the room.

Constance looked at her appreciatively. "Thank you, Mma," she said, adding, "You must find that person. He cannot be allowed to get away with it. You must find him."

"We shall," said Mma Makutsi. Mma Ramotswe could not help herself—she sighed. She would need to talk to Mma Makutsi.

CHAPTER FOUR

WHAT THE SHOES SAID

MMA RAMOTSWE might have felt that she would need to talk to Mma Makutsi, but there was another matter waiting to be aired. That conversation would not be a difficult one for Mma Makutsi, although for Mma Ramotswe it would be slightly harder, which was why she waited until the next morning to broach the subject, although, as she put on the kettle and opened some letters, looking somewhat anxiously at her watch, she wondered if she might have to wait even longer.

Life had been going well for Mma Makutsi. As a general rule, she was not one for excessive reflection—she prided herself on being a *doer* rather than a *ditherer,* a distinction based on another of her magazine articles, *Are you a doer or a ditherer? Fill in our questionnaire below and find out the truth about yourself!* She had complied, and had been pleased to discover that she was in the top two per cent of life's *movers and shakers,* as the magazine labelled this privileged group. She had taken to using the expression, *mover and shaker,* not in any self-congratulatory way, but referring to others whom she had identified as being in the same category. Mma Ramotswe had noticed this, and had passed what Mma Makutsi considered a slightly less than helpful comment on how, while she could see how movers could be helpful, shakers could just get in the way with all their shaking. "Do we need these people to go round shaking things all the time? Or is that how they walk, Mma? Shaking, or even quivering?"

Mma Makutsi had smiled tolerantly. "They do not shake *themselves,* Mma. You must not take these things too literally."

"I am pleased to hear it," said Mma Ramotswe. "I had an aunt who used to shiver a lot. She was always shivering if the tiniest cloud appeared in the sky. She would shiver and say, *Here it comes. The cold weather is upon us.* It never was, though, because Botswana is a warm country, after all."

Mma Makutsi had repeated that shaking was an attitude, rather than a physical matter.

"Just as well," muttered Mma Ramotswe. "What would happen to Mr. Polopetsi if somebody started to shake him? You know that he's slightly built, Mma. He would not cope with being shaken too much—or at all, really."

Mma Makutsi had felt that the discussion was treating a serious subject with excessive levity, and had stopped using the expression. She still took pleasure, though, in the magazine's assessment of her abilities, and in particular she liked the thought that she was a *doer.* Looking back on her life, she was inclined to agree: she had come a long way from Bobonong, her home town in the remote north. It had been a hard battle—firstly, studying at school when she had been expected to help in the family's fields, and then, again by dint of hard work, securing her place at the Botswana Secretarial College. That had involved sacrifice by the wider Makutsi family, who had contributed to her fees, often at the cost of going short themselves. She would never forget that sacrifice, and had managed in due course to repay those uncles and aunts tenfold, thanks to the generosity of her husband, Phuti Radiphuti, owner of the successful Double Comfort Furniture Store. Phuti was another of life's *doers,* although he had completed no questionnaire to find that out about himself.

She took quiet satisfaction in reflecting on how she had come to be where she was. Not only had she met and married the kindest of men, he was a comfortably off one at that, with a considerable herd of cattle and a total of sixteen people working for him. That total was reached by counting the people in the store as well as the cattle-men and herd boys, a herd boy counting for half a man. That resulted in an employee total of fifteen and a half, and she rounded it up to sixteen: you could not talk, she decided, of half-employees, not these days, when people were so sensitive. Although there were some people who behaved as if they were not quite full people: Charlie, for one, did not *think* as much as a full person should think. He was always jumping to conclusions or saying foolish things, none of which a full person would do or say. And then there was Mr. Polopetsi, who was so apologetic in his manner, so mousy. He referred to himself as *just me* or *only me,* which suggested that he did not see himself as being of the same weight as those around him. And he was not, come to think of it: Mr. Polopetsi probably weighed less than half of what Mma Ramotswe weighed; which meant that there was almost twice as much Mma Ramotswe as there was Mr. Polopetsi . . .

This led to another thought. Up in Bobonong there had been a man—a quite ridiculous man, Mma Makutsi recalled—who had said that large people should be allowed to talk for longer at the local community meeting, the *kgotla*. This man, a butcher, was of a generous build, a fact put down by many to his profession and its ease of access to steak. But that was no grounds for his claim to have greater attention paid to his views. Bigger people often thought they should be listened to more than smaller people, and that, unfortunately, was what did sometimes happen. But it should not be like that, thought Mma Makutsi; each of us had a voice that should be listened to with the same attention and courtesy as any other voice, not with any amplification just because of who we happened to be.

But here was Mma Makutsi, an identified and admitted *doer,* lying in bed, thinking about these matters, and not actually *doing* anything. Phuti was an early riser and would already have set off for the Double Comfort Furniture Store, not even bothering to have breakfast before he started the working day. Of course, he would have something to eat when he reached his office—his secretary always bought fat cakes on her way into work, serving one of these with the cup of strong coffee that she made for him as her first duty of the day.

Mma Makutsi could have stayed in bed longer if she wished; one consequence of being married to Phuti was that she had not only one helper in the house, but two—Naledi, a young woman from Molepolole, barely nineteen; and a more senior person, Mma Poeli, herself a grandmother of five grandchildren, who had come on the recommendation of Sister Banjuli of the Anglican Hospice. The young woman's job was to keep the house clean, a task she tackled with a vigour that Phuti occasionally found excessive. "She polishes the floor too much," he said. "It looks very nice and shiny, but floors are meant to be walked on—they should not be too slippery."

Mma Makutsi had been tactful. She remembered the zeal with which she had approached her work when she had first been appointed to the No. 1 Ladies' Detective Agency. There had been very little actual work to do in those early days, and she had put body and soul into the few tasks that there were, in case Mma Ramotswe should decide that there was really no need for a secretary. She had spent hours checking and then re-checking her filing system, creating file after file for letters that were merely hoped for rather than actually received. She was so proud of her job, and would arrive for

work half an hour earlier than necessary, waiting patiently for Mma
Ramotswe to drive up in her white van and open the doors for the
business that seemed so slow to materialise. They had become busier,
of course, as the reputation of the agency spread and more people
came to realise that they would benefit from the services of a private
detective agency. But she had not forgotten those early times, and
how she felt about the job. So now, to Naledi, for whom the position
as maid in the house of Phuti Radiphuti and his wife was a matter of
such status, she explained that, while hard work was always appreciated, it was not necessary to overdo things. She suggested that more
time might be spent on ironing rather than polishing, and this, for
a time at least, seemed to work. But then Phuti complained that,
although it was always a pleasure to put on a well-ironed shirt in the
morning, it was not necessary to have underpants, trousers, *and* socks
so stiffly starched.

Both Naledi and Mma Poeli helped with the Radiphutis' son,
Itumelang Clovis Radiphuti, who was now eighteen months old and
enjoying mobility with all the gusto of that age. He had been an early
walker, and an enthusiastic one, and it was a full-time job for Mma
Poeli to supervise him in his explorations of the world. In the house
itself that was not too much of a problem, as Naledi's efforts meant
that there were no dusty corners in which dangers might lurk; no
spider would find a peaceful haven there, nor any other potentially
harmful insect that might bite incautious young fingers. Outside in
the garden, it was another matter, and vigilance was always required,
particularly in the hot weather, when snakes might migrate from the
stretch of scrub bush that adjoined the Radiphuti plot. Phuti had
created a small pond in the garden, and this attracted frogs, which in
due course interested snakes. Most of these would keep well away
from people, but some, particularly the lethargic and slow-moving
puff adder, would be slow to get out of the way and could inflict a

devastating bite. Itumelang loved being outside, but vigilance was required.

Both Naledi and Mma Poeli lived in the small servants' block at the back of the main house. In Botswana, any house of any size—even relatively modest, suburban houses in the main towns—might be expected to have such accommodation in the garden. More often than not these places were cramped in their dimensions—single rooms in which there was little natural lighting, four roughly distempered walls topped with a flat cast-iron roof. These were mean quarters for anyone, reminders of a time when domestic servants were treated with little consideration. That had changed, of course, and people were now obliged to meet certain minimum standards in their treatment of those whom they employed; but the legacy of mean-spiritedness remained in the hovels in which people were obliged to live.

Phuti would have none of that, and neither would Mma Makutsi. In his case, he had never lived in poverty: the Radiphutis had been well-to-do—starting in a modest way—for three generations. Phuti's grandfather, Edward Radiphuti, had been the headmaster of a school, while his father, Thomas Radiphuti, had grown the family fortunes—and cattle herd—through his hard work in the furniture business. Thomas had taught Phuti a valuable lesson in how to deal with people less fortunate than oneself. "Think of what *you* have," he said. "Then think of what *they* have. See what that does to the way you think about other people." He had found this simple act of imagining had the desired effect: from the well of security it is not hard to draw the water of generosity.

Mma Makutsi, of course, had come from a very different background. She had known poverty and knew very well what it was to have no money—just no money at all—and to wonder where the next meal would come from. That experience could either make people grasping and selfish once their fortunes changed, or it could have the opposite effect. In her case it was the latter. Naledi and Mma Poeli were not expected to work long hours, and were given both Saturday and Sunday off, something that few domestic servants enjoyed. Then there was the money: although she was canny in her housekeeping—Mma Makutsi did not believe in waste—she insisted on paying Naledi and Mma Poeli well above the rather pitiful minimum wage that many people paid their domestic helpers. This was topped up with generous food allowances, and with gifts of furniture that Phuti would occasionally bring back from the store. These were items he described as *shop-soiled*—tables with scratches on the surface, chairs with discoloured coverings because somebody had left them too long under a window in the warehouse and the sun had done its damage, beds with legs that had unaccountably broken between factory and store. There was not much room for such items in the servants' quarters, which were already furnished, but they were gratefully received by relatives. There was always somebody who would appreciate something—always: an aunt, a cousin, or one of that strange, unlimited category of distant, unspecified connections. To these people Naledi and Mma Poeli would pass on Phuti's gifts, with Phuti's blessing, because he too understood the way in which things worked—the way in which people looked after one another.

Lying in bed that morning, Mma Makutsi heard the sound of Mma Poeli's voice drifting through from the kitchen, where she would be feeding Itumelang. She was telling him to eat up; sometimes, though, she would be singing, as grandmothers did to small children, and Mma Makutsi would recognise the song from somewhere back in her own childhood. A few days earlier she had heard Mma Poeli singing the song of the wedding of the baboons, and had told Mma Ramotswe about it over the first office cup of tea. Mma Ramotswe had smiled and remembered: she knew the words, about how the baboons had celebrated their wedding and dressed each other in scraps they had managed to steal from human houses—an old hat, a dishcloth made to serve as a skirt, a torn handkerchief making the groom's shirt.

Mma Makutsi stretched out in her bed. She knew that there was no need to get up if she felt disinclined to do so. Her hours at the agency were flexible now, as she did not have to work for a salary and could choose when she went in. Mma Ramotswe paid her, it was true, but only for one-third of her time—the figure they had agreed upon after Mma Makutsi's marriage to Phuti. She had no need of that money now, and occasionally, after a slack period in the agency, she would tacitly fail to draw what was owing to her. This was a gesture very much appreciated by Mma Ramotswe; although she too could rely on Mr. J.L.B. Matekoni's income, she still liked to avoid the business going into the red at the end of the month.

Mma Makutsi looked at her watch. It was now almost eight, and Mma Ramotswe would be sitting at her desk, attending to the mail that had been collected the previous afternoon, too late to be dealt with before the close of business. It was usually Mma Makutsi's job to slit open the envelopes and log the contents in a large ledger labelled *Mail In*. She would give each letter a reference number—a vital component in any good filing system, she believed—and then glance at its contents before passing it on to Mma Ramotswe. This was the way things had always been done, although Mma Makutsi believed that there was no reason why the mail should not be divided into two piles, one for Mma Ramotswe to deal with and one for herself. Passing on every letter to Mma Ramotswe might have made sense in the days when she was simply the secretary, but now that she was a director—no, joint managing director—there was no reason why she should not respond to correspondence in her own words, and under her own name. She would suggest that to Mma Ramotswe at some point, even if not just yet. There was still a feeling that the No. 1 Ladies' Detective Agency was Mma Ramotswe's creation and therefore she had a greater say in its affairs. Mma Makutsi could not argue with that: Mma Ramotswe had started the agency; she had chosen its name; she had determined where its office would be, which happened to be under a roof shared with her husband's garage, Tlokweng Road Speedy Motors. And yet there must come a time, Mma Makutsi thought, when the centre of gravity in a business shifted from the old guard to the new, and up-and-coming people could assume control.

Up-and-coming . . . she savoured the sound of the expression as she lay there in bed. *Up-and-coming* . . . She was definitely up-and-coming, and the next time she was interviewed for a newspaper profile—as had happened a few months ago—she would suggest that form of words to the journalist. *Grace Makutsi, Up-and-Coming Powerhouse in the World of Detection.* That would be a very satisfactory heading for an article, not that one wanted to be too presumptuous in these things. *Powerhouse* might be a bit much, perhaps; *figure* might be better, or *prospect,* that had a good ring to it, and was suggestive of the future; so perhaps she might propose that, if the interview ever took place, that was. The last profile had been a bit dull for Mma Makutsi's taste, and had given excessive weight, she felt, to her origins. *A Long Way from Bobonong* was not a particularly complimentary title for the piece, in her view, and there was far more to her career than a rags-to-riches story. There were her successful cases, for instance—her *triumphs,* as Mma Ramotswe had generously called them; Mma Makutsi had told the interviewer about them, in some detail, but there had been no mention of any of this in the newspaper article, other than a vague reference to "certain satisfactory results." Instead there had been a whole paragraph on the fact that nobody of any note had ever come from Bobonong before and that it was a pity that people up there seemed completely unaware of Mma Makutsi's stellar progress. Then there had been something about Mma Makutsi's alma mater, the Botswana Secretarial College, which had been described as an "office school" where "office workers learned basic skills." That had incensed Mma Makutsi, and understandably so. Basic skills? Did that journalist have any idea—the slightest idea—of just what was taught at the Botswana Secretarial College? Did he know, for example, that there was a full course entitled Advanced Accountancy? Not just accountancy, but *advanced* accountancy. Did people like that know the first thing about Filing Theory, Part One, a course in which Mma Makutsi had achieved a grade of one hundred per cent? She had mentioned in the interview that her examination paper in that subject had, with her permission, of course, been used by the college as a model paper for subsequent students. There was nothing about that in the final article, but that was the way that journalists behaved. Unless you gave them a positive steer, they could go off in some odd direction of their own.

She closed her eyes. She could easily drift back to sleep, she thought, and then wake up again at nine, or even later. She knew that sleep was good for one, and in particular helped the skin. She needed to watch her skin; it had a tendency to excessive oiliness, although she managed to keep that in check by using a special lemon-based balm she ordered by post. That came all the way from Cape Town and would arrive in a small parcel marked *Strictly Confidential*. She did not think that was necessary—oily skin was not something she felt she had to be ashamed of; it was better, surely, to have what she called a "well-irrigated skin" rather than to have a dry skin or, even worse, a flaky skin. A flaky skin was particularly bad if you were a criminal, she had read, as it meant that you left a great deal of DNA at the scene of the crime. That had amused her. That would teach any flaky-skinned housebreakers to burgle people's houses. "You really need to do something about your skin," the police might say to such people when they arrested them.

What was that? She opened her eyes, sure that she had heard something. From the kitchen she heard Mma Poeli's voice, and this was followed by a brief exclamation in Itumelang's high-pitched tones. Then Mma Poeli once again, saying something to Naledi, who must have been in the kitchen with them. But it was not this that Mma Makutsi had heard, but something quite different.

She was wide awake now, and slipped out from under the sheet to stand on the bedside mat. Had she imagined it? No, she was sure she had not. She knelt down and looked cautiously under the bed. Caution was always required when you looked under a bed—anybody's bed, even your own. You never knew. She had heard of somebody who had looked under her bed to discover an intruder concealed there. That would have been a terrible shock—the sort of thing from which you might never recover. Other people had found snakes there—for some reason, snakes liked to curl up under people's beds—or a scorpion nest, which would be almost as bad; or money, of course. There were still people who kept their money under their bed. It was not a wise thing to do, but these people somehow felt more secure if they knew they were sleeping over their savings.

There was nothing under Mma Makutsi's bed—thanks to Naledi, not even a sign of dust. Relieved, she stood up again and crossed the floor towards the cupboard in which she kept her clothes. And again she heard it: a tiny, almost inaudible voice, one that she recognised immediately. It was a voice she had not heard for some time, but now it had something to say once more. *Careful, Boss! Don't get mixed up in politics!*

It was her shoes. They were in the bottom of the cupboard, and that was why they sounded so faint. Her shoes.

She opened the cupboard door gingerly. There had been cases of intruders hiding in cupboards, but there was nothing like that now. Just her clothing, and below that the shoes, staring up at her with the innocent look of shoes that would never take it upon themselves to address anybody about anything, let alone issue what sounded like an unambiguous warning.

Mma Makutsi sighed. Imagination was an odd thing. It made you see things that were not there and hear things that were not said. Although sometimes the things that were not there or the things that were not said were things to which you should pay close attention. Sometimes, she thought, but not always.

_____

CHAPTER FIVE

SIGN HERE, PLEASE, AND HERE . . .

IN SPITE OF her tardiness that morning, Mma Makutsi still arrived
at the office in time to forestall Mma Ramotswe's switching on the
kettle for the second cup of tea. "You must let me do that, Mma,"
she said. "That is my job, you know."

Mma Ramotswe glanced at her watch—not too pointedly, she
hoped, but sufficiently obviously for Mma Makutsi to notice.

"I know it's rather late," Mma Makutsi said. "It's just that . . ."

Mma Ramotswe relented. "Oh, I know, Mma. A small child. A
husband. A house to run." Mma Ramotswe was keen not to offend
her colleague; she knew that Mma Makutsi did not need to work
and that her continued involvement with the agency came from the
goodness of her heart. She appreciated that, and she could not imagine what the No. 1 Ladies' Detective Agency would be like without her. Mma Makutsi might say some strange things from time to
time, she might be prickly on occasion, she might wind Charlie up
the wrong way and even frighten Mr. Polopetsi, but she was part of
the agency, in with the brickwork, and it would be inconceivable to
lose her.

Mma Ramotswe went on to explain. "It's just that, if it were possible to let me know whether you would be coming in or not, that would be useful. I'd know, then, whether I could go out, or whether I'd have to leave Charlie looking after the office. And then Mr. J.L.B. Matekoni would know whether he would need to allocate Charlie's time to us or to the garage."

Mma Makutsi pursed her lips, making Mma Ramotswe fear that she had gone too far.

"It's just an idea, Mma," Mma Ramotswe said hurriedly. "Just a thought, really. Everything's working fine—in general, that is. There is no problem with anything, come to think of it."

Mma Makutsi busied herself with the making of the tea. "I'm glad to hear that, Mma," she said. "And I'm very happy too."

"Good," said Mma Ramotswe, relieved that the moment had passed. She looked at her watch again—this time not in censure. "Mma Potokwane is dropping in," she said. "She phoned earlier and asked if she could call on us."

"Should we wait to have tea, then?" Mma Makutsi asked.

Mma Ramotswe did not think that was a good idea. The body expected tea, she believed, and the rhythms of the body, its anticipations and requests, should not be ignored. "We can have another cup of tea when she arrives. That is the best thing to do."

Mma Makutsi agreed, and the two women sat down to enjoy their brew. It was a warm day, but not too warm, as the hottest months had passed and a body of cooler air had moved up from the south: air that had started its travels far down over the southern oceans, then swept up over the Cape of Good Hope, over the dry reaches of the Karoo, and into Botswana itself; air that brought a hint of something unfamiliar to the nostrils, a hint of salt and iodine, of something beyond the land, of something beyond Africa. Mma Ramotswe sensed it. "This weather, Mma, is from somewhere else, I think."

Mma Makutsi agreed. "Phuti has ordered some firewood," she said. "He says that you should always be prepared."

"Very wise," said Mma Ramotswe.

She thought of the fireplace in her own house, for much of the year left empty, but prepared for service during the relatively few chilly weeks of the year. The weather in that cold season was only occasionally overcast—grey days were virtually unheard of in Botswana—but even a clear sky, drenched in sunlight, could be chilly once the sun went north. At such times, the dry cold could penetrate to the very bones, and in the early morning people would huddle about such fires as they could make, rubbing their hands to keep them warm. And in the evenings, when the sun disappeared, a fire would again bring comfort. She remembered the fire outside her aunt's house in Mochudi; she remembered sitting beside it as a young girl and looking up at the night sky, with its fields of stars, its spilt-milk galaxy, and asking her aunt whether that was Botswana too, or whether it was England or India or somewhere else altogether. And her aunt laughing and telling her that there were places where there was nothing, just air and more air, and that what she was looking up at was one of those. "England is far away," her aunt had said. "They used to be here, you know, but now they have gone back to their own place. There was the Queen, and then there was Seretse Khama and our own people. That is called history, you see."

"But who asked them here?"

The aunt shook her head. "There are some guests who do not knock."

"That is very rude."

"Yes," said the aunt.

How many years ago was that? And why should such a memory— a brief snatch of conversation—lodge in the mind when so much else of childhood was irretrievably lost? That was what was in Mma Ramotswe's mind when Mma Makutsi suddenly stood up and peered out of the window beside her desk. "Mma Potokwane is coming," she announced. "I shall put the kettle back on."

MMA POTOKWANE settled in the client's chair, her cup of tea placed before her on Mma Ramotswe's desk. "I have had a very successful morning," she announced breezily. "So far. And I'm sure it will get even better."

Mma Ramotswe smiled. Her friend had always been an optimist, and with good reason; but there were also times when her bright view of life had not been justified. "So, Mma?" she encouraged. "Tell us what has happened."

Mma Potokwane turned to include Mma Makutsi in the conversation. "You'll be interested in this, Mma Makutsi," she said. "I went to see the people who sell those photocopying machines. The office equipment people. Over in the industrial sites."

Mma Makutsi nodded. "I know that firm. They are very big."

"And generous—as it turned out." There was a note of triumph in Mma Potokwane's voice as she continued. "They're sponsoring one of the children. They've just confirmed it. Completely. Everything. School uniform. Books. Food. The lot."

Mma Ramotswe clapped her hands in delight. "That's wonderful, Mma. Wonderful."

Mma Makutsi looked proud. This reflected well on the whole secretarial world. "That is very good news for the child," she said. She paused before she went on, "And maybe one day that child will even go to the Botswana Secretarial College. Who knows?"

"Anything is possible," agreed Mma Potokwane. "That little boy is very lucky."

There was a brief silence, bringing with it a slight drop in temperature, as if the cool air outside had suddenly penetrated the office itself. Then Mma Makutsi asked, "Boy, Mma?"

Mma Potokwane had not noticed the effect of her words. "Yes, I have already chosen the boy."

Mma Makutsi's glasses flashed, throwing a tiny reflected chit of light on the office wall. It was, as Mma Ramotswe knew very well, a sign of disapproval.

"Why not a girl?" And then came Mma Makutsi's point: "There are very few boys who go to the Botswana Secretarial College." *Very few* was an overestimate. There were, she thought, none at all.

Mma Potokwane frowned. "That may be, Mma. But there are other forms of training."

"But you said the child could go to the Botswana Secretarial College, Mma. You said that."

Mma Potokwane was firm. One did not argue with a matron, and, if one did, the result was a foregone conclusion. "No, Mma. I did not say that—not in so many words. I did not. I said that it was *possible,* and that is completely different from saying that something will definitely happen." She turned to Mma Ramotswe for support. "Isn't that so, Mma Ramotswe?"

Mma Ramotswe glanced in Mma Makutsi's direction. "Does it matter?" she asked. "The important thing is that this money is being made available for a child. Does it matter which child?"

"Yes," said Mma Makutsi. But then she relented. "Maybe no. All children are deserving."

"There you are," said Mma Ramotswe, relieved at the defusing of the disagreement.

"And yet," said Mma Makutsi, "I'm sure that firm would have liked to think that the child could maybe grow up to use their equipment."

"I'm very grateful, whatever happens," said Mma Potokwane.

Mma Makutsi cleared her throat and turned to Mma Potokwane. "Who is this boy, Mma?" she asked.

Mma Potokwane explained that it was a small boy whom Mma Ramotswe had met. "Oh," said Mma Ramotswe. "He is the one who stole the eggs?"

Mma Makutsi was quick to react. "Stole eggs? Why is a boy who steals eggs being given that chance? Are there not plenty of children—including girls, I might add—who have not stolen eggs? If you have to choose between those who steal eggs and those who do not, then surely you should reward those who do not steal eggs?"

Mma Ramotswe tried to explain. "They were guinea fowl eggs, Mma. They were in the bush . . ."

"That is no excuse, Mma," snapped Mma Makutsi. "It doesn't matter if the eggs belonged to a bird or to a person."

"And he is a very small boy," interjected Mma Potokwane. "Boys do silly things—all the time, Mma." She paused. "I will use some of the money to buy him new shoes. His current shoes are old—and too small for him, I think. I shall get him some shoes with rubber soles because he is very frightened of lightning."

They waited for further explanation.

"If you wear shoes with rubber soles," explained Mma Potokwane, "you are much better protected against lightning strikes."

Mma Makutsi considered this for a few moments. She still took issue with favouring a boy who had stolen eggs, even if the theft was being made light of by Mma Potokwane. There were standards to be kept up here, she thought, and it seemed to be falling to her to do that. "It is very wrong to take eggs from a bird," she muttered. "There will be no birds left if everybody starts doing that, you know."

Mma Ramotswe pointed at her teacup. "You must not let your tea get cold, Mma. In this cooler weather, you know, it gets cold rather quickly."

They all took a sip of tea, and Mma Ramotswe tried to think of something to divert the conversation into safer territory. Before she had the opportunity, though, Mma Potokwane took the initiative. "I had the opportunity to call in at the council offices this morning," she said. "I obtained the form."

Mma Ramotswe looked puzzled. "Form, Mma?"

"The nomination form," the matron replied, digging into the bag she had brought with her. "Here it is. You just have to sign it. It's very simple. Then it needs two signatures of registered voters." She turned to face Mma Makutsi. "That could be Mma Makutsi and myself. Or even Mr. J.L.B. Matekoni, if he's not too busy." From the garage there came the sound of a car engine being revved. "Perhaps he is too busy."

"What is this form?" asked Mma Makutsi. This may have been business between Mma Potokwane and Mma Ramotswe, but if she was going to be asked to sign anything, she felt she had the right to know.

Mma Potokwane turned to give her answer, holding up the form for Mma Makutsi to see. "It's the nomination for the council elections. If Mma Ramotswe is to be a candidate . . ."

Mma Ramotswe shook her head vigorously. "No, Mma. I do not want to . . ."

Mma Potokwane seemed not to have heard. "If she is going to be a candidate," she continued, "then she must fill this in. I'll return it to them for you. I have put my own name down as your election agent."

Mma Makutsi's eyes were wide with astonishment. Her glasses flashed. "You're going to stand for election to the council?"

The answer came from Mma Potokwane rather than Mma Ramotswe. "Yes, she is. There's a vacancy coming up, and Mma Ramotswe will surely win it."

"I won't win," protested Mma Ramotswe. "I don't want to stand, Mma."

Mma Potokwane shook a finger at her friend. It was a playful gesture, but its point was a serious one. "That's defeatism, Mma. That's giving up before you've even started. And if we all took that approach, where would we be? Where would *anyone* be, Mma?"

"I am not being defeatist, Mma. I'm simply saying that standing in an election is not what I want to do. There are plenty of people who like that sort of thing, but I am not one of them."

That should, she believed, have clinched the argument, but Mma Potokwane had the bit between her teeth. "But if you don't stand, Mma, then who will show these people that they can't get away with it?"

Mma Makutsi now joined in. "Get away with what?" she asked.

Mma Potokwane waved a hand airily. "With all their nonsense."

Mma Makutsi snorted. "Oh, there is always a lot of nonsense. Nonsense about this thing; nonsense about that thing. A lot of nonsense."

"Precisely," said Mma Potokwane. "And now we can do something about it. Not a big thing, maybe, but electing Mma Ramotswe would mean there'd be at least one sensible voice on the council." She paused. "And it would be a good thing for women in general. We need to have more women in politics, rather than all those men."

"With all their nonsense," Mma Makutsi chimed in. This was very much what she had always thought, even if it had not occurred to her that Mma Ramotswe, of all people, would be the one to lead the charge. Still, somebody had to take the first step . . . She stopped herself as she remembered what had happened earlier that morning. *The shoes* . . .

Mma Potokwane was talking. "I know you may have reservations, Mma, but I'm sure you'll get used to it. In fact, you'll enjoy yourself, I think. Most people in politics enjoy themselves very much."

The shoes, thought Mma Makutsi. The shoes. *Don't get mixed up in politics!* Why should her shoes say that on the very morning when Mma Potokwane came into the office and produced a nomination form? It was an unsettling coincidence. She cleared her throat. "But if Mma Ramotswe doesn't want to, Mma Potokwane . . . If she doesn't want to . . ."

"I don't," interjected Mma Ramotswe. "I don't."

Now it was simple. Mma Ramotswe needed Mma Makutsi's support, and she would give it. "I don't think you should press her," said Mma Makutsi. "Politics may not be for everybody."

Mma Ramotswe looked at her colleague gratefully. "That's what I think," she said. "I'm glad there are people who stand for these things, but it's not me. I have other work to do, Mma Potokwane."

It was at this point that Charlie entered the room. The young man had been helping Mr. J.L.B. Matekoni in the garage, but had been told that he was now free to see if there was anything for him to do in the office. This was the arrangement they now had: Charlie was a part-time trainee detective and a part-time unqualified—but enthusiastic—mechanical apprentice. Whether his apprenticeship would ever be finished was uncertain, but the set-up suited him as much as it suited both businesses, neither of which could afford to give him a full-time position.

"*Dumela,* ladies," Charlie said cheerfully, wiping his hands on a blue paper towel. "I hope I'm not interrupting anything." He crossed the room to pour himself a mug of tea.

Mma Potokwane had a soft spot for Charlie. She knew about his irresponsibility, she knew he had an eye for girls, she knew about his fecklessness, but all young men were like that, she thought, to a greater or lesser extent. Now she detected an ally, and so she said, "Mma Ramotswe is thinking of standing for the council, Charlie. I'm sure you'll vote for her, won't you?"

Charlie stopped in his tracks. He stared at Mma Ramotswe. "You, Mma? You, go on the council?"

Mma Ramotswe shook her head. "We talked about it, but—"

He did not let her finish. "But that's fantastic, Mma. I'll vote for you. Fanwell will vote for you too. I'll get all the girls to vote for you. There are hundreds of girls, hundreds, who'll give you their vote." He shook his head at the thought of hundreds of girls, all lining up to vote for Mma Ramotswe, marshalled by himself.

This was exactly what Mma Potokwane had wanted to hear. "There you are, Mma Ramotswe. I told you that there'd be plenty of people to vote for you."

Mma Makutsi was scornful. "Who are these girls, Charlie? Where do they come from, these hundreds of girls?"

Charlie looked smug. "Wouldn't you like to know, Mma Makutsi?" he snapped back.

"That's why I'm asking." She paused. "And if they're the sorts of girls you know, Charlie, they won't be interested in politics. Hair, maybe. Fingernails. Dancing. But not politics. Girls like that, you see, don't vote."

Charlie opened his mouth to respond, but Mma Ramotswe, keen to avoid disharmony, gave him a warning glance. "It doesn't matter," she said. "Since I'm not going to be standing, it doesn't matter whether Charlie's friends vote or not." She turned to Charlie. "But thank you anyway for your support, Charlie."

Mma Potokwane had been observing this *contretemps* without intervening. Now she made her move. "Of course, if Mma Ramotswe doesn't stand, then somebody else will get in." She sighed. "That will be most unfortunate, in view of who the other candidate is likely to be."

This remark was greeted with complete silence. Mma Makutsi looked up sharply. Her glasses caught the light again. Mma Ramotswe frowned. Charlie, who had been fiddling with a paper clip he had found on top of the filing cabinet, tossed it aside.

Mma Potokwane appeared to relish the drama of the moment. "Yes," she said, lingering over what she had to say. "Most unfortunate indeed. In fact . . ." She saw that they were all hanging on her words. "In fact, very bad."

Mma Ramotswe spoke next. A name had come to her immediately after Mma Potokwane had spoken. Now she sought confirmation. "Violet Sephotho, by any chance, Mma?"

Mma Potokwane inclined her head sadly. "I'm afraid so, Mma."

From Mma Makutsi's corner of the room there came a sound that could have been anything. It could have been some sort of uncontrolled stomach eruption—a belch of distress, perhaps—or it could have been a growl of unsuppressed anger, or a moan of extreme despair. Whatever it was, it left nobody in any doubt that this was not welcome news. And, when the power of speech returned, all she could do was to hiss, "Her!"

"Yes," said Mma Potokwane, her voice grave. "I heard from somebody in the council office. She told me that Violet's papers are already in. She's standing as an independent. No party—just an independent. And I heard, too, that there are no other candidates." Now came the most shocking disclosure of all. "And so, if Mma Ramotswe doesn't stand—and of course she has a perfect right to say no, I'd never dispute that—but if she doesn't stand, then Violet Sephotho will be elected to the council unopposed."

"Without anybody voting?" asked Charlie. "Just like that?"

Mma Potokwane nodded. "That's the way it works, Charlie."

Charlie looked directly at Mma Ramotswe. "But you can't let that happen, Mma. She's a terrible woman."

On this, if on no other subject, Mma Makutsi and Charlie saw eye to eye. Now she rose from her chair and went across the room to the kettle. More tea, and more thought, would be required if the bombshell that was this new disclosure were to be dealt with. And there would have to be a realignment of views.

She did not turn to speak to Mma Ramotswe; instead, her remarks appeared to be addressed to the teapot. "That makes everything different," she said. "There are times when you have to put personal feelings to one side. There are times when you have to do your duty to Botswana."

Mma Potokwane agreed. "Well said, Mma Makutsi."

Charlie looked thoughtful. "That's probably true."

"So," continued Mma Makutsi, "we must all stand together."

Charlie liked that. "Together," he muttered. "United. Together."

Mma Potokwane flourished the nomination form. "This is all that stands between us and . . ."

Mma Makutsi spun around. "Disaster," she said, her voice rising with emotion. "Oh, Mma Ramotswe, you cannot let this happen."

Mma Ramotswe gestured helplessly. "But surely there must be other people who could stand," she said. She looked at Mma Potokwane. "What about you, Mma Potokwane?"

The response came quickly. "Impossible, Mma. I would love to be able to help, but I have the Orphan Farm to run. That is a double full-time job."

Mma Ramotswe was not ready to give up. "Or you, Mma Makutsi? How about you?"

"Out of the question," said Mma Makutsi. "Phuti would not want me on the council. He doesn't like that sort of thing."

"Or even Charlie," tried Mma Ramotswe. "Charlie, you would get the young vote. All those hundreds of girls would love to vote for you."

In spite of the united front that seemed to be developing, this was too much for Mma Makutsi. "Charlie? Charlie, stand for election?" she mocked.

"Why not?" snapped Charlie.

Mma Makutsi said nothing.

"I don't think we should put Charlie under any pressure," said Mma Potokwane rapidly. "He is still a young man and has many other things to do."

"You see," crowed Charlie. "So don't look at me."

Silence returned. Mma Potokwane held out the form. "I think you should sign, Mma," she said gently. "You will be a very good member of the council and you will save us all from that woman." Then she added, almost inaudibly, "I think it's your duty, Mma."

Mma Ramotswe looked at the piece of paper and made her decision. Up until that moment she would have stuck to her guns, but Mma Potokwane had said something that changed everything. It was one word that did it: *duty*. If her friend thought it was her duty, then it was her duty. Mma Potokwane was the one person she thought was entitled to speak about duty with unchallengeable authority. That was because she herself had never swayed in discharging what she saw as her obligation to all the children she had looked after. She had never, not for one moment, questioned or complained about that. It was simply her duty, and she had carried it out, and would continue to do so until she could do it no more. That was the sort of woman Mma Potokwane was, and that was the sort of person who was now asking her to do something which, by comparison, was a small thing indeed. How could she refuse?

"Mma Makutsi," she said. "I'll need a pen, please."

How easy it was, she thought, to sign your life away. Just a few strokes of the pen on paper, and your life could take a different, and wholly uncharted, course. Just like that.

CHAPTER SIX

UNTIL AFRICA IS FULL OF CHINA SHOES

CHARLIE STEPPED OUT of the minibus that had taken him a short distance down the Tlokweng Road in the direction of town. It was the same minibus that he normally caught at the end of every working day to travel home to Old Naledi, but on this occasion he disembarked well short of his usual stop. It was shortly after five o'clock, and he was due to meet a young woman in the coffee bar near the parking lot at the Riverview Mall. Any meeting with a young woman was important in Charlie's eyes, but this one was especially so, and before he left work he had been careful to ensure that the front of his shirt was clean, that his hands were well scrubbed, and that any grease under his fingernails—something that all mechanics were used to—had been prised out with a sharpened matchstick. It was so much easier to keep presentable if you were an office worker, Charlie thought; they did not have motor oil dripping down on their heads when they had a car up on the ramp, nor dust sticking to their clothing when they wrestled with the changing of a tyre. They could look as neat and tidy at five o'clock in the evening as at eight in the morning, never having to work up a sweat, but sitting quite comfortably under the cooling blades of an office fan, not exerting themselves in any way—except mentally, of course, but thinking never made you sweat, nor stained your clothing, nor led to bruises and bumps. No wonder that men who worked in office jobs—civil servants, bank managers, and the like—seemed to find so little trouble in meeting and marrying glamorous, eligible girls. Such men had no *personal freshness* issues; such men found it only too easy to look cool, collected, well groomed, and presentable, even on the hottest days of the Botswana summer.

As he made his way over to the coffee bar, Charlie gave an appraising glance at the cars in the parking lot. This was a mechanic's habit, at least one of the things he had picked up during the years of his unfinished apprenticeship—and retained, unlike so much else that had been so quickly lost. While most people saw the person first and then the car, with mechanics it was different: the car was recognised before its driver. Indeed, Charlie had seen Mr. J.L.B. Matekoni himself instinctively appear to greet a car before he enquired of a client about his health and whether he had slept well, and all the other things that a formal greeting in Botswana might entail. Charlie had seen this, and had smiled; he had always been a wry observer of human foibles, and was becoming all the more so now that he had embarked on his training as a part-time detective. *A part-time detective . . .* The words thrilled him. *I am not just a mechanic,* he thought. *I am not just any old person who has to get under cars for a living; I am an actual detective, engaged in investigative work for Botswana's premier detective agency—indeed, for Botswana's* only *detective agency.* And since that was the No. 1 Ladies' Detective Agency, and therefore staffed by ladies, he was the only male private detective in the whole country—or probably in a whole number of countries, if you included Zambia to the north and Swaziland and Lesotho off to the east—and you should include them, he thought, because he did not think much was happening in any of them from the detection point of view. The Zambians were perfectly nice people, but he did not think they had many issues of the sort that would require the services of a detective agency, and the same, he decided, could be said of Swaziland and Lesotho, both very small countries where everybody would be presumed to know everybody else's business anyway. There was little call for discreet investigation when you already knew the answer to the issue you were addressing. So, thought Charlie, he really was an international private detective, and if somebody in Zambia, for instance, wanted something looked into, he would have to come to Botswana to find the necessary *trained operative*. That was a lovely expression that Charlie had heard Mma Makutsi use on one occasion and that he had purloined for his own use. *Trained operative* . . .

And yet, and yet . . . In spite of all this, in spite of having been plucked out of the garage by Mma Ramotswe and being given the chance of a new career, in spite of being able to call himself an international private detective (in training), life was still not quite what Charlie would have liked it to be. For a start, he had no car, and surely if there was anything that an international private detective should have it was a car. Could you imagine any of those people—the people you saw in films—agreeing to meet a client somewhere as soon as he managed to get there by *bus*? That would impress nobody—least of all the client. And then there were his clothes. International private detectives tended to wear well-cut suits, and Charlie had no suit at all, well cut or otherwise. On most days he made do with a pair of khaki trousers that would be protected against grease—he hoped—by the work overalls provided by Mr. J.L.B. Matekoni. When not working in the garage and assigned to the agency, he would abandon these overalls and make do with the khaki trousers, one of the four shirts he possessed, and the better of his two pairs of shoes. He was allowed to keep these shoes behind the filing cabinet in the office so that he might change into them when he moved between his mechanic's job and his detection role. They looked smart enough, but they had a fatal flaw: a crack in the left sole; and that sole, being made of a toughened rubber substance, could not be fixed.

"Leather's different," said the shoe-repair man who plied his trade under an acacia tree on the other side of the Tlokweng Road. "Leather you can take off, see. Then you put on a new bit of leather that you can cut from a bigger piece. You nail it on, see, but this stuff"—he gestured contemptuously to the exposed sole of Charlie's shoe—"this stuff can only be fixed by some special glue. It has to dissolve rubber. Sorry."

Charlie enquired whether supplies of the special glue might be obtained.

The repair man shook his head. "No," he said. "They make those things over in the China place and they don't send us any. You have to go and ask those China fellows if they have any." He sighed. "And they wouldn't give you any, because if we can fix their shoes like that, then we won't buy any new pairs. They want us to be buying their shoes all the time—more and more China shoes, all the time, until Africa is full of China shoes and things. All China stuff."

Charlie resigned himself to living with his damaged footwear. The crack was a small one and only occasionally let in a small grain of sand. That could be irritating—and sharp against the sole of the foot—but it was not something that would be detected by anybody else, and it would certainly not diminish him in the eyes of any client. The khaki trousers were a greater cause for concern in that respect; if there was any colour that an international detective did not choose for his trousers, then Charlie imagined it would be khaki. But his situation was what it was, and his trousers were the colour they were, and Charlie decided to accept the situation, at least for the time being. Things would improve—he was sure of that—and for the time being he had a new girlfriend, and an attractive one at that. Oh, yes, things would improve, even if your left shoe had a crack in its sole, your trousers were the wrong colour, and you had to travel everywhere by crowded—and badly maintained—minibus. You could put up with the indignity of all that if you had a girlfriend called Queenie-Queenie who was head-turningly pretty and who had a good job in the This-Way Fashion House, a shop that advertised itself as *the* place for "ladies in executive positions" to choose the clothes that would help them to get where they wanted to get "in every department of life." Queenie-Queenie wore a badge that announced her as a *Senior Sales Consultant,* a job title that sounded almost as good as *International Private Detective,* although, as Charlie remarked to himself, no private detective would ever wear a badge announcing his occupation. That was a pity, perhaps, as it would certainly impress those with whom one came into daily contact—particularly on that crowded minibus, where fellow passengers were frequently so careless as to where they put their elbows.

QUEENIE-QUEENIE, who was already in the coffee bar waiting for Charlie, glanced first at her watch and then at the group of four young men who were occupying the neighbouring table. She had not seen them before, and there was something about them suggestive of some-where other than Botswana. Perhaps it was their clothing; perhaps it was the way they talked—they were speaking Setswana, as far as she could hear, but there was an unfamiliar note to their voices. There were plenty of people over the border in South Africa whose mother tongue was Setswana, but there were differences, both subtle and unsubtle, in intonation and even vocabulary. These young men looked as if they might come from Johannesburg, or somewhere like that—there was that ring of the big city to them, and in their eyes Gaborone, for all its new buildings and its prosperity, was nowhere much. Well, let them think that, Queenie-Queenie told herself. She could have gone off to live in Johannesburg if she had wanted to, but she did not. Better to be a big fish in a small pond, she thought, rather than a small fish in a big one. What happened to small fish? Everybody knew the answer to that: they were eaten by bigger fish.

Queenie-Queenie thought of the very obvious contrast between these young men and Charlie. It could not have been more marked: the boys at the table—and that was how she thought of them, as boys—were dressed flashily, and expensively. Charlie would arrive in his khaki trousers and his plain shirt. They would have money in their pockets; Charlie usually had little of that, sometimes only just enough to pay for two cups of coffee, and, if he did that, he would sometimes find himself short of the tiny amount—no more than a couple of pula—that he needed for his minibus fare home. The contrast went further than that. If they had known about Charlie's comparative penury, these young men would probably have merely shrugged, or even smiled. They would never guess that she would find that penury attractive; that Charlie's struggles added to, rather than detracted from, his appeal. Charlie had character, she thought, and character so often came from having to battle for what you had in life. Well-off young men—like those at the nearby table— would not know what it was like to scrimp and save. And that, she thought, made them Charlie's inferior—at least in all the things that counted.

People might have thought it surprising that an elegant, attractive young woman—especially one named Queenie-Queenie and working in a fashionable dress shop—should favour the underdog rather than his flashy contemporaries. People might also have thought that somebody like Queenie-Queenie would have lamented Charlie's inability to give her what many young women of her age group might consider a good time—meals eaten out at a restaurant; evenings in one of those bars where they played the latest music so loudly as to inhibit all but the most basic conversation; presents of those violet-scented chocolates, Lovers' Choice, that they sold in the Pick 'n' Pay supermarket. But the absence of these things was a matter of complete indifference to Queenie-Queenie; she did not bother about any of this, because her real and over-riding concern was family. She was deeply and unconditionally attached to her parents, her various uncles and aunts, and her only sibling, her brother, Hercules, one-time runner-up substitute in the Mr. Botswana Competition, an annual muscle-building prize challenge sponsored by the country's principal maker of traditional beer. She was also determined that, as soon as she was able, she would find a suitable young man to marry, and present her parents with grandchildren and Hercules with nephews and nieces. That such a domestic set of ambitions should have existed in the breast of a young woman who looked as glamorous as Queenie-Queenie was something that the casual observer would not even guess at—and that was precisely Charlie's position when he first met her: he had no idea.

Charlie did not know it, but the family to which Queenie-Queenie was so attached was one of the wealthiest in Botswana. It was also one of the most closely knit, and most cautious—in a nation renowned for its reticence and general caution. The head of this family was Lucas Modikwe, the son of a small-scale road haulage contractor from Ghanzi. The contractor had been the *fons et origo* of the family's prosperity: he had started with one vehicle, a pensioned-off Bedford truck of uncertain and possibly illegal provenance, and had progressed by dint of hard work to the ownership of a fleet of sixteen cattle trucks. These had plied their trade between Ghanzi and other cattle-raising districts in the west of the country and Lobatse, the headquarters of the national livestock industry, down in Botswana's southeastern corner. The cattle trucks had been followed by buses, and eventually by refrigerated transport to bring vegetables and other frozen foods from factories as far away as Durban, on the Indian Ocean. By the time that the grandfather died, the family business had become large enough to support four uncles—the husbands of Lucas's sisters—and their total of eleven sons, all working in one capacity or another in the office and marshalling yards in Gaborone. Presiding over all this, though, was Lucas Modikwe, father of Queenie-Queenie and Hercules, and husband of Mma Tippy Modikwe. He owned eighty per cent of the company's shares, the remainder being held, in diluted holdings, by the uncles and their sons. Everybody understood what the share register would anyway reveal: Lucas Modikwe could do as he liked with this sprawling and prosperous company. He also decided, in a general way, what the family's attitude would be towards those with whom they came into contact, whether as employees, customers, supplicants, or suitors.

Hercules was the first-born child of Lucas and Tippy. The arrival of a son was a source of great pride to Lucas, particularly since the baby was the largest child of either sex born that year at the Princess Marina Hospital in Gaborone. The sheer weight of the baby—twelve pounds and one ounce—meant that the labour was long and arduous: thirty-two hours, and at the end of it Tippy had not been in a fit state to share her husband's delight at the birth. He saw this, and generously assured her that, having presented him with such a fine son, he would not expect her to go through the gruelling experience again. "We can be a small family," he said. "We do not need to have many children."

In spite of this resolution, Tippy wanted a daughter, and assured Lucas that a second pregnancy and delivery would be altogether easier. "The first time is a big problem," she said. "The second is always much easier."

But it was not, or at least it was only very slightly less traumatic.

Queenie-Queenie arrived after a shorter labour and weighed considerably less than her brother, but the delivery led to severe complications for the mother, and these were sufficient to resurrect the parents' earlier resolve. There would be no more children. "We have one of each," said Lucas, "and we shall be very satisfied with that. God has sent us two children, and we shall not ask him for any more."

Hercules was two years older than Queenie-Queenie, but he showed none of the resentment or rivalry that older children might feel on the arrival of a younger sibling. He seemed immensely proud of his sister, and this pride grew with each fresh achievement of the young Queenie-Queenie. Her first steps, taken in his presence, led to whoops of delight and shouted claims that he had taught her to walk. In the same way, he solemnly told relatives that it was he who should get the credit for her first real achievement at school: a prize for a drawing she did of a hoopoe. "I have taught her everything," he announced with an eight-year-old's solemnity. "I am her teacher, you see."

The pride and affection Hercules showered on his sister was fully reciprocated. In her view, there was nothing he could not do; no feat of strength was beyond him, no task too daunting, no problem too difficult to admit of a solution at his hands. His disapproval, rarely shown, would send Queenie-Queenie into the deepest despair—would turn off the sun, she felt, until she was forgiven and the natural equilibrium of their relationship was restored.

Hercules was not the name given to him as an infant. In the Register of Births for the Gaborone district there was no Hercules Modikwe; there was, however, a Muso Ketakile Modikwe, Muso being the name of his maternal grandfather, and Ketakile being the family name of his paternal grandmother. The name Hercules was first used by an aunt, a teacher at a school in the north, who called him this when she first met him. The boy was then just over two, but already had the stocky, muscular constitution that was to become so evident later on.

"He is a strong one, this," she said, admiringly. "He will be a very strong man, just like Hercules."

Neither Lucas nor Tippy had heard of Hercules, and they had listened with interest to the aunt's version of the legend. She had a book of Greek and Roman stories, she explained, and had learned of Hercules from that. "I do not think he existed," she said. "These tales are all false. They are nonsense, really, like some of the stories the grandmothers tell here. You know—those stories about talking birds and so on."

"Maybe there was a really strong man some time ago," said Lucas. "Sometimes these stories are about something that was almost true."

"That's possible," said the aunt. "But one thing is certain: this boy will be just like Hercules—very, very strong."

The name stuck, and by the time Muso went to school Hercules was the only name to which he would answer. That was entered into the school register as the child's name, and no more was heard of the names he had been given at birth. It proved appropriate, as nicknames often do: Hercules was by far the strongest boy in his age group at school, his strength being an effortless expression of his underlying muscularity. Yet he was not satisfied with the endowments of nature, and by the time he reached the teenage years he had begun a course of muscle-building, following manuals he had ordered from a body-building institute in Durban. These manuals showed *before* and *after* pictures of the transformation that could be expected, many of the successful body-builders being photographed on one of the beaches near Durban, muscles rippling under a glistening layer of the oil with which such people liked to anoint themselves. Hercules had less work to do than these young men to achieve the same result: he was already muscular and had only to look forward to an increase in muscle bulk, encouraging that strange bodily look in which small muscles seem to grow on the surface of underlying muscles, creating an undulating topography of ridges and valleys, dunes of tissue like the sandscape of the Namibian desert.

Lucas encouraged his son in his body-building. "If you're strong," he said, "you need never be afraid. Nobody will try to push you around. It is very good to be strong."

Tippy agreed, although she felt there were limits. "You do not want to end up with too many muscles," she warned. "If you have too many muscles, you will seize up. You can't move if you are made entirely of muscle."

Hercules listened, but was not deterred. By the time he was sixteen he was already becoming well known at the body-building competitions that were occasionally held at the Sun Hotel, and when he left school at eighteen, going straight into the family transport business, he already had two titles to his credit. For a year he had been Mr. Teenage Botswana, as well as runner-up in the Southern African Power Man competition held over the border at a popular South African resort. Now his sights were firmly set on the Mr. Botswana contest. This was still fourteen months away, a period during which Hercules would redouble his efforts to increase his already prodigious strength.

Queenie-Queenie followed his progress with special pride. It had been the greatest moment of her life, she felt, when she had read the *Botswana Daily News* headline: *Big Hope for Botswana Body-Building*. And there, beneath those echoing, dramatic words, had been a photograph of her brother—her own brother—the upper part of his body exposed, his muscles exhibited for the whole country to marvel over. "Yes," she said to those who enquired, "that is my brother, as it happens. Yes, he is very strong, but he is also very kind and gentle. Strong men do not need to throw their weight around. Strong men have nothing to prove, you know."

Queenie-Queenie had mentioned to Charlie that she had a

brother, but had not said much about him. Certainly she had not mentioned the body-building, nor the titles, nor the fact that she spent at least an hour a day preparing for him the special high-protein foods that he ate in place of regular meals. These required close attention to temperature and had to be served in a special order at particular intervals, often between bouts of intense weight-lifting. Queenie-Queenie kept a record of all this, complete with graphs and tables to show body-mass index, body temperature, liquid consumption, and so on.

"Making the perfect body is a science," pronounced Hercules. "You are a scientist now, Queenie-Queenie."

Hercules took a protective interest in his sister's life. He had been a stout defender of her interests at school, where, if there were occasional incidents of bullying, none of these was ever directed at Queenie-Queenie—for obvious reasons. He could see that his sister was attractive, and would come to the attention of boys, but he let it be known that any boy who wanted to approach her would have to come through him, and such interviews proved to be rare. One unfortunate boy who asked whether he could invite Queenie-Queenie to accompany him to the cinema was left in no doubt that such requests would be given short shrift. He was lifted up, given a good shaking, and then told to ask the same question once he had a job, a car, and twenty thousand pula in the bank. Word of that soon got round, and there were no further requests made to Hercules.

Queenie-Queenie was vaguely aware that Hercules was acting as some sort of gate-keeper. She did not mind this—indeed she was flattered by her brother's concern. She found boys interesting enough, but was in no hurry to start seeing any one boy in particular. There would be time enough for that in the future, she thought, when she imagined that a suitable man would present himself, propose to her, and agree to a proper Botswana wedding with a great deal of feasting, music, and smart clothing. Then she would carry out her long-cherished plan to present her parents with the grandchildren they were hoping for, while at the same time continuing to cook high-protein meals for her brother. Queenie-Queenie was a home-loving person, and these ambitions were quite enough for her.

Charlie was not her first boyfriend. Shortly after she had taken up her first job, as an assistant in another, less fashionable dress shop, she had been asked out by a young man working in a domestic appliance shop next door. She liked him, and had begun to see him without telling Hercules or her parents. Then, quite abruptly, the young man had broken off the relationship without any explanation other than a mumbled excuse about being too busy and having to work on the book-keeping course he was pursuing at night school. The real reason, unknown to Queenie-Queenie, was that her brother had made an adverse assessment of the suitor's intentions. Hercules had heard of the relationship, made enquiries, and discovered that the young man had had four girlfriends in the previous eighteen months. Drawing his own conclusions from this, he had visited the young man in his lodgings and made it clear to him that he should no longer see Queenie-Queenie. The young man, who recognised Hercules from his photograph in the *Botswana Daily News,* did not argue, and was quick to give the necessary assurances.

This habit of intimidating his sister's would-be friends might suggest that Hercules was a bully. But he was not: in most of his dealings with people he was courteous, even slightly diffident; it was only when it came to the protection of what he saw as his family's interests that he used the undoubted leverage that his superior strength gave him. He was sure that in time a suitable young man would appear, and when that happened he would give the liaison all the support he could muster. But for the time being Queenie-Queenie needed protection from predators, of which there were considerable numbers, Lotharios all, circling any beautiful—and rich—young women. It would be folly,

Hercules thought, for a brother or any other close relative to ignore the danger that such men posed to Botswana womanhood.

As for the parents, they remained unaware of any young men whom their daughter was seeing. They lavished attention on Queenie-Queenie, whose photographs in various poses adorned every wall of their house; they spoke of her to their friends to such an extent that all but the most intimate, loyal friends dreaded the subject; and it was only reluctantly that they agreed to her finding work outside the safe confines of the family firm. She was adamant, though, that she wanted to earn her own living; she did not want people to know that her father was well off, and she never mentioned the fact to anybody—and especially not to Charlie.

"My father drives a truck," she said to him when he had asked her about her family. "He moves cattle—and sometimes other things."

Charlie had concluded that Queenie-Queenie's father was a long-distance truck driver of the sort one encountered on every journey from the north down to Lobatse, carting cattle to market. It was good enough work, if nothing special, and no further mention was made of it.

"You should tell him I'm a mechanic," he said. "If his truck needs fixing, I can do it cheaply. Tell him that."

Queenie-Queenie smiled. She was about to explain that her father already employed six mechanics. But she did not do so. If a boy liked her in the belief that she was just an ordinary girl, then his motives would be clear. The last thing she wanted was a boy who liked money more than the promptings of his heart. She had once read a magazine story about just that problem, and she had felt appalled by the plight in which the heroine found herself. How could anybody live with the suspicion that her partner, her spouse perhaps, had only taken her on because of the dowry that came with her? She could not; not for one moment, and for this reason she said nothing more to Charlie about her parents and steadfastly declined his suggestions that he could run her home.

"But you don't have a car, Charlie," she pointed out. "How can you run me home?"

"I can use one from the garage," said Charlie. "There is a truck that Mr. J.L.B. Matekoni lets me drive."

Queenie-Queenie smiled. "You're sweet, Charlie. But I won't be driven back in a truck. No, that would not be a good thing."

"It's a comfortable truck," said Charlie. "And I could put a blanket over the front seat—to protect you from grease."

But she shook her head, closing the subject. "No. I wouldn't want that, Charlie."

He did not press the point, but he found himself wondering about the house she lived in. Was it shame over humble conditions that made her unwilling to show him her home? He could understand that—many people were ashamed of the conditions in which they lived their lives. Poverty was grubby, dirty even, and people did not like its taint, even if it was not in any way their fault. But how did you convince them that it didn't matter, that what counted was the person rather than the surrounding circumstances? Charlie was still a young man, and young men do not always grasp that, but his outlook was maturing—even if rather late, according to Mma Makutsi—and he understood how Queenie-Queenie might feel. That surprised him; he had never taken girls particularly seriously—another of Mma Makutsi's charges against him—but with Queenie-Queenie he found it was different. He found himself worrying about how she might feel about things; he imagined what she would be thinking; he found himself thinking of how she looked at the world, and he wanted to think about it in the same way. Charlie was growing up.

QUEENIE-QUEENIE allowed him to take her hand when he arrived. He pressed it gently, before she withdrew it. They were not at the stage of kissing one another in public which, anyway, was still frowned upon by some. "So, Charlie," said Queenie-Queenie. "What's new?"

Charlie waved a hand. "We've got a big case coming up," he said. "I can't really talk about it too much. A hit-and-run case."

Queenie-Queenie's eyes widened. "Oh," she said. "Will you find the driver?"

Charlie waved a hand insouciantly. "I'll do my best. I can never guarantee results, you know."

Queenie-Queenie smiled. "I'm sure you're very good at all this, Charlie."

"I get by," said Charlie, thinking about how Mma Makutsi never told him he was good at being a detective. Yet here was somebody who knew nothing about his work expressing confidence in him. And it cost you nothing, thought Charlie, to say something nice to somebody.

"And the garage?" asked Queenie-Queenie. "You were working there too?"

Charlie nodded. "I lend a hand," he said. "I help them out when they're busy. The boss relies on me, I suppose."

He swallowed. These were not real lies; they were exaggerations, perhaps, but they harmed nobody, and anyway, if only people treated him fairly, they would probably be true. If Mr. J.L.B. Matekoni would let him get on with his work without constantly telling him he was doing it incorrectly, then he would become good enough to be relied upon. So it was not *really* untrue.

Charlie now asked Queenie-Queenie about her day.

"Very busy," she replied. "There's a big wedding coming up and they're coming to us for dresses. All the guests, or most of them. Big dresses. Big shoes. These people are spending a lot of money."

"Weddings . . . ," mused Charlie, leaving the sentence unfinished. Then he went on, "Who's getting married?"

Queenie-Queenie shrugged. "Some guy—I don't know him. But the bride works at the President Hotel. She arranges their functions— you know, business dinners and so on. She has lots of friends and they all want a better dress than everyone else."

Charlie laughed. "That's because they'll be looking for husbands. Weddings are a good place to meet a husband."

Queenie-Queenie thought about this. "Many of them, maybe," she said at last. "But not all. Not all girls want a husband, you know. Not all."

Charlie looked sceptical. "What do they want, then?"

"They want the same as men want. A good job. Money to buy food. A good time."

"And a husband," added Charlie.

"Not all," Queenie-Queenie repeated.

There was a bright checked tablecloth covering the table at which they were sitting. Coffee, ordered by Queenie-Queenie, had been brought to the table. Charlie fingered the edge of the tablecloth. He was not sure whether he should say what he wanted to say, but he decided to take the risk.

"And you, Queenie? Do you want a husband?"

Queenie-Queenie did not blink. "Yes, I'd like a husband."

There was a silence.

"What sort of husband?" asked Charlie.

She shrugged. "I haven't made my mind up yet. But he would have to have a good sense of humour."

I have, thought Charlie.

"And he would have to be kind."

I'm definitely kind, thought Charlie. *Ask Fanwell. Ask anybody. They'll all say the same thing.*

"And it would be nice if he's good-looking . . ."

No difficulty there, thought Charlie.

"And likes lots of children."

Children, thought Charlie. *Well, there's nothing wrong with children.*

He noticed that Queenie-Queenie was staring at him. Was she expecting a response? Was she trying to say something other than to list the requirements of the ideal husband? But then he saw that she was not so much staring at him, but beyond him. He half-turned in his seat. Queenie-Queenie muttered something, and he turned back to look at her.

"What, Queenie?"

Now her voice was clearer. "My brother."

Charlie twisted around again, just as Hercules reached their table. He rose to his feet, awkwardly and uncertainly, bringing himself up against the slightly taller, but considerably more muscular, figure of Hercules. He glanced down at Queenie-Queenie, who had shifted unhappily in her seat. Hercules was looking at his sister too, an eyebrow raised in unambiguous puzzlement. Eventually Queenie-Queenie broke the silence. "This is Charlie," she said. "Charlie, this is my brother, Hercules." And then to Hercules, "You can sit down, Hercules. You can have coffee with us."

Charlie shot her an agonised glance. He did not want Hercules to join them for coffee. Everything was ruined now, ruined utterly. Hercules, though, did not hesitate to accept the invitation. "I'm glad I was passing," he said. "It is good to see you, sister."

Queenie-Queenie nodded. "It is good to see you, brother."

The formalities over, Hercules turned to Charlie. "So, Charlie," he said. "So what brings you here?"

Charlie frowned. What sort of question was that? What right had one person to ask another person, met in a public place, what brought him there? He was as entitled as anybody, he felt, to be sitting in that coffee bar, drinking coffee. He did not have to answer the question, *What brought you here?* He decided that a light-hearted response would be the best.

"A minibus," he said.

It took Hercules a few moments to deal with that answer. Then he said, "So, a minibus."

Charlie grinned nervously at Queenie-Queenie. "Yes, I took a minibus from my work. Along the Tlokweng Road. I got off on the other side of that road over there, and then I walked."

Hercules pursed his lips. "So, you walked?"

"Yes," said Charlie. "I walked." He grinned again at Queenie-Queenie, who said nothing.

Now Hercules said, "You're a friend of my sister's, then?"

Charlie nodded. "Yes, I hope so." He looked at Queenie-Queenie. He felt it was time for her to become involved in this conversation, but she remained silent.

Hercules was still staring at him, his outward expression one of interest rather than hostility. But, just beneath that, Charlie detected a current of antagonism: this was clearly not a friendly encounter, in spite of the outward civility.

Hercules now asked a different question. "Your work, Rra—you mentioned your work. What work do you do?"

Charlie took a deep breath. "I'm a detective."

The effect on Hercules was immediate. The truculent tone in which the question had been asked was replaced with a note of admiration. "A detective! So you are police then, Rra? CID?"

Charlie shook his head. "Private," he said. "None of that police business. Private investigator."

Hercules let out a low whistle. "Here in Gaborone? There are private detectives here in town? Right here? True as God?"

Charlie's manner was nonchalant. "Of course. There are many people who have problems, you know. They come to us."

Queenie-Queenie appeared to be reassured by her brother's change of tone. "It's very important work," she said. "He is with the No. 1 Ladies' Detective Agency."

Charlie nodded. "I am a partner there."

He said this without thinking, and immediately regretted it. He looked away. *I should be a partner,* he thought. And then he thought: We are all partners in the business—in a sense. Everybody who works with others is a partner in the thing they did together. That was common sense.

But this was not what interested Hercules. "Ladies?" he said. "No. 1 Ladies' Detective Agency?"

Charlie made a careless gesture. "Oh, that is just the name. We have always used that name so that ladies will come to us for help with their problems." He leaned forward, as if to impart a confidence. "You know how it is with ladies, Rra? They worry about many things. Is their husband behaving himself? Has he got a secret girlfriend? Is he giving money to somebody and not bringing it home? There are many problems in a lady's life, Rra—many big problems."

Hercules frowned. "So you only help ladies?"

Charlie explained that this was far from the case. "We have many men who come to us too. They come because they think that anybody who can solve the problems that ladies have will be able to solve men's problems too."

"So the people who work there are not just ladies, then?"

Charlie shook his head. "I have some lady colleagues," he said. "But . . ."

Hercules finished the sentence for him. "But you are the manager, and the ladies work for you?"

Charlie laughed. "We all work together, Rra. That is the modern idea, isn't it? This business of men being the boss and the ladies being the secretaries is long gone. We all work together now—and the ladies have a big part to play."

"But you must have a secretary," Hercules persisted. "There must be somebody to type the letters and open the mail, and so on. My father has such people in his business."

Charlie was confused. Did a truck driver need a secretary? And then there was the reference to *such people*. This suggested more than one secretary. Even if a truck driver had one secretary—which was unlikely—he would certainly not have need of two or more. But there was Hercules' question, which needed answering, and so Charlie, having dug the beginnings of a hole for himself, burrowed deeper. "A secretary, Rra? Yes, we have a secretary. There is a lady called Mma Makutsi, who is a trained secretary. She does all the filing and so on . . ." His voice dropped away as he added, ". . . for me."

Hercules appeared satisfied. "Every good business needs a Mma Makutsi," he said. "There is nothing worse than having papers filed in the wrong place. True as God."

"Yes," said Charlie enthusiastically. "There is nothing worse than that." *And nothing worse than telling big lies,* he thought.

Hercules looked pensive. "We sometimes have problems in the business," he said. "My father gets very worried if he thinks that somebody is cheating us. Maybe we should come to your place, Rra, and get you to sort things out for us. Should I come around tomorrow? Where exactly is your office, Rra?"

Charlie froze. He looked mutely at Queenie-Queenie, but she was looking at her nails, having seemingly lost interest in what Hercules was saying.

"Well, Rra? How far down the Tlokweng Road is it?"

Charlie swallowed. "We are very busy at present," he said, his voice sounding oddly strangled. "We cannot take on any new cases right now." He paused, before adding lamely, "Perhaps some time in the future, Rra. I'll let you know."

Hercules looked disgruntled. "You shouldn't turn away business," he said gruffly. "If my father had done that, then where would we be today?"

Charlie was relieved that an immediate crisis had been averted. He could afford to be magnanimous now. "You're right, Rra. I shall raise that with my colleagues. Perhaps we need to expand."

"Expansion is the thing," said Hercules. "That's right, isn't it, Queenie?"

Queenie-Queenie abandoned her study of her nails. "Yes, brother, that's right. Expand, expand, expand."

A mug of coffee had now been delivered for Hercules, and he swallowed this in a single draught. Then he looked again at Charlie. "Arm-wrestle?" he said.

Charlie was confused.

"He wants you to arm-wrestle with him," explained Queenie-Queenie. She looked at Charlie with concern. "I have to warn you: he's very strong." She turned to her brother and admonished him. "Don't hurt Charlie. He's not used to it."

"Of course I won't hurt him," Hercules reassured her. "Nobody gets hurt in an arm-wrestle. True as God. Okay, Charlie? Arm-wrestle?"

CHAPTER SEVEN

AN ASSISTANT TO AN ASSISTANT

THE FOLLOWING DAY Mma Ramotswe made one of her lists. These were sometimes entitled *Things to be done today;* on other occasions they were headed *Things to be done soon,* and, rather more rarely, simply *Things to be done.* The descending order of urgency was matched by a descending rate of fulfilment. *Things to be done* tended to be merely aspirational—catalogues of things that would be done if conditions were right or if there was nothing else more pressing to be done. *Things to be done today* were, as Mr. J.L.B. Matekoni once wryly observed, those tasks that should have been done yesterday but which, not having been done, were now weighing heavily on Mma Ramotswe.

"Perhaps you might have another list altogether, Mma," he suggested. "This could be called *Things I'll never do.* You would not feel uncomfortable reading that list, as you will have already admitted that these are things you do not want to do—and will not do."

Mma Ramotswe laughed. "It would include many wishes," she said. "It would have all those things that it would have been nice to do."

Mr. J.L.B. Matekoni warmed to the theme. "And you could have yet another list," he said. *"Things that other people should do, but don't seem to be doing."*

Mma Ramotswe thought for a while. "That could be a very long list," she said. "There are many people who do not do what they should be doing."

"They probably have no lists," said Mr. J.L.B. Matekoni. "If they did, then they might do some of the things they should be doing but are not."

But now, on that particular day, she set off to the office from her house on Zebra Drive, her tiny white van coughing and spluttering in the cool air of morning, like a person clearing his or her throat of the furriness of the night. The van was due for a service, and she would speak to Mr. J.L.B. Matekoni about that, although she always dreaded raising the subject with him. Her husband, although tolerant of just about everything, had limited understanding of why anybody should wish to drive an aged and ailing vehicle when there were modern vehicles looking for a home. He had heard the argument about character—and he could go along with that to an extent. He readily agreed with those who said that modern cars lacked individuality—he understood exactly what they meant—but at the same time his view as a mechanic could hardly be anything other than that when the time came for a car to be put down, it had to be put down. That was what vets did with animals that had no chance of recovery: to save them suffering, they would be painlessly eased out of this world. A mechanic, he thought, should do the same thing with a vehicle that had reached the end of its natural span of years. The owner might be attached to it, just as people were attached to their pets, but there was a point at which the heart should be stilled and the hard decision be made. It was the last kindness an owner could show an animal or a machine. As she drove into work, Mma Ramotswe made a mental note to talk to Mr. J.L.B. Matekoni about a service for the van, but did not dwell on the matter. Her thoughts were focused rather on the two items that topped her current *Things to be done today* list. Indeed, these two tasks were the *only* items on that list, and each of them, in their own particular way, was weighing heavily on her mind. Neither required much expansion. First there was *Election: notify council of withdrawal.* That, surely, was clear enough. Then came: *Marang case: think of something (anything).* That, too, was unambiguous, and yet, like the first task, it was easier said than done.

The election issue would probably have to be put off until the afternoon, when, as she had found out, the relevant council official, who only worked part-time, would be in her office. She would seek an appointment and explain that regretfully she had decided to withdraw from the council election. Since signing the paper, she had been thinking—it had kept her awake last night—and she had become more and more certain that she had made a grave error of judgement. She was really not the right person for this important and very public role. She felt uneasy about changing her mind, but it was her life, after all, and, although she had always been prepared to do her civic duty, she now felt that there must be others who would have more time for council affairs. She understood the danger of a Violet Sephotho victory, but surely there would be others who would step forward once they realised that Violet was the alternative. She hoped that they would understand, but, even if they did not, there was not much they could do about it. A person could not be forced to stand for office—that would be absurd. She imagined the scene. An official might call on some poor unfortunate citizen and say to her: *I'm terribly sorry, but you have been elected President of Botswana. I know you don't want to do it, but there you are: this is a democracy, and that is how democracies work.*

She allowed herself a smile at the thought. How would Mma

Potokwane react if that happened to her? Would she be able to excuse herself on the grounds that she had quite enough to do in running the Orphan Farm, without taking on the country as well? That would be a cogent and powerful excuse: the children relied on Mma Potokwane, as did the housemothers who looked after them. If she were to go off to live in State House, then who would make the duty rosters, who would order the food for the kitchens, and who would cajole local businesses into sending out the support they gave—the surplus equipment, the spare food, the blankets and toys—all of that? Of course, Mma Potokwane might be delighted to accept, and might come up with some substitute matron from somewhere. She would make, Mma Ramotswe was sure, a very fine president, if perhaps a little bit—just a touch—on the bossy side. With Mma Potokwane installed in the president's office, she would be able to go and visit her and talk about how things were going in the country. They would eat Mma Potokwane's fruit cake, which would be delivered from the presidential kitchens—wherever they were—in a police car, with its lights flashing . . . And woe betide any politician who broke ranks on Potokwane policy: he would be given a dressing-down that he would not forget in a hurry—oh, yes, he would. There were many politicians, come to think of it, who could do with such treatment right now, and it would be a fine spectacle for the country as a whole to watch.

But then she stopped thinking these satisfactory thoughts and turned her mind to the other pressing matter—the Marang case. The problem there was that she had no idea at all how even to start that investigation. There were no witnesses to whom she could speak, no physical evidence of any sort; and, in the absence of these, she could not see what she could do. Perhaps she could go up to Mochudi— as she thought she certainly would have to do at some point—and speak to people. But what would she say? She imagined going to the market there and asking people whether they had seen a blue car being driven suspiciously. She could do that easily enough, but the problem with such a question was that it was most likely to provoke either a look of bafflement or, more likely, a gale of laughter. *A blue car being driven suspiciously, Mma? What do you actually mean by that? Driven slowly, by somebody wearing dark glasses? Creeping along the side of the road as if the car knew that it had no business being there? Going everywhere in reverse rather than in forward gear?* That last would surely be suspicious, unless, of course, it was a car that could only go backwards rather than forwards. She had heard Charlie and Fanwell talking about such a car some time ago but had assumed that it was just part of their usual nonsensical chatter—and anyway, that was a mechanical issue rather than anything bearing upon guilt.

She reached her destination—the acacia tree at the back of the agency office. Under the shelter of its delicate grey-green foliage she parked the van, switching off the ignition with a deeply felt sigh. And the van, as if in sympathetic response to its owner's burden of cares, gave a few final splutters before its engine became silent. "Don't worry, old friend," she muttered, "I shall never allow them to scrap you." She looked at the van, and it looked back at her with its small, rather lopsided headlights, mute in its gratitude, as old and trusty machinery could be. Such machinery was happy to serve, and did, until at last its valiant heart could serve no longer.

Mma Makutsi was already in the office, as was Charlie, who had his arm in a sling. Mma Makutsi was examining the injury and asking him how it had happened.

Mma Ramotswe could tell that Charlie was embarrassed. He glanced at her as she came in, and then quickly looked away again.

"See this, Mma?" said Mma Makutsi. "Charlie's got his arm in a sling."

Mma Ramotswe crossed the room to her desk. "So I see." She put her bag down on the floor. "Poor you, Charlie. I hope you're all right."

Charlie nodded. "I only have to wear it for a day or two," he said. "That's what they told me at the clinic."

"I was just asking Charlie what did it," said Mma Makutsi. Turning to him, she asked again. "So, Charlie, why is your arm in this sling?"

"I hurt it," Charlie replied tersely. "It's nothing serious. Just a pulled muscle maybe."

"Picking something up?" asked Mma Makutsi. "Lifting something? You have to be careful about that sort of thing, you know. Phuti had somebody at the shop who thought that he could lift a sofa all by himself." She turned to face Mma Ramotswe as she described the incident. "Not a small sofa, Mma. Not one of those two-person sofas—the ones that Phuti calls a *starter sofa*. Not one of those, but a four-seater, one that we call an *executive sofa*. He picked up one of those—silly man—and pulled something in both his shoulders, his back, and somewhere down in his legs—the bit that makes your legs go backwards and forwards, that bit. He couldn't move for weeks, and Phuti had to pay him all the time he was off work because it was an *industrial injury*."

Charlie said nothing; he was adjusting the white cloth of his sling. Mma Ramotswe was silent too; sometimes these stories of Mma Makutsi's went off at a tangent.

"I don't think," Mma Makutsi continued, "that people should be able to get compensation for doing something stupid. If you do something stupid—like try to pick up an executive sofa—then I think you can't go to your boss and say, *It's all your fault, Boss.* I don't think that at all. You shouldn't get compensation for doing something stupid, and nor should you get compensation for *being* stupid." She paused. "You wouldn't have done anything stupid, would you, Charlie?"

As Mma Makutsi asked this question, and as Charlie reacted to it, Mma Ramotswe realised that in all probability Charlie had indeed done something stupid. But this realisation only made her want to defend him. Of course young men did stupid things—it was part of being a young man—and if you saw a young man with an arm in a sling, then you had every reason to assume that his injury was the result of some act of folly. But even if you reached that entirely feasible conclusion, you might still wish to spare the young man his embarrassment, and she wanted to do that for Charlie.

"I'm sure that Charlie has not done something stupid, Mma Makutsi," she said. "I think that we—"

She was not allowed to finish. "Oh, I'm not so sure, Mma. How did you get it, Charlie? Why won't you tell us?"

"I twisted my arm," muttered Charlie. "I hit it on something."

Mma Makutsi was quick to sense a contradiction. "Twisted it? Or hit it? You can't do two things at the same time, can you?"

"Twisted it," Charlie replied.

"How?" pressed Mma Makutsi.

"Let's not worry about that," said Mma Ramotswe. "Spilt milk is spilt milk. It doesn't matter how you spill it."

"That's right," said Charlie, relieved at the support he was receiving.

"But I don't see why you won't—"

It was Mma Ramotswe's turn to cut Mma Makutsi short. "Mma Makutsi," she said, raising her voice slightly, "I think we should have tea. And then we can talk about this Marang business. I have some important news to give you." She did not have any important news, but she thought that this at least would get Mma Makutsi off the subject of Charlie's arm, saving the young man further interrogation.

"YOUR TEA," said Mma Makutsi, placing Mma Ramotswe's mug on the desk in front of her. "Red bush for you, Mma, and special English

Breakfast for me and Charlie." She placed Charlie's mug on a filing cabinet where he could take it with his good arm.

"English Breakfast," mused Charlie. "Why do they call it that, Mma Makutsi?"

Mma Makutsi made a gesture to suggest that everybody should know the answer to that. "Because that is what they drink for their breakfast over there," she said. "English people are always drinking tea. That is something they brought to Africa. They said, *Why don't you drink tea like us?* And we said, *Yes, that's a good idea, we'll drink tea.*"

"And then we said, *Go back to your place and drink tea there,*" said Charlie. "That's what people like Nkrumah said to the English people, way back. I learned about that at school."

Mma Ramotswe took a sip from her mug. "There is enough tea for everybody," she said. "There is enough tea for everybody in the world, if we share it properly."

"Yes, if we share it properly," said Charlie. "But do we? There are some people who take too much tea, Mma. I learned about that too."

"Yes," said Mma Makutsi, lifting her mug to her lips. "There are. There are people who want more than their fair share of tea." She looked out of the window, and the sun briefly caught the lenses of her large round spectacles. If ever there were a warning to those who would take more than their fair share of tea, then this was it. She put down her cup. "Now, Mma," she said, "what was this news you have for us?"

Mma Ramotswe had to think quickly. "It's news that there's no news," she said. "The news is . . ." She faltered. She should have tried to distract Mma Makutsi in some other way—now it was too late. "The news is, I'm afraid, that I have no news. In other words, I cannot think of what to do in the Marang enquiry. I have thought and thought, but no ideas have come to me. That's the news, Mma."

Mma Makutsi frowned. "That is not very helpful, Mma. Forgive me for saying that, but it doesn't bring us any closer to a solution."

Charlie, who had gulped down his tea, as he usually did, suddenly raised a finger of his undamaged hand. "I have an idea," he announced.

They both turned to look at him.

"I have a friend in Mochudi," he said. "He and I go back a long, long way. Six years—maybe more. He works for a cattle-feed company."

They waited.

"He's always been very keen on cars," Charlie continued. "He wanted to be a mechanic, but he wasn't accepted for training, and so he became one of those people who fix the bodywork of cars when they have an accident. He takes out dents. He spray-paints cars."

Mma Makutsi pointed out that Charlie had said that his friend worked for a cattle-feed company. Where did cars come into it?

"He fixes cars in his spare time," said Charlie. "There was nowhere up there to have dents taken out. His uncle has a workshop, and my friend does it with his uncle. It's cheaper than bringing your car down to Gaborone."

Mma Ramotswe broke into a broad smile. "I can see where this is going, Charlie. Well done. You think that if the car was damaged in the accident—even just a small dent where it hit poor Dr. Marang, then . . ."

Charlie nodded enthusiastically. "Yes, then the driver would have wanted the evidence covered up. He'd want the dent fixed, wouldn't he?"

Mma Makutsi clapped her hands together. "Very clever, Charlie!" she exclaimed. "Very, very clever!"

Charlie basked in the admiration of the two women. "It's just an idea, of course," he said. "He may not be able to tell us anything, but he could, you know."

"It's just an idea," echoed Mma Ramotswe, "but it's the only idea we have at the moment. It gives us something to work on." She paused. "I think that you should go to see this friend of yours up in Mochudi, Charlie. You could go today, if he's there."

Mma Makutsi agreed. "I could go with him," she said. "I could go with him to supervise."

Mma Ramotswe was tactful. "It's very good of you to offer, Mma, but I think maybe we should give Charlie the chance to conduct an independent investigation. You would be able to do it much more quickly than he would, Mma, because you are so senior—and generally so successful. But I think it would be good for Charlie to spread his wings a bit, don't you think?"

Flattered at the tribute, Mma Makutsi was quick to agree that Charlie should go to Mochudi by himself.

"Take my van," said Mma Ramotswe. "I'll go home with Mr. J.L.B. Matekoni."

Charlie smiled. "I will be very careful, Mma Ramotswe."

"Of course you will be, Charlie," she said. "And Mma Makutsi will give you some expenses money out of the petty cash."

Charlie's face suddenly fell. "My arm, Mma. I'd forgotten about my arm."

Mma Ramotswe thought for a moment. "How about Fanwell? I can see whether Mr. J.L.B. Matekoni will give him the afternoon off. He can be your driver—your assistant, so to speak."

Charlie thought this a very good idea, as did Fanwell when he was approached. "I will be an assistant detective for an afternoon," he said, rubbing his hands together.

"Assistant to an assistant to a detective," corrected Mma Makutsi. It was important, she felt, to get terminology right, especially when it came to job descriptions and positions. You had to watch people—if you were not careful, all sorts of people would promote themselves well above their real station in life, causing nothing but confusion and uncertainty. That this principle should apply to her as well was not something she had given much thought to—in fact, she had given it none, which was just as well, given her own record.

Talk about criticising others for the things you do yourself! remarked her shoes, but in a voice so muted, a tone so reedy and slight, that it might have been the sound of the wind in the acacia, the sound of dust blowing over the land, the sound made by the beating of a bird's wing on the yielding air.

_____

CHAPTER EIGHT

THE REAL VOICE OF BOTSWANA

MMA RAMOTSWE had planned to go to the council offices at three that afternoon. Her mind was now firmly made up: she would hand in her letter of withdrawal, explain herself to the official, and then telephone Mma Potokwane and tell her that, much as she appreciated the faith the matron had shown in her, a political career was just not for her. She would present Mma Potokwane with a *fait accompli,* and thus prevent her friend from exercising any of her undoubted persuasive powers. She told Mma Makutsi of her decision shortly before lunch. "I have thought very hard about this," Mma Ramotswe said. "I have gone over all the pros and cons, Mma, and I feel that on balance I should not do this."

Mma Makutsi stared at her in disbelief. "But you said you would, Mma. You said so. I was there. I heard you."

Mma Ramotswe acknowledged that this was so, but pointed out that a person had a right to change her mind. "You've changed your mind in the past, Mma—we all have. If we aren't allowed to change our minds, then where would we be?"

But Mma Makutsi was not to be put off. "Yes, we can change

our minds, Mma, but not in very important matters. There are times when, if you change your mind, all will be lost. This is one of them."

"All will not be lost," said Mma Ramotswe, trying to calm her down. "The world will go on. The council will get by without me."

Mma Makutsi's voice rose. "But what about Violet Sephotho? What about her? If she wins, then we may as well all pack up and leave."

"Oh come now, Mma," said Mma Ramotswe. "Even if Violet wins—which she may not do—there are many other people on the council. They won't all be like her. She won't end up as mayor."

This was an unfortunate tack. "Mayor!" screamed Mma Makutsi. "Violet Sephotho as mayor of Gaborone! Oh, Mma, we are lost; we are completely lost. It is the end. The end. I shall move to Francistown. I'll get Phuti to transfer the business . . ."

Mma Ramotswe struggled to be heard. "Nobody said Violet would be mayor, Mma. Nobody. So, please calm down."

Mma Makutsi looked at her reproachfully. "It's all very well for you to ask me to calm down, Mma, but it's not every day that you're . . ." She paused, and there was now another reproachful look. "It's not every day that you're betrayed."

Mma Ramotswe sighed. "I have not betrayed you, Mma. I have not betrayed anybody. I am simply saying that I do not want to be on the council. That is my decision."

"Then we need not discuss it any further, Mma," said Mma Makutsi. "I shall try to get over my disappointment—my deep disappointment. I shall try not to mention this very sad thing ever again." She busied herself with a pile of papers on her desk. "I shall not talk about it again, even though I am very, very upset."

"I'm sorry about that," said Mma Ramotswe. "I'd never want to upset you, Mma Makutsi."

Mma Makutsi sniffed. "We need to deal with some correspondence, Mma Ramotswe. There are bills to be sent out. Life has to go on in spite of things like this—in spite of major setbacks and defeats. We have to ignore those things—those betrayals and what-not—and look forward. That is the only way, Mma."

Mma Ramotswe sighed again. "Let's start with the bills," she suggested.

MMA POTOKWANE arrived at two-thirty, just as Mma Ramotswe was putting the final touches to an important business letter. The matron usually gave them some warning of her visits by telephoning to check up that they were free to see her, but on this occasion she was unannounced. *"Ko, ko!"* she called as she pushed open the door. "I hope I'm not disturbing anything."

Mma Makutsi looked up from the pile of envelopes she was addressing. Then she glanced across at Mma Ramotswe. This was going to be interesting.

Mma Ramotswe did her best to conceal the fact that she was considerably put out by this unexpected visit. It could not have come at a worse time: her plan had been to visit Mma Potokwane and present her with a done deed; now she would have to explain her change of mind without having the assurance of a signed-and-sealed withdrawal. But she tried not to show her dismay, welcoming Mma Potokwane warmly and gesturing for her to sit down in the client chair.

"I thought we could have a preliminary planning meeting," Mma Potokwane began as she lowered herself onto the chair. "There is a great deal to do, Mma Ramotswe." She turned to face Mma Makutsi, whom she had greeted perfunctorily. "And it's good that you're here too, Mma Makutsi. There will be an important role for every one of us. Even Charlie, if he wants to be involved."

Mma Potokwane laughed as she referred to Charlie and his possible involvement. She was surprised, though, when neither Mma Ramotswe nor Mma Makutsi seemed to be amused. For Mma Ramotswe, of course, an initial difficulty was that of getting a word in edgewise; once Mma Potokwane got the wind in her sails, it could be difficult to stop her, and they might be well into the meeting before she had the chance to disabuse her friend of the fundamental assumption that she was still standing for election. She would have to act—and she would have to act quickly.

"Mma Potokwane," she began, "I have been thinking very hard—"

She did not have the chance to finish. "So have I, Mma Ramotswe," interjected Mma Potokwane. "I have been thinking of little else, in fact, and I have come up with a plan. I hope you will—"

Mma Ramotswe tried again. And she would raise her voice. "I have changed my mind, Mma," she all but shouted. "I have decided that—"

Mma Potokwane brushed the attempted intervention aside. "No, Mma, let's not reach any firm decisions until we have looked at the various possibilities. So if you've changed your mind about strategies, that is something we can talk about a bit later on."

"Not about strategies . . . ," Mma Ramotswe struggled to say, but it was hopeless: Mma Potokwane had extracted a page from her notebook and was beginning to talk about an agenda.

It was left to Mma Makutsi to bring matters to a head. "Mma Potokwane!" she said, her glasses flashing as she spoke. "You have not been listening. Mma Ramotswe is trying to tell you something, and you are not giving her the chance to speak."

The reproof struck home. Mma Potokwane, momentarily taken aback, assured Mma Ramotswe that she had been listening all along—it was merely her own excitement over the campaign ahead that had made her a bit too enthusiastic. "But now I'm listening very carefully, Mma Ramotswe. Now I am going to let you say exactly what it was you wanted to say. After all, you are the candidate, and your views are more important than anybody else's."

Mma Ramotswe drew in her breath. "I have decided not to stand," she said. "And perhaps I should repeat that, just in case there is any misunderstanding. I have decided not to stand after all."

Mma Potokwane's eyes widened. "But you said, Mma—"

It was Mma Ramotswe's turn to interrupt. "I know I said I would, Mma, and I'm very sorry that I have misled people. But I feel that on further consideration I just cannot do this, Mma. I cannot. I am just an ordinary person, you see, and there is a limit to what I can take on."

Mma Potokwane lapsed into silence.

"I am very sorry, Mma," repeated Mma Ramotswe. "Very sorry."

Mma Potokwane turned to Mma Makutsi in mute appeal, but Mma Makutsi shook her head. "I tried to persuade Mma Ramotswe to change her mind," she said. "I pointed out the danger of Violet Sephotho becoming mayor, but I'm afraid she has decided."

Mma Potokwane turned back to face Mma Ramotswe again. Her hands were folded together in her lap, and she lowered her gaze to stare at them. Now, almost imperceptibly, her not-inconsiderable frame began to heave as she started to sob.

"My Botswana," she muttered through her tears. "My Botswana. What can we do to stop it falling into the wrong hands? What can we do to stop those greedy men who want to make everything into a place where they make money? What can we do to stop our country being sold?"

Mma Ramotswe did not know what to say.

"Because," continued Mma Potokwane, wiping her eyes, "if good people like you, Mma Ramotswe, will not stand up to those people, then they will win. They will win hands down and our town will be run by people who will not think of others, who will not care what they do, who will allow all sorts of people to build whatever they want, wherever they want, as long as it makes them money. Money, Mma. Money. Money. Everything will be judged by money—not by what people want, or what they feel, or what they believe in—just by money."

Mma Ramotswe rose to her feet and put an arm around her friend's shoulders.

"Can't we find somebody else?" she asked. "Isn't there anybody who could stand instead of me?"

Mma Potokwane shook her head. "There is nobody, Mma, who would stand a chance of winning. Violet will go out and get all her young men to vote for her. She will bribe the rest. You are the only person who is well enough liked to defeat that sort of thing. People trust you, Mma Ramotswe; they know that, when you speak, it is the real voice of Botswana speaking. They can hear that. You can always tell when it is the real Botswana speaking—always."

"Oh, Mma Potokwane," wailed Mma Ramotswe. "I do not want to let anybody down—it's just that I am not a person who wants to spend years and years on committees arguing about things."

Mma Potokwane looked up. "Years and years, Mma? No, no, no! You will not have to spend years on the council. Just one year. Maybe eighteen months. Then you can resign."

"I can resign?"

"Of course you can. Lots of politicians resign . . ." Mma Potokwane paused. "Mostly because they've done something that requires them to resign, but there are others, Mma, who resign because they want to spend more time with their families. That is what they say, Mma—I have heard them say that."

Mma Makutsi joined in. "One year, Mma Ramotswe. Just enough time to stop the Big Fun Hotel."

Mma Potokwane had now detected the chink through which her point could be made. "Yes, Mma," she said. "The Big Fun Hotel . . .

Nobody wants that, Mma—or at least nobody except a few greedy men. You can stop it, Mma. You can, you know."

Mma Ramotswe hesitated, and Mma Potokwane pressed on. "And here's a promise for you, Mma. If you decide you don't like it—that you really don't like it—you can come to me at any time—at any time, Mma—and say, *I want to give it up.* And I will not say anything to persuade you otherwise—not one word."

"Not a single word," added Mma Makutsi for emphasis.

They waited. Mma Ramotswe had been so certain, but now it seemed to her that it would be churlish to refuse something that would not bind her for too long and from which she could, if she really wished to do so, honourably resign.

"All right," she said. "I will do it, Mma Potokwane. But it has to be on the terms you have just laid down."

"Of course, of course," gushed Mma Potokwane. "All that is agreed—and Mma Makutsi is my witness."

"God too," said Mma Makutsi solemnly. "He heard what Mma Potokwane said and will hold her to her words."

Mma Potokwane threw a sideways glance at Mma Makutsi. "That too," she said. "That too."

THE NEXT SURPRISE came from Mma Makutsi. Once tea had been poured and they were all seated around Mma Ramotswe's desk, she announced that she had, in fact, spent the previous evening writing a manifesto for Mma Ramotswe's campaign and that she had it with her to read out for approval.

"I have already typed it out. It is here." She unfolded two sheets of paper. "Should I begin, ladies?"

"Yes," said Mma Potokwane. "I was hoping to follow an agenda, but this is a very important matter, Mma, and you should read it now."

Mma Makutsi took off her glasses and polished them carefully.

"Those are very fine spectacles," observed Mma Potokwane. "My husband needs bigger spectacles—he is missing seeing things at the sides. I have said that bigger spectacles will give him a wider field of vision."

"So he can see all of you," said Mma Makutsi.

It was a casual observation, not intended in any insulting way, but Mma Ramotswe gave her a sharp look. Mma Potokwane appeared not to notice.

"Please carry on," said Mma Ramotswe. "I am very eager to find out what I think."

Now Mma Potokwane looked at her sharply.

Mma Makutsi began. *"Ladies and gentlemen,"* she read out, *"this is a very important election."*

Mma Potokwane raised a finger. "Not ladies and gentlemen, Mma. This is a not a speech at a school prize-giving. This is talking to the people of Botswana, Mma."

"And are they not ladies and gentlemen?" protested Mma Makutsi.

"Yes, they are," Mma Potokwane replied. "They are ladies and gentlemen, but you don't speak to them like that in a manifesto. This is a manifesto, Mma—that is, a sort of mission statement. You start by saying: *Dear voters.* Or maybe you say: *People of Gaborone.* Something like that."

Mma Makutsi pouted, but reached for a pencil and altered her text. *"Dear voters,"* she intoned. *"This is a very important election. It is historic."*

"That's very good," applauded Mma Potokwane. "People like to think they are making history."

"Even if they're just choosing a councillor," said Mma Ramotswe.

Mma Potokwane smiled. "Even then, Mma. Even then. People like to think they are important."

Mma Makutsi continued her reading. *"In this election,"* she went on, *"you can choose what sort of person you want to have to represent you. You can decide whether you want a woman who has worked tirelessly for the benefit of humanity over many years—"*

Mma Ramotswe raised a hand. "Oh, Mma, you cannot say that. It is very kind of you, but it is not true. I have worked hard, but mostly I have been working for the business. Or I have been growing beans in my garden and cooking meals for the family and repairing Mr. J.L.B. Matekoni's work overalls. Things like that, Mma—not working tirelessly for the benefit of humanity."

Mma Potokwane proposed a compromise. "Write: *a woman who has been working very hard over many years,* Mma. Write that instead. That is certainly true."

Mma Makutsi reached for her pencil. *"Over many years,"* she intoned, *"or a woman who is one of the worst people in the country. This Violet Sephotho may not be known to some of you, but let me tell you . . ."*

Mma Potokwane was shaking her head vehemently, but it did not stop Mma Makutsi.

"Just let me read to the end, Mma. Then you can make any suggestions . . ." She emphasised the word *suggestions.* "So I shall continue, Mma. *But let me tell you what sort of person she is. Let us start at that most distinguished educational institution, the Botswana Secretarial College. How Violet Sephotho secured a place in that college has been a matter of discussion for years, but there are many who believe that she may have bribed her way in. I am not saying that is what I think, ladies and gentlemen . . .* No, I shall put in *dear voters* instead of that. *So, that is not what I necessarily think, dear voters, but there are many who do, and it is probably true. Once she was there, did she work hard? She did not. Once she was there, did she sit there in the lecture room, painting her nails and thinking about men? She most certainly did. Once she was there, did she get over ninety per cent in the final examinations? She most certainly did not. She got barely fifty per cent. She was lucky to pass. And yet here she is putting herself forward for election to public office on the basis of a mark of barely fifty per cent! What will History have to say about that?*

"I now turn to what she did afterwards. While other, more meritorious candidates found it hard to get a job, Violet Sephotho found herself being offered first-class jobs in more than one firm. How did she do it, if not by using her charms to work on the men who made the hiring decisions? She did not say anything specific, of course; oh, no, that woman is not so foolish as to leave any trail in writing, or even in words. She would go to the interviews in the most immodest dress; she would cross her legs in a way that weak men cannot resist; she would flutter her eyelashes— they are artificial, by the way, ladies . . . I mean, dear voters . . . and she would get the job on the spot while other candidates, wearing modest clothing and thinking only of the things they learned at the Botswana Secretarial College, were turned down again and again.

"And, since then, she has not hesitated to use underhand means to get what she wants. She has also tried to entice other people's husbands away from their wives. Ladies . . . and I will have to leave that reference to ladies in place, I think . . . ladies, if you want to keep your husbands, make sure you don't vote for a proven husband-stealer! Do not be fooled by this woman. Do not think, just because she is wearing the clothing of one of those harmless sheep you see grazing in the fields, that she is not a jackal underneath. Or a hyena, perhaps. Either of those. Both will bite you, dear voters, and the only way you can make sure that doesn't happen is to vote for the lady who is not a jackal, nor a hyena, but is a real woman who represents all the women of Botswana—and the men too—and who will bring prosperity to this town and all its inhabitants, with the exception of those who do not deserve it. That is the choice before you, dear voters: so think very carefully before you go into the

voting booth, and once you have thought very carefully, put your mark against the name of Mma Ramotswe. That is what God wants you to do. That is what the late Seretse Khama would have done, if he were still with us. Vote the right way so that—"

It was too much for Mma Potokwane. "Mma Makutsi," she said. "That is a very powerful manifesto, but I think we need to talk about it."

"Yes," said Mma Ramotswe. "I think we do."

LATER THAT AFTERNOON, sitting on the verandah with Motholeli and Puso, Mma Ramotswe told the children of her decision.

"There is going to be an election," she said. "You know what that is, don't you?"

Motholeli nodded; Puso looked uncertain.

"It is about choosing," said Mma Ramotswe. "It is about choosing people to run the country—or the town."

"I know that," said Motheleli.

Puso decided to look knowledgeable. "I know that too," he said.

"You will see some posters," Mma Ramotswe continued. "They may even have a picture of me, I think. That is because I am standing in this election."

Motholeli smiled. "Everyone will vote for you, Mma. You will get all the votes."

Mma Ramotswe laughed. "I don't think so, Motholeli."

"Yes, they will," said Puso.

Motholeli looked thoughtful. "Who will be the other people, Mma?"

"There is a lady called Violet Sephotho. She is going to stand too."

Puso's eyes narrowed. "I hate her," he said.

His sister gave him a sideways look. "You've never met her, Puso. You don't know who she is."

"I don't care," said Puso. "I hate her. She is very smelly."

Mma Ramotswe put an arm around the boy's shoulder. "We don't hate people, Puso. We don't hate anybody."

He looked at her sullenly. "Why?" he asked.

"Because hate makes you very tired," said Mma Ramotswe. She wondered whether there was more to say, but suddenly she felt tired herself.

"She'll lose," said Motholeli.

Mma Ramotswe smiled. "Let's wait and see," she said. And then she said, "I have some fat cakes. They are in the cupboard."

They had been sitting down during this conversation; now she rose and made her way to the kitchen cupboard. There were four fat cakes on a plate—delicious, greasy, tempting. She took them out and offered the plate to the children. She closed her eyes. Temptation nudged at her, a soft, persuasive tap on the shoulder. She returned to the verandah. "One and a third each," she said.

CHAPTER NINE

AN EIGHTY-FOUR-HORSE-POWER HEROINE

FANWELL WAS a more cautious driver than Charlie, and, as they made their way to Mochudi in Mma Ramotswe's white van, he resisted Charlie's encouragement to drive faster. "This vehicle is not designed to go fast," he insisted. "We'll get there when we get there, not before."

"You can't get there before you get there," Charlie said.

"No," said Fanwell. "That's what I meant."

The road was quiet in the mid-afternoon heat. To their right, broken acacia scrub stretched out to a distant, flat horizon. On fences and on telephone wires, the occasional bird perched—a hornbill with its yellow beak, a hoopoe with its waistcoat of brown and tiny stripes, a grey Cape dove calling for its partner. The earth was dry, baked by months of waiting for rain, beaten flat where animal tracks had made winding paths, crumbling elsewhere, where the erosion of wind and ancient rain had worked its effect.

To their left there stretched out much the same terrain, but with a hint of something different in the distance. Not too far away in that direction—fifty miles perhaps—the real Kalahari began, that vast dry land that ran all the way to the Okavango and the western limits of the country: Botswana boiled down, distilled, into a place of dryness, a place of air and light and human loneliness. Here and there along the way were farmhouses, scattered across the land seemingly at random but obeying a code of ownership and title, observing human claims to be where grandfathers and grandmothers, and others before them, had been. These houses were the sites of many stories: stories of men who worked there, and of those who travelled for work in distant places and never came back; of women who stayed and nurtured the children and bore the world upon their backs.

Fanwell asked Charlie about his friend in Mochudi. Who was he? Where did he learn to fix car bodies? Did he have a girlfriend?

"His name is Eddie," said Charlie. "He's tall. We used to call him Giraffe, but he did not like that, and so people went back to calling him Eddie. He has a Setswana name too, but I've forgotten what it is. Only his mother ever calls him that. Mothers are like that, aren't they? They give you some stupid name, and then they're the only ones who use it."

"They don't think it's stupid," said Fanwell.

"Well, it often is." Charlie paused. "Your name, Fanwell—where does that come from? Why do they call you that?"

Fanwell did not answer immediately. He was Charlie's loyal friend, but there were times when he thought Charlie could think a bit more before he spoke.

"It was my father's name," he said at last. "He was Fanwell too."

Charlie shrugged. "Odd name, isn't it? I'm not saying it's stupid— I'm just saying it's odd."

Fanwell said nothing.

Charlie grinned. "We could give you another name, of course, if you like. What about Pilot? Would you like to be called Pilot? I heard of some guy called that the other day. The girls loved it. *Oh, buy me a drink, Mr. Pilot . . .*"

"Was he a pilot?" asked Fanwell.

"No, he worked in the tax office. Some rubbish job. But he called himself Pilot and he had a lot of girls hanging around him, I'm telling you."

Fanwell smiled. "Pilot? Yes, maybe, but maybe not. I like being Fanwell. Girls don't mind that name, you know."

"In that case," said Charlie, "keep your name. Hold on to it. Big asset."

They drove on. Then Fanwell said, "What about girls, Charlie? Do you have a girlfriend at the moment?" He had always stood in awe of Charlie's way with the girls; he himself had difficulty in making the girls take notice of him, whereas Charlie made it all seem so easy.

"You're asking me whether I have a girlfriend, Fanwell?" said Charlie. "Is that what you're asking me?"

Fanwell nodded. "I haven't got one at the moment, I don't mind telling you. I wondered if you had one."

Charlie whistled. "No girlfriend? Are you remembering to wash every day?" He laughed. "Only joking, Fanwell, but it's something that some guys don't think about. Women don't like men who smell. There's been research into that. It's been proven."

Fanwell smiled weakly. "I wash every day. Every day."

"Yes," said Charlie. "And don't worry, Fanwell. If you really did smell, I'd be the first to tell you. That's what friends are for, isn't it? To tell you if you smell."

"So, is there a girl?"

"Could be," said Charlie.

Fanwell pressed him. "What does that mean?"

Charlie gazed out of the window. They were nearing Mochudi now, and the first houses were appearing. Goats wandered in the dusty yards, sniffing out the tiniest piece of vegetation to nibble upon. A child pushed a model car, made out of wire, along the side of the road. A cyclist, dressed in the blue robe of the African Zion Church, wobbled erratically along a track leading off to a cluster of buildings.

At last Charlie answered. "I'm seeing a girl called Queenie-Queenie. She works in a dress shop. I really like her."

The car swerved as Fanwell registered this information. He recovered quickly. "I know that girl," he said. "I have heard about her."

Charlie frowned. "Have you actually met her?"

Fanwell replied that he had not, but he knew somebody who knew her. "I haven't actually seen her," he said. "But I have heard all about her."

Charlie looked at him sideways. "So, what have you heard?"

"Her father is very rich," said Fanwell. "Her father's a big man."

Charlie was silent.

"Very rich," repeated Fanwell. "Very big."

Charlie shook his head. "I don't think it can be the same person. Her father has a truck. He delivers things."

Fanwell laughed. "A truck, you say? Fifty trucks, more like it. A whole fleet of trucks. He carts cattle down from Francistown to Lobatse. They go up to Maun as well. And up north too. Zambia. The Congo as well. They're everywhere."

"Are you sure? Has this girl you know got a brother?"

Fanwell replied that she had. "He does body-building," he said. "He's one of these strongmen."

"Then that's Queenie," said Charlie.

Fanwell was silent. If only he could meet a girl like that, who would change his life. She would lift him out of poverty—the poverty that seemed to stretch out in front of him no matter how hard he worked. How could he ever afford, on his mechanic's pay, a place of his own to live in when Gaborone was becoming so expensive? The people who had houses had these houses because they had bought them a long time ago. If your parents had a house, then that made it easier, because you could share their house with them and then, when they became late, it would be yours. Or if your parents were rich, they could help you find the deposit to buy somewhere of your own, or at least to get a lease. But Fanwell did not have parents in that position, and so he would have to continue to live in a small room, shared with another. How could you ever find a wife if all you had to take her back to was a shared room? Lucky Charlie, he thought. If he played his cards right, he would be able to marry this girl, Queenie-Queenie, and live in a large house paid for by his father-in-law. He would even be invited to join the family business and help run the fleet of trucks.

Charlie cleared his throat. "I didn't know about her father," he said. "That's not why I've been seeing her. Word of honour."

"I didn't say you had," said Fanwell.

Charlie sounded sullen. "But you thought it, didn't you?"

"Just for a short while," said Fanwell. "But I don't think it now."

THEY FOUND EDDIE at his uncle's workshop, tucked away behind the hill that dominated the village. It was, like so many such businesses, an eyesore: several cars, well beyond repair, had been abandoned to the side, clearly cannibalised for their parts, occupied in one case by chickens. Elsewhere in the yard were piles of bodywork parts: mudguards, side panels, half of a truck's cab, what looked like the side door of an ambulance.

Eddie was standing beside his uncle, who was using a welding torch. Both wore protective visors, but when Eddie saw Charlie he moved away, took off his welder's helmet, and walked over to meet him.

"So, Charlie," he said. "What brings you to the sticks?"

They shook hands. "I thought it was time to look you up, Eddie," Charlie said. "I wanted to see if you'd grown any taller."

Eddie looked at Fanwell and grinned. "Your friend's got a great sense of humour, hasn't he?"

Fanwell laughed nervously. Eddie was certainly very tall—at least a head and shoulders above him and Charlie.

"Who's this?" asked Eddie, gesturing to Fanwell. He might not have intended to sound rude, but that was the effect. Fanwell looked down at the ground in embarrassment.

"This is my assistant," said Charlie, avoiding Fanwell's eye.

"Ha!" exclaimed Eddie. "You've got an assistant these days, Charlie? What does your assistant do—make you your lunch? Polish your shoes?" He laughed at his own wit. Charlie smiled patiently.

"I'm not just working in the garage these days," Charlie said. "I'm also working as a private detective. You may have heard of the place— the No. 1 Ladies' Detective Agency."

"Never heard of it," said Eddie abruptly. "Working for ladies? You wouldn't catch me working for a lady."

Fanwell looked up sharply. "Mma Ramotswe is a very good detective," he said. "She is very well known . . . to people who know what's what."

It was as stout a defence of Mma Ramotswe and the No. 1 Ladies' Detective Agency as he could manage, but it did not seem to have a conspicuous effect on Eddie, who simply ignored it.

"So where did you learn to be a private detective?" Eddie challenged.

"It's a practical training," said Charlie. "Like training to be a mechanic."

"Sounds like a girl's job," said Eddie.

Fanwell looked at Charlie, wondering whether he would respond to this provocative series of comments. Charlie returned the glance, making it clear that he did not want a confrontation.

"I'm making certain enquiries," Charlie continued patiently. There was pride in his voice; the words had been mentally rehearsed several times on that day's journey.

Eddie pointed to two white plastic chairs that had been placed under the shade of a nearby tree. "We could sit down," he said. "It's easier to talk if you're sitting down." There was no question of offering both chairs to the visitors; Eddie secured one for himself and then gestured for Charlie to occupy the other. Fanwell was left standing.

Charlie started the conversation. "A month or two ago there was an accident here in Mochudi . . . ," he began.

Eddie shrugged. "There's an accident every day around here, if you count the small ones. People reverse into other people. They don't look where they're going and they scrape the side of somebody's car. They stop too quickly and somebody hits them from the back. There are many different types of accidents."

Charlie nodded. "This one involved a vehicle. And a person. There was a person knocked down."

The effect of this on Eddie was immediate. The bemused, slightly bored expression was replaced by a sudden, wary attentiveness. "I didn't hear anything about that," he muttered.

Charlie stared at him. "People must have talked about it," he said. "Nothing happens in a village without everybody hearing about it sooner or later."

"Well, I didn't," said Eddie truculently. "Nobody told me about this."

"The person who was knocked over was a well-known man," Charlie continued. "Dr. Marang. Do you know him?"

Eddie shook his head quickly. "Never heard of him," he said. And then, rising to his feet, he asked if Charlie had any other questions before he went back to work. "I can't leave my uncle to do all the work," he said. "Not while I sit around and talk about minor accidents."

"Not minor," interjected Fanwell.

Eddie threw him a glance. "Minor accidents," he repeated. "When you see what we see in this workshop, you know what's minor and what's major. Some old guy being knocked down by a car is minor, believe me. Nothing to get worried about."

"That's for us to judge," said Charlie testily. He had been a friend of Eddie's in the past, but now he found himself wondering what he saw in him. "So, what I'd like to know is this: Did you get anybody bringing in a blue car for repair?"

Barely a second or two elapsed before Eddie gave his response to Charlie's question. "No, never. Sorry."

"Can you think really hard?" asked Charlie.

Again, the answer came immediately, and forcefully. "I've thought. No. No blue car."

Charlie looked at Fanwell, who bowed his head. This meeting with Eddie was proving very unproductive.

Charlie stood up. "I don't want to waste your time, Eddie."

"No. Lots to do."

Charlie hesitated. "You remember how I helped you once. Remember?"

Eddie looked flustered. He stood up, towering over Charlie. "That was a long time ago."

"Yes," said Charlie, "but I haven't forgotten, Eddie."

Eddie looked about him furtively. Inside the workshop, his uncle had finished welding and taken off his protective clothing. He turned towards the three young men and began to walk towards them. Eddie pointed an accusing finger at Charlie. "You said you wouldn't—"

He did not finish. Charlie grabbed his finger. "All I'm asking is that you try to find out some information for me. Look around, Eddie. You know most of the cars in this place."

The uncle had almost reached them now. Eddie leaned forward and muttered to Charlie, "All right. I'll do that. Now you can go home."

THAT EVENING, while Mma Ramotswe and Mr. J.L.B. Matekoni were sitting on the verandah of their house on Zebra Drive, she told him of her change of mind. "I had decided not to stand," she said, "and then, I'm afraid I changed my mind today. I have now decided to be a candidate after all." She paused. That was not strictly true; Mma Potokwane had decided that she should be a candidate—it was the matron's decision rather than hers. "Or rather, Mma Potokwane has changed my mind."

Mr. J.L.B. Matekoni heard this in silence. Then he sighed. It was not the first time that this had happened; this was what Mma Potokwane did—she decided *for* people, but did it in such a way that they thought they were making their own decisions. But they were not, and once they reflected on what had happened they often realised that they had ended up doing exactly as Mma Potokwane wanted them to do. He remembered, in particular, the occasion on which Mma Potokwane had enrolled people for a sponsored parachute jump in aid of the Orphan Farm. He himself had been one of those targeted—not as a sponsor, but as a jumper—and he had spent an unpleasant period of time in utter terror at the prospect. Then, on another occasion, Mma Ramotswe had been inveigled into baking two hundred scones for sale at an Orphan Farm fund-raising bazaar. When he heard about this, Mr. J.L.B. Matekoni had queried the figure of two hundred. Was Mma Ramotswe sure that she had not agreed to baking *twenty* scones? It was very easy to add a zero to any sum, and perhaps that had been done here. But no, it was two hundred, and Mma Ramotswe had spent an entire Sunday mixing the ingredients and sliding the baking trays into the oven. That was another case of what he now called *the Potokwane effect,* and here it was again.

"But you don't want to do it, Mma," he said. "You told me that, just last night."

Mma Ramotswe sighed. "You're right, Rra. But you know how it is. Or rather, you know how *she* is."

Mr. J.L.B. Matekoni's dismay at the thought of his wife being forced to do something against her will was mitigated by his admiration for Mma Potokwane's persuasive ability. "At least she's on the right side of things," he said. "Imagine what it would be like if she were on the other side."

"You mean, if she were selfish? If she were just out for herself and what she could get?" asked Mma Ramotswe.

"Yes. If she were a property developer, for instance." And then he added, hurriedly, "Not that I'm suggesting that all property developers are selfish or out for themselves. They aren't."

"No, of course not," agreed Mma Ramotswe. "But some . . . well, some are clearly very bad people who will do anything to turn a profit. Some of them would not hesitate to knock down their own grandmother's house if it got in the way of their schemes."

Mr. J.L.B. Matekoni laughed. "You would be surprised, Mma, to know that that is just what happened down in Lobatse once. There was a builder down there who bought up old houses and knocked them down. One of those houses really did belong to his grandmother. She did not want to move, and they say that he had to put a snake into her house to shift her."

Mma Ramotswe's eyes opened wide in astonishment. "A snake, Rra? In his own grandmother's house?"

"Yes," he said. "He put a mamba underneath the floorboards. Those old houses have a space under the floor to let the air circulate. That is a very good place for a snake to live."

Mma Ramotswe shuddered. "But a mamba, Rra! Those snakes will never move once they decide to live somewhere. And if you anger them . . ." It did not bear thinking about. Of all possible nightmares, encountering an angry mamba was undoubtedly the worst. Most snakes would do their utmost to avoid human contact, would slide discreetly away when they heard—or felt—footsteps approaching, but some snakes did not. Puff adders would refuse to budge because they were too lazy and sluggish to get out of the way, waiting until you trod on them before they sank their fangs into your leg. Mambas, although they were as fast as any other snake, if not even faster, would defend their territory rather than avoid contact. They knew that they had a decisive weapon in their arsenal—a venom that could kill a grown human within an hour of its injection. And they had copious quantities of it too, as they used it in their hunting, swiftly reducing their prey—a rat or a similar creature—to the paroxysms that precede an agonising death.

"So what happened, Rra?" she asked.

Mr. J.L.B. Matekoni explained how he had only heard the story second-hand, and that sometimes these stories tended to be exaggerated in the re-telling. But he had been told that the girl who worked in the grandmother's kitchen had seen the snake watching her through a small hole in the floor and, panicking, had fetched the grandmother. After that, every sound the grandmother heard— and an old house is full of sounds—she imagined was the sound of the mamba moving around beneath her feet. It was not long, then, before she begged her grandson to find her a new house. This new house was some way out of town, and much smaller and cheaper than the one she had been living in. There had been no cash adjustment, said Mr. J.L.B. Matekoni; the grandson had pocketed the profits he made when he knocked the old house down and erected a new one.

"And the snake?" asked Mma Ramotswe.

"What would you like the answer to be, Mma?"

She thought for a moment. "I would like to hear that it moved out of the old house when the bulldozers came to knock the house down. I would like to be told that it ran off and searched for another place to live. I would like to hear that the first house it came to was the grandson's, and that it moved in there, under his bed perhaps, or just behind the laundry basket in the bathroom."

Mr. J.L.B. Matekoni laughed. "And bit him?"

"No," said Mma Ramotswe. "I would not wish that on anyone— even on a man who knocks down his own grandmother's house. Just frightened, Rra. Badly frightened him."

"I didn't hear what happened," said Mr. J.L.B. Matekoni. "And that makes me think the story is a true one. It is often only those stories that are made up that have endings in which bad people get what they deserve."

Mma Ramotswe's disappointment showed in her tone of voice. "So he got away with it?"

"Yes," he said. "A lot of people get away with a lot of things. We don't want them to, and we think that somewhere there is justice to be found. But they get away with it—time after time."

Mma Ramotswe said nothing. She was thinking of the issue that had triggered her candidacy—the building of the Big Fun Hotel. The thought made her skin prickle. The people who were planning that should not be allowed to get away with it. And that made her think that, even if Mma Potokwane had browbeaten her, what she was doing was the right thing. She would fight the election even if she found the whole process distasteful. She had to, because this was not a fight from which one could walk away and feel easy. This was a line in the sand, drawn as clearly and unambiguously as any line could be drawn.

She looked at Mr. J.L.B. Matekoni. "Is it a bad thing to change your mind?" she asked.

He was in no doubt about the answer. "Not if what you end up doing is the right thing." He paused. "And I think I can say, Mma Ramotswe, that what you're doing—and I suppose also what Mma

Potokwane is doing—is exactly the right thing. And I am very proud of that."

She reached out to touch him on his forearm. "Thank you, Rra. It will be easier for me if I know you are with me."

"I am," he reassured her. "You are a heroine, Mma. You are an eighty-four-horse-power, six-cylinder heroine—you really are."

It was the highest praise a mechanic could ever give, and he meant every word of it, every single word. He said nothing about upholstery, or suspension, or any of those matters pertaining to cars: a metaphor should not be strained, lest praise be diluted and made less glowing.

CHAPTER TEN

TELL THEM YOU BELIEVE IN PROGRESS

THE FIRST MEETING of the Elect Mma Ramotswe committee
took place at mid-morning the following day, chaired by Mma Potokwane. As well as Mma Makutsi, of course, who had agreed to act as
secretary to the committee, the membership had expanded to include
Mr. Polopetsi, who had been extremely excited to hear of Mma Ramotswe's nomination, and Charlie and Fanwell, who had promised to
devote their evenings to leafleting and going from house to house
to canvass votes. Mma Ramotswe herself was on the committee, of
course, although Mma Potokwane now insisted on calling her "the
candidate" rather than "Mma Ramotswe." Only Mr. J.L.B. Matekoni
did not participate. He had been invited, but had thought it better to
distance himself. "We do not want people thinking that we're trying
to start a dynasty," he explained. "You know how you get those politicians who are sons of other politicians and grandsons of even more
politicians. I do not think that is very democratic, and so I shall not be
involved in this campaign, even if I fully support it and put the whole
resources of Tlokweng Road Speedy Motors behind it."

That was a fairly long speech for Mr. J.L.B. Matekoni, and nobody had wanted to argue with the logic—or the dignity—that underpinned it. And so the leadership of the group, which he, as spouse of the candidate, might have been expected to assume, passed naturally to Mma Potokwane, whose idea the whole thing had been in the first place.

There was an air of almost palpable excitement in the room when Mma Potokwane entered. She was the last to arrive, and the others were all in their places when she came in and seated herself in the chair beside Mma Ramotswe's desk. Mma Makutsi was in her usual place, Mr. Polopetsi was standing by a filing cabinet, and Charlie and Fanwell were squatting on the ground in that effortless pose adopted by those who hamstrings had yet to seize.

Mma Potokwane cleared her throat, looked about her, and then, in a voice that Mma Makutsi thought was a little bit louder than the occasion required, called the meeting to order.

Charlie looked sideways at Fanwell. "But there was no disorder," he said. "I didn't see any."

Mma Potokwane gave him a warning glance. "That's how meetings begin, Charlie," she said. "The chairman calls the meeting to order. That's the signal for everybody to stop talking."

"But nobody was talking," protested Charlie. "Nobody said a thing, did they, Fanwell?"

Fanwell did not want to be drawn in. He looked away.

"And anyway," Charlie continued, "there is no chairman here, Mma. You are a lady. You are not a man."

Mma Makutsi drew in her breath. "Charlie," she hissed. "There is no call for disrespect."

"It was not disrespect, Mma Makutsi," Charlie retorted. "I'm just pointing something out. You yourself have often said it's important to be accurate."

Mma Makutsi sighed. "You don't understand, Charlie. The word *chairman* covers both men and women." She paused. "Mind you,

Mma Potokwane, many people these days just use the word *chair*. Perhaps you'd like—"

She was not allowed to finish. "Certainly not, Mma," said Mma Potokwane. "I am not a chair—I am a person."

Mma Makutsi did not press the point. Mma Potokwane's protestations were all very well, but, now that she came to mention it, she did look remarkably like a chair—a great, accommodating upholstered armchair. You could certainly sit on Mma Potokwane and feel perfectly comfortable: she was the sort of chair into which one might sink after a hard day's work—sink, and possibly not reappear until hours later, emerging from voluminous feather-filled cushions. That was the sort of chair that Mma Potokwane would be, whereas poor Mr. Polopetsi, if he were ever to be a chair, would be a wooden kitchen chair, hard and uncomfortable, because he did not carry much spare flesh; unlike Mma Potokwane, who had more padding and spare flesh than the Bank of Botswana had currency reserves—and those reserves, as everybody knew, were considerable.

It was a delicious train of thought, this chairing of people, but it was a distraction from the business of the moment, and so Mma Makutsi said, "I think that you have order now. As long as Charlie keeps quiet."

Mma Potokwane unfolded a piece of paper and laid it on her knee. "I've made some notes," she said. "There is an agenda of matters we need to discuss." She picked up the paper and peered at it. "*Number 1: Strategy. Number 2: Tactics. Number 3: Leaflets. Number 4: Posters. Number 5: Any other relevant business.*"

She looked out over the meeting. Everybody seemed to be nodding their agreement. Then Charlie raised a hand. "Excuse me, Mma. There's another item: money. What about money?"

Mr. Polopetsi, who had said nothing so far, nodded sagely. "A very good point, Charlie. Strategy and tactics may be free, but leaflets and posters require money. What are we going to do about that?"

Nobody said anything. Behind her desk, Mma Ramotswe shifted uncomfortably in her seat. She had not given any thought to financing her campaign, and this only increased her misgivings over the whole thing. She hoped that Mma Potokwane was not assuming that she, the candidate, would cover the costs; if that had been the assumption, then the matron should have mentioned that to her before persuading her to stand.

At last Mma Potokwane cleared her throat. "Money is very important," she pronounced.

This was greeted with silence. Charlie looked at Fanwell, and Fanwell looked out of the window.

Mr. Polopetsi raised a finger. "May I say something, Mma Potokwane?"

That was typical of Mr. Polopetsi's timidity, thought Mma Makutsi. It was, in general, a good thing that he was not a pushy man, as there were far too many of those around, but she wondered whether being timid was the best quality to have if you were involved in politics.

Mma Potokwane made an encouraging gesture. "Think of this as a *kgotla*." That was the traditional village meeting, the bedrock of Botswana's democracy, a firm rule of which was that everyone could have a say. "Of course you may speak, Rra. It is very important that people should be allowed to speak. That is the way we all get to hear useful ideas." She paused. "Have you an idea, Rra?"

Mr. Polopetsi looked like a rabbit caught in the headlights of a car. "No, Mma," he stuttered. "It wasn't so much an idea as a question. May I ask a question?"

"Perhaps that's his question," said Charlie, in a stage whisper. "Perhaps his question is whether he can ask a question."

Mma Potokwane glared at Charlie. "It is very important that people do not interrupt other people," she said. "If we have constant interruptions—with comments from the floor . . ."

"But I am on the floor," said Charlie. "If we cannot hear from the floor, then I will be able to say nothing."

Mma Makutsi sighed. "Sometimes you just don't understand, Charlie. The floor of a meeting is not the actual floor you're sitting on. The floor is all the people who are there—that is the sort of floor that Mma Potokwane was talking about." She sighed again, and for a few moments remembered the lectures on meeting procedure at the Botswana Secretarial College, where the taking of minutes had been explained in great detail and the finer points of recording proceedings extensively discussed. It was long ago now, and the lecturer who had taught them all that was now late—she had seen the notice in the newspaper and had been saddened at the snapping of yet another link with that part of her past, her student days. *One day,* she thought, *we should have a reunion, and all of us who sat together in the college's classrooms could meet once again and compare notes* . . . Except for Violet Sephotho, of course, who could be left off the list of those invited.

But now it was time to get back to money and to the question that Mr. Polopetsi had raised.

"Mr. Polopetsi," said Mma Potokwane, "you may certainly ask a question. Please go ahead."

Mr. Polopetsi looked around him nervously. "How many people are there in this room?" he asked.

Charlie sniggered. "If you can't work that out, Rra . . ."

"Hush, Charlie," said Mma Potokwane. And then, to Mr. Polopetsi, "Is that your question, Rra?"

"No, I can count how many people there are in the room, Mma. What I wanted to say was, if you think of how many people there are in this room, and then you imagine that each of those people gave one hundred pula to the campaign, that would end up being quite a large amount. That would cover the printing bills if we can find somebody who has one of those big office photocopiers."

Once again there was silence as people digested this suggestion. Then Fanwell spoke. "I don't have one hundred pula," he said.

Now Mma Makutsi had an idea. "We need to have a sliding scale," she said. "I have always said that sliding scales are a good way of doing things."

They waited for her to expand.

"So," she went on, "people who earn less than other people will give, say, twenty pula, and those who have more money than the people who have less money will give more money than the people with less money."

"That sounds very clear," said Mma Potokwane. "I will give one hundred pula and Fanwell can give ten."

"That will be very fair," said Fanwell.

Mma Potokwane was decisive. "In that case, that is the money issue dealt with. Now we need to talk about strategy."

Fanwell, relieved by the financial settlement, raised his hand. "I think we need to be both positive and negative," he said. "That will be the key to success here."

They all looked at him.

"Just like a battery," Fanwell continued. "A battery has a positive terminal and a negative terminal. You put the two of them together and you get a strong current. That's how batteries work."

"There is a lot of truth in that," said Mma Potokwane. Then she added, in a slightly puzzled way, "But how does that apply here, Fanwell?"

Fanwell thought for a few moments before he explained himself. "I think we should tell people what we are going to do if Mma Ramotswe gets elected. That will be the positive terminal. But then we should tell them about how bad the other candidate will be. That will be the negative terminal."

"Very, very good," enthused Mma Potokwane. "I think that is exactly what we should do." She turned to Mma Ramotswe. "What do you think, Mma? Do you agree? You're the candidate and you'll be putting these messages across. Do you agree?"

Mma Ramotswe's mind had been wandering and she had not followed every detail of the proceedings. But she had taken in the gist of what Fanwell was suggesting, and it seemed to her that there was a fundamental issue here as to what she would do in the unlikely event of her being elected. What was she to say? Did she have any policies? All politicians, it seemed to her, had a long list of policies. She was not sure if she had any—other than to veto the building of the Big Fun Hotel.

"I agree with the positive part," she said. "I am not so sure about being negative, but we can come to that later." She paused, and looked about the room. "The problem, though, is this: What exactly *am* I going to do? What are the policies that I can put to the voters?"

"Progress," said Mr. Polopetsi. "You must tell them you believe in progress."

Mma Ramotswe considered this. She was not sure whether she agreed. Most people would not hesitate to say that they believed in progress, but was *all* progress necessarily a good thing? The people who wanted to build the Big Fun Hotel would undoubtedly claim that their plans were an example of progress in operation, but if that was so, then it was not the sort of progress that Mma Ramotswe would like to see. Progress was more and better schools, better clinics, less poverty in general; progress was not riding roughshod over people's wishes, pursuing profit at all costs, building large and noisy hotels in places where people wanted there to be quiet—in places where there were important memories of late people and what they meant to us. That was definitely not progress.

"Not all progress is good, Rra," she said mildly.

Mma Potokwane looked thoughtful. "There's truth in that, Mma. Yes, there is truth in that."

Mma Makutsi thought that it would be possible to put across that message by talking about going forward. "Why not say, *Let's go forward together with Mma Ramotswe?*" she suggested. "That would be a good message for people to get."

"Yes," said Mma Ramotswe. "But where am I going?"

"Forward," said Charlie. "Not backwards."

"I think it's becoming clear what we must do," declared Mma Potokwane. "There are problems with progress because there is obviously good progress, which we like, and bad progress, which we do not. We can come back to this question of a slogan some other time, once we have had time to think a bit more. For now, I think we need to concentrate on tactics."

The debate continued. There were many good ideas, and others that were generally agreed not to be all that good. Then there were one or two suggestions—mostly from Charlie—that were firmly vetoed by Mma Potokwane. One of these, which was that they should find somebody to break into the other side's headquarters and find out what their plans were, attracted particular opprobrium. "This is not a game, Charlie," warned Mma Potokwane. "We must be very careful to do everything correctly and legally. We are not Violet Sephotho, remember!"

At length the meeting came to an end. Everyone had been given a task of some sort, and everyone was keen to get on with it. Only Mma Ramotswe remained somewhat detached. Her doubts about the whole venture had only grown during this meeting, and now they weighed heavy upon her. It was too late now for her to withdraw, but her heart was far from being in this campaign, and there was a niggling feeling in the back of her mind that it would all end unhappily—or, even worse, messily. There were some people cut out for politics, but she was sure she was not one of them. She believed in reconciliation and compromise; politicians seemed to believe only in the routing of their opponents. That was not the way she saw the world. It was not the way her father, the late Obed Ramotswe, had seen it, either. It was not the way, she was sure, that the ancestors had viewed things. It was not the Botswana way . . . And yet, there were battles to be fought precisely because there were people, right there in Botswana, who were not doing things the Botswana way. The people who were proposing to build that hotel were a prime example of that. If they were to be defeated—because that progress was the wrong kind of progress—then perhaps it was necessary after all to engage in this unpleasant business of politics, with all its talk of positive and negative approaches, of strategy and tactics and the communication of messages. What was the difference, she wondered, between strategy and tactics? They both sounded very much the same to her. And why did people have to refer to *communicating with* others rather than talking to them? She sighed again, and joined in the general applause that followed Mma Potokwane's closing of the meeting—but she did so with reservation, and with a heavy heart.

CHAPTER ELEVEN

PHUTI AND GRACE EXCHANGE WORDS,
BUT REGRET IT

As MMA MAKUTSI drove home later that afternoon, her mind was full of the task that had been allocated to her at that morning's meeting. It was, she thought, the most sensitive of the assignments that Mma Potokwane had allocated. While Mr. Polopetsi was charged with the task of designing the posters, and Mma Potokwane had undertaken the wording that would go on these, she had been entrusted with the far more onerous responsibility of assessing the company behind the hotel project. This had been Mr. Polopetsi's idea. He had pointed out that, if the Big Fun Hotel was to be a campaign issue, then it was important for them to know more about the people behind it. "It is important to know your enemy," he said. "If you know who he is and what he wants to do, then you can plan your defences. That is something that any soldier will tell you. He will say: *Know who you're up against.* That is what he will say."

Everybody at the meeting had been impressed with this, although Mma Makutsi had secretly wondered how Mr. Polopetsi knew what soldiers would say. If she were to think of the least likely person to mix with soldiers and to know their ways, then that person would undoubtedly be Mr. Polopetsi. But perhaps people did not mind too much about authenticity when it came to quoting others; Mma Ramotswe, after all, regularly quoted Seretse Khama although she had never met him. Mma Makutsi had long suspected that these quotes were entirely made up, even if she had to admit that the sentiments they expressed were, on the whole, consistent with that late great man's philosophy of life. On the one occasion when Mma Makutsi had raised this issue, Mma Ramotswe had responded by saying that, even if Seretse Khama had not used the exact words suggested, and even if one could not be certain that he had ever expressed a view on the matter in hand, she was nonetheless sure that he would have said something similar had he had the opportunity to do so. Perhaps it was the same with Mr. Polopetsi's quoting of soldiers. Even if he had never heard any soldiers talking about knowing one's enemies or knowing what one was up against, he could be reasonably certain that this was the sort of thing that soldiers would say.

From Mr. Polopetsi's suggestion to a definite plan was but one short step. Mma Makutsi would pay a visit to the headquarters of the hotel's developers. She would speak to the manager there and find out as much as she could about their plans for the site. She would also find out who the hotel's backers were, with a view to discovering some chink in their armour, some weakness that they could exploit in the arguments that were now sure to follow.

Charlie had seen a flaw in this plan. "But how are you going to do that, Mma?" he asked. "You can't just turn up and ask: *Who are you people and what are you planning to do?* They will say, *But who are you, Mma, and what makes you think you can come here and ask us questions like this?* That is what they may say, you know. People don't like to be asked personal questions by complete strangers."

This was a valid objection, and it was a few minutes before Mma Makutsi was able to respond. "That's a very good point, Charlie," she said. "But I have a perfect excuse to go and see these people. It will be a commercial visit."

They waited for her to explain.

"You see," she went on, "if you build a hotel, you have to put furniture in it. They will need to buy chairs and beds and all sorts of other furniture. And where will they buy that from? From furniture shops."

Fanwell emitted a sigh of discovery. "Ah, I see where this is going now. The Double—"

"Yes," interjected Mma Makutsi. "Phuti's company—the Double Comfort Furniture Store. We have supplied many hotels with many chairs. Many."

"So they won't be suspicious," said Fanwell. "That is very clever, Mma. That is a very good trick."

"It is not a trick," sniffed Mma Makutsi. "It is a strategy. Or even a tactic. I will go to talk to them about a contract for chairs, but I shall try to find so much more than that."

Mma Ramotswe looked out of the window. She did not like subterfuge of any sort, but there were times when, as a private detective, you needed to have what Clovis Andersen called *credible cover.* If you could assume such cover without telling direct lies, then there was nothing too much to worry about. This situation was on the borderline, she thought. However, Mma Makutsi could say with complete truthfulness that she was from the Double Comfort Furniture Store—she was . . . in a sense. And it was also true—just— that she could claim to be discussing the possible purchase of chairs because Phuti's company might well be interested in selling furniture to the developers. So she put aside her concerns and wished Mma Makutsi luck in what could be a very delicate operation. "It's just as well you're so experienced, Mma," she said. "This is not an assignment for an inexperienced person."

If Mma Ramotswe had had her doubts about the propriety of Mma Makutsi's plan, then such doubts were more than shared by

Phuti Radiphuti. When Mma Makutsi explained to him that evening that she would be speaking to the management of the proposed Big Fun Hotel, he listened intently. When she finished her explanation, he was silent for a while before he responded. She noticed this, and looked at him with concern.

"Don't you think it will work?" she said.

Phuti was hesitant. "It might," he said. "I don't know those people very well, but they will certainly talk to you. They'll know who you are, you see."

She was surprised. "Will they? I was going to tell them I worked for the store. I don't think they'll know who my husband is."

He shook his head. "No, Mma, you're wrong there. They'll know. This is not a great big city—this is quite a small town, even if it has grown and grown. Inside it's small, Mma; inside it's still one of those places where everyone is somebody's cousin or friend, and where there are not many secrets."

Mma Makutsi listened to what he had to say, but she disagreed. "I am not saying you're wrong, Rra," she said. "But even if they know who I am, will that make any difference?"

"It will," said Phuti. "They will think that I have sent you. And if they find out that you were there on behalf of somebody who is opposed to their scheme, then they will think that I have put you up to it."

Mma Makutsi was not prepared to accept this. "But women are no longer under their husbands' thumbs, Rra. That's all over now."

Phuti was not one to question women's rights, and he knew that what his wife said was, to an extent, quite true. But at the same time he knew how people thought about things, and he knew his concerns were well founded. He waited, though, for a few moments before he delivered his plea. "I'm asking you, Mma: please don't do anything that will embarrass me in my business. I am asking you that."

This conversation took place in the kitchen, where Mma Makutsi was preparing the evening meal. Now she stopped what she was doing and stood quite still at the sink, the pot in her hand half-filled with water. Phuti had never spoken to her in such an impassioned way—he was a mild man, not given to shows of emotion, but now this was something different. For a few moments she thought of agreeing without hesitation—it would be easy for her to say that she would abandon the plan—but then something within her resisted the idea. Phuti was not an overbearing man—in fact, he was the opposite—but the truth of the matter was that women in Botswana had for years been subject to male domination. Women had been told that men would make all the decisions; women had been told that their place was doing exactly what she was now doing—preparing a meal in the kitchen—and not trying to run the country, or even any small part of it; women had been obliged to take a back seat in everything, even those areas where they did all the real work. It was not that Botswana was particularly bad in that respect—it was not. Botswana had a good record on most matters, and great strides had been made in bringing about equality of the sexes. But there were still many battles to be fought against male assumptions, and now she felt that this was one of them. She was sure that Phuti's fears were groundless and that there was no risk to his business if she were to do as she planned. She would persuade him; she would make him see things from her perspective, and in this way she would be saved the indignity of going back to Mma Potokwane—Mma Potokwane, of all people!—and confessing to her that her husband had vetoed her plan. That would be a major humiliation, thought Mma Makutsi: *I cannot do what you wanted me to do because my husband says I must not.* No, she would not put herself in that position; she simply would not.

Mma Makutsi put down the saucepan. She drew in her breath, fixing Phuti with a look that was half understanding and half determined. "Nonsense," she said. "Nonsense, Phuti."

Phuti frowned. "I am not talking nonsense, Grace. I never talk nonsense."

"But, Rra," she said, "there is no grounds for what you say. That is why I call it nonsense."

He frowned again—more deeply this time. "No, no, Grace. You are the one who's talking nonsense, not me. I'm not talking nonsense."

"I am *not* talking nonsense, Phuti. It is not nonsense to carry out a decision approved by Mma Potokwane *and* Mma Ramotswe." She felt herself becoming heated. These two ladies were pillars of the community—standard-bearers for the women of Botswana. She would not have them described as talkers of nonsense; she would not.

Phuti, rather unusually, was also deciding to dig in. For years, he said to himself, the men of Botswana had been dominated by strong women telling them what to do; this was just another example. That Mma Potokwane was a prime example of the problem—if ever there was a bossy woman, it was the matron of the Orphan Farm. Poor orphans! Or, rather, poor *boy* orphans, who would be ordered about endlessly by a regiment of women, at the apex of which sat Mma Potokwane, the ultimate arbiter of their fate. Well, freedom might not be a prospect for those poor little boys, but out in the wider world, at long last, men were beginning to run their own lives without being manipulated by these ladies. It was time for men to stand up for themselves.

He steeled himself. "Mma Potokwane," he said quietly, "is a cow."

Mma Makutsi gasped. "What did you say, Phuti? What did you call Mma Potokwane?"

He almost recanted, so shocked was he by his own temerity. But it was too late; the men of Botswana—the patient, long-suffering, henpecked men of Botswana—were counting on him, he thought, and he could not let them down by retreating in the face of the first tirade.

"I said that she was a cow, Grace. And I said that because it's true.

That is what Mma Potokwane is. She is just like a cow that stands in the middle of the road with a stupid expression on its face. She reminds me of a cow."

Mma Makutsi steadied herself by holding on to the edge of the sink. She had never heard Phuti use language like this. "You cannot say that, Phuti," she hissed. "You cannot."

He was like a small boy emboldened by sudden daring. "But I have said it," he retorted. "And I'll say it again if you like."

Mma Makutsi moved away from the sink. "Then you can make your own dinner," she said, adding, "if you can. Men can't cook, of course."

It was a gratuitous, childish insult, tossed into the situation with as little thought as usually accompanied such insults. She immediately regretted it, and would even at this point have stopped herself and apologised, but the momentum of the argument was too great.

"Then I shall go out for dinner," said Phuti. "There are plenty of restaurants where men can go without being treated like this."

He left the room. Mma Makutsi looked down at the abandoned pot in the sink. She did not know what to do. It was the first real argument of their marriage, and she wondered, appalled, whether this was the way that marriages ended: with fights about little things, with an exchange of harsh words, with little patches of hurt feelings that became swamps of resentment. She started to cry, her large spectacles misting up with her tears.

HE WAS BACK before nine that evening. Mma Makutsi had taken to her bed, and was lying in the darkness when Phuti entered the room. She heard him cross the floor, and she closed her eyes in a pretence of sleep. He sat down on the edge of the bed, awkwardly, and reached out to her. She felt his hand upon the blanket that covered her shoulder; she shifted slightly, involuntarily.

"I am a very unhappy man," he whispered. "I am a very unhappy man who has been very rude to his wife. Now I am coming to say how sorry I am."

She opened her eyes wide, and sat bolt upright. He was not expecting this, and he almost fell off the side of the bed. She took his arm to steady him and save him from the tumble.

"Oh, Phuti," she said. "I am the unhappy one. I am the unhappy one who has been unkind to her husband and who is now very, very sorry."

"No," he said. "I am the one. It was my fault."

"No, it was my fault."

He laughed, and with his laughter the tension that had filled the air seemed to fade away. "We must not start another argument about whose fault it was."

Her relief was palpable; it was as if a light had been switched back on. "No," she said. "We must not do that."

Phuti now made his declaration. He had given the matter thought; indeed, he had thought about nothing else over his solitary dinner in the restaurant—not a good dinner, he said, as everything was cold and lacked the taste of Grace's cooking. He had thought about what she proposed to do and had decided that it was not for him to object to any scheme endorsed by Mma Potokwane and Mma Ramotswe. "I am very sorry that I said unkind things about Mma Potokwane," he confessed. "I'm ashamed of the words I used."

Mma Makutsi had to admit that his words were surprising, and quite unlike him. But, she thought, we all *think* such words from time to time, and occasionally thought stronger words than that; and she felt that one should not be too hard on those who actually uttered them. Even Mma Ramotswe must have her moments when . . . She stopped herself. No, she could not imagine Mma Ramotswe ever thinking uncharitably about somebody else—although, now that she came to think about it, there were occasions on which Mma Ramotswe became quite short with people. But that was only when they deserved it, and she was always, always prepared to forgive.

There were, of course, people who used strong language all the time. Mma Makutsi had noticed this and had wondered why it was that such people were always swearing. Was it frustration with the world? Was it because they found that nothing worked as they wanted it to work, with the result that they felt they had to express their anger in this way? When she had been at school up in Bobonong, she remembered that there had been a teacher who had been particularly strict when it came to swearing. This woman, who taught mathematics, kept a bar of carbolic soap and a jug of water in the cupboard behind her desk and would publicly wash out the mouth of any child reported for the use of bad language. The soap treatment would also be applied in cases of lying, and in such cases would even be performed twice in quick succession, to deal with any lingering untruths. This had been extremely effective, as the soap, a large bar of Lifebuoy, with its smell so redolent of hospital corridors, had a stinging astringent taste that took a long time to fade.

Then it had all stopped rather suddenly. A schools inspector, nosing about in cupboards, had come across the soap and had somehow elicited an account of what was going on. This, he declared, was not the sort of educational practice that should be encouraged in a modern country, and it must stop. The soap went, and the level of bad language went up accordingly. That should surprise nobody, thought Mma Makutsi: if people think they can get away with something, they do it. That was a simple and, she thought, self-evident proposition. By and large, people will not do things that they know will bring disapproval. If you know that somebody might wash your mouth out with carbolic soap if you should use bad language, then you will avoid the use of bad language. If, however, you know that you can say what you like and there will be no consequences, then you will say what you like.

Now Mma Makutsi knew that there were people who took the view that children should be allowed to behave as they wanted to behave. There were people who said you should never tell a child that he or she could not do something, because that would crush the child's spirit. Mma Makutsi could scarcely believe that anybody would say something so obviously wrong as that, but they did. And she had heard somebody on the radio, somebody described as an expert in the raising of children, saying exactly that, and the interviewer from Radio Botswana actually agreeing with her. Mma Makutsi had listened in complete disbelief and had later told Mma Ramotswe of what she had heard. Mma Ramotswe had shaken her head and said, "There are many people these days who think that the sun goes round the moon." That, thought Mma Makutsi, was a good way of putting it. Everybody knew that the moon went round the sun or . . . She had decided to ask Charlie, just to see whether somebody of his age would know about things like that. He had not hesitated to give his answer. "The sun goes sideways," he said. "It goes from east to west. That's the way the sun goes." He had then said, "Everybody knows that, Mma; I am surprised you didn't."

But now, here was Phuti saying that he was ashamed of his words, and she just wanted to reassure him that she understood and that there would be no need for anybody to say anything more about the incident. She also wanted to tell him that she was prepared to drop the plan altogether, and that there would be no further mention of it. But that was not what happened, and, rather than prolong the issue, she quietly agreed that she would go to see the developers as planned, but would be more than careful in what she said.

"Then that is settled," said Phuti. And added, "You are my darling, Grace. You are truly my darling."

Phuti, like so many men, was undemonstrative. He did not use romantic language very much; in fact, he had never used it, and for him to say this came as a complete surprise to Mma Makutsi. But what a wonderful thing it was for a husband to say to his wife: *You are truly my darling*. A man who said that would not have to say much more; indeed, he could remain silent for the rest of the day, for the rest of the week, and his wife, basking under the light of such words, would surely feel that he had said enough to last for months and months.

She said, "You are my darling too." And in that way their day, troubled as it had been, drew to a gentle close.

CHAPTER TWELVE

EDDIE IS ONE FOR THE LADIES

THE GENERAL AIR of excitement that had prevailed since the announcement of Mma Ramotswe's standing for election did not, of course, eclipse the tasks of everyday life, including those of running the No. 1 Ladies' Detective Agency. Mma Makutsi had to deal with a difficult ongoing case connected with the affairs of an elusive trading company that was being pursued, with every justification, by its creditors; Mma Ramotswe was busy with a report on an allegedly errant husband; and Mr. Polopetsi was engaged in the background vetting of prospective junior employees of a diamond-cutting firm. Of these three cases, the simplest one was the one Mma Ramotswe was handling. She had discovered that the husband whose fidelity was being impugned was, as far as she could tell, completely innocent. His private life, it was emerging, was really rather dull. He went out only infrequently, and when he did, it was almost always to go to the Gaborone Golf Club, where he either played golf with the same male friend or sat in the bar and read the newspaper until it was time to go home. To Mma Ramotswe fell the difficult task of telling the suspicious wife that her husband was really rather dull, and that she had no cause for concern. She wanted to say that she did not think any other woman would find him in the least bit interesting anyway, and that this should allay any wifely anxiety, but she felt that would be tactless. That information would have to be conveyed in some other way.

If the investigations of the three more senior members of the firm were proving routine, the same could not be said for that with which Charlie was concerned—the case of Dr. Marang and the hit-and-run motorist. He had told Mma Ramotswe about the visit that he and Fanwell had paid to Mochudi, and about his conversation there with Eddie.

"He is the right man to talk to about this," said Charlie confidently. "He said he would get in touch with me."

Mma Ramotswe smiled. There were many people who said they would get in touch but who did not—the world, it seemed, was full of people who made idle promises. And one of the things about getting on a bit in life was that you came to realise that half of what people agreed to do would never be done. Charlie was still too young to know that, but he would find out before too long. Of course, Mma Ramotswe did not approve of cynicism—she still took people on trust, she still gave them the benefit of the doubt, but at least she had learned not to be disappointed when people failed to do what they said they would do. She hoped that Charlie would come to understand that too, and that he would not become distrustful in his dealings with others. *Poor Charlie,* she thought: *he has so many lessons to learn about the world and its problems.* He was still at the optimistic stage in life; he still believed that there was nothing that he could not do, that life would get better and better. For most people, Mma Ramotswe thought, the discovery that this was not so happened some time after their thirtieth birthday. That meant that Charlie, who was . . . Now how old was Charlie? she wondered. She had to admit that she still thought of Charlie and Fanwell as being about eighteen, which was how old they had been when she had first met them. They had been junior apprentices then, in Tlokweng Road Speedy Motors, and the bane of Mr. J.L.B. Matekoni's life. "There are some things that are sent to try us," he had once remarked to her, "and in my case it is apprentices." But years had passed since then, and so Charlie would be about twenty-five, possibly even twenty-six—on the outside, that is; how old you were *inside* was another matter altogether.

Now she said to him, "Well, Charlie, that is very good. Although, this friend of yours, this . . ."

"Eddie," Charlie supplied.

"Yes, this Eddie—he may not get in touch with you, you know. Sometimes people don't keep their promises, I'm afraid to say."

Charlie shook his head vehemently. "No, Mma. He will get in touch. He will not dare not to."

Mma Ramotswe was amused by his certainty. "You shouldn't count on things like that, Charlie," she warned. "That is not the way a detective works. Do not put all your eggs in one basket—especially if that basket has a hole in it."

Charlie looked puzzled. "What have baskets to do with this, Mma?"

"It's just a way of saying things," answered Mma Ramotswe. "It is not about real baskets."

"Or eggs?"

"No, it is not about eggs—or it is, maybe, in a general way." She sighed. "It is not about actual eggs, Charlie. It's about things that you want to happen—that sort of egg. So what it means is this: don't count on just one answer to your problems."

Charlie saw the point. "Well, why didn't you say that, Mma?"

"I did, Charlie. But let's not spend too much time on baskets . . ."

"Or eggs."

Mma Ramotswe laughed. "Or eggs. All I'm telling you is that we must have some other line of enquiry in case this friend of yours . . ."

"Eddie, although we used to call him Giraffe, because he's so tall,

Mma. He was the tallest boy in the school, even when he was quite young. You saw his head sticking up no matter how many people were around. There was Giraffe, just like a real giraffe."

"If Eddie doesn't come up with anything, then we must think of some other way of tackling this case."

"But I told you, Mma," Charlie protested. "I told you: he will. I *know* he will." He paused. "I know he will because he thinks that, if he doesn't, I will do something to him."

The disclosure worried Mma Ramotswe. Charlie was keen to learn the art of detection, but could he be trusted to adhere to proper procedures? She had entertained doubts about that, and now here he was more or less confessing to having threatened a contact. She would have to sit down with him one day and give him some basic lessons in the ethics of the profession, as set out by Clovis Andersen in that superlative first chapter of *The Principles of Private Detection*. That chapter, entitled "Behaving Properly," laid out the basis of professional ethics in investigation. And it almost went without saying—Clovis Andersen did actually say it, though—that one should never use threats or violence. It might be tempting, Clovis Andersen admitted, to *lean* on a recalcitrant source or a witness, but you never do that because, as he so succinctly put it, "leaning on somebody can very quickly become pushing somebody, or even twisting somebody's arm behind his back." That would not do, he said, because evidence obtained in that way was forever tainted. And at this point Clovis Andersen had even quoted Shakespeare, and the anguished attempts of Lady Macbeth to cleanse the blood from her sullied hands. Mma Ramotswe knew about Shakespeare, of course, and somebody had once mentioned *Macbeth* to her, but she had not encountered before the image of somebody wishing away a taint quite so strongly. Clovis Andersen, she thought, was a whole education as well as being a practical manual.

Looking at Charlie with a certain seriousness, she now asked him directly whether he had threatened Eddie. "Because you must never, never do that, Charlie. It is what we call *unethical*. That means you must not do it."

Charlie seemed unmoved. "I didn't threaten him," he said. "I just reminded him. There is a difference between threatening and reminding, Mma—even I can tell that."

"So what did you remind him of?" she asked.

Charlie grinned. "Eddie is one for the ladies," he said. "I know you don't approve of that sort of thing, Mma, you being a lady . . . But there are some men who are called ladies' men, Mma. They are ones who like many pretty ladies and like to have them as their friends."

Mma Ramotswe resisted the temptation to laugh. Charlie could have been describing himself.

"So," Charlie went on, "old Giraffe was seeing this girl a long time ago. This is years I'm talking about, Mma. She liked him, I think, because he was so tall. There are some girls who think that tall men are attractive. They like them. I have seen it happen, Mma Ramotswe—I've seen it with my own eyes.

"Anyway, Giraffe was seeing this girl, and I'm sorry to say that one day she came to him and said, *Eddie, I'm going to have a baby*. He was very upset about this, Mma—very upset."

"I'm not surprised, Charlie. A baby is a big commitment, and if you're one for the ladies, as you say Eddie was, you may not be thinking of marriage and babies and commitments in general."

"Oh boy," exclaimed Charlie. "Eddie was certainly not thinking of commitments."

She waited for the tale to unfold. It was not going to end well, she imagined.

"Her father was not happy," Charlie continued. "He was a big man in the ostrich business. He had an ostrich farm with hundreds of ostriches. You should see those places, Mma—all those stupid birds running around in circles. Ow!

"He didn't like the thought of his daughter not being married and having a baby. So he sent a message to Eddie that he should get married quickly—in one week's time, I think he said—or he might find himself dumped in the middle of a whole lot of ostriches. Now, Mma, you may not know how dangerous those birds are. Some people think they're just like chickens and chickens can't harm you. Big mistake, Mma. An ostrich has a big claw where its toes should be, and if it kicks you with that, it can split you in two. I'm not making this up, Mma Ramotswe—those birds are bad news.

"The trouble was that Eddie was not ready to commit. That's what he said to me, Mma. He said, *I'm not ready to commit.* So he came to see me and asked me if he could stay at my place until the heat died down. I said yes, and then straightaway thought better of it. Those ostrich people traced him and they came to talk to me at the garage. Eddie had told me to tell them that he had gone to South Africa and that I wasn't sure exactly where, but it was down near Durban somewhere. He gave me a story to tell them, which was that he had a cousin down there who was a big man with the Zulus. You don't mess about with the Zulus, Mma Ramotswe—try that and you'll regret it big time. I gave them this story and added a few details. I said that the cousin down there was a senior gangster who ran twelve shebeens in Durban and Pietermaritzburg. I said that Eddie had gone to work in one of the shebeens, but that I didn't know which one it was.

"That stopped them, Mma. They looked cross and went off. I think they knew they wouldn't be able to chase after him there, what with all those Zulus and the cousin being a gangster and so on. So they went back and told that girl's father, and he found another husband for her instead of Eddie.

"Now I can see you looking at me, Mma Ramotswe, as if you're thinking—Charlie is a big liar who told lies to those men to save Eddie. But I think I did the right thing there: they would have forced him to marry somebody he didn't want to marry, and that would not have been good for anybody, would it, Mma? So it was the right thing to do, I think."

His story finished, Charlie looked defiantly at Mma Ramotswe. She did not upbraid him, but simply said, "I wasn't thinking that, Charlie. I was wondering, though, what you reminded Eddie of the other day."

Charlie looked pleased with himself. "I just reminded him, Mma. I reminded him of what I had done for him and also . . ." He hesitated; he had now noticed Mma Ramotswe's expression. "Also, I wanted him to think about what would happen if I went to that girl's father and told her that Eddie wasn't down in Durban, but was in Mochudi. I think he might still have something to say to Eddie—if he knew where he was."

Mma Ramotswe stared at the floor in silence. Watching her, Charlie shifted in his seat. "You do know that what you have done is blackmail, Charlie," she said. "You do know that?"

Charlie looked at his hands. "I do not see what is wrong with that, Mma." He looked up again. "Think of Dr. Marang, Mma. Just think of him. I am just trying to help that old man. That is why I had to . . . to remind Eddie." He watched for signs of her being persuaded, but she was still gazing down at the floor. Charlie persisted. "And remember, Mma, Eddie is a no-good sort of person. He is very selfish—and he docs not treat women well. I can tell you that, in confidence, Mma. Ladies need to look out when Eddie is about."

Mma Ramotswe sighed. "All right, Charlie. I will not mention it again. But please be careful—and never, never think that you are justified in doing something wrong just because you are trying to do something right."

Charlie was pleased to have been let off. Sometimes he felt that Mma Ramotswe could make you feel bad just by looking at you; she did not have to say anything, she just looked, and her look was impossible to ignore, because it said so much without actually saying anything. "So you see, Mma," he concluded breezily, "that is why I am so sure that I shall hear something from Eddie. I am one hundred per cent sure, Mma, that he will come and tell me who was driving that car on the day that poor Dr. Marang was knocked over."

Mma Ramotswe said that she hoped for the same thing, even if she still felt that Eddie might not call back. "I hope he does, though," she said, "because I'm afraid I don't have any ideas at all as to how we can take that particular investigation any further. You don't have any ideas, do you, Charlie?"

"I do not," he said.

CHARLIE WAS PROVED RIGHT rather sooner than he had expected. The next morning, when he was working in the garage with Fanwell and Mr. J.L.B. Matekoni, a red car, throaty in its exhaust, drew up at Tlokweng Road Speedy Motors. The arrival of this car was noticed by Mma Makutsi through her window in the office, and she drew Mma Ramotswe's attention to it.

"Are you expecting anybody in a noisy red car, Mma Ramotswe?" she asked.

Mma Ramotswe barely glanced up from the file before her on the desk. "I do not know anybody who drives a noisy red car," she replied. "Cars like that are just for young men—they are never for ladies. It will be somebody for the garage, I think."

Mma Makutsi got up from her chair to get a better view. "It's a very tall young man," she said. "He's getting out. Very tall."

Mma Ramotswe looked up. Very tall? And then she remembered: Giraffe.

"And now Charlie is going out to see him," reported Mma Makutsi. "Charlie is wiping the grease off his hands. They are greeting one another."

"I think I know who that is," said Mma Ramotswe. "That is the young man from Mochudi. Charlie spoke to him the other day about that Marang business and—"

Mma Makutsi interrupted her. "Now he's saying something to Charlie. He's pointing his finger at him. He has some sort of message, I think." She paused. "Now Charlie is taking a step back. I don't think he's happy."

And in that respect, Mma Makutsi was right. Eddie had brushed aside Charlie's greeting and had gone straight to the point.

"That thing you asked me to do, Charlie," he said. "I've done it."

Charlie was casual. "Oh, yes? And?"

Now came the pointing of the finger. Eddie raised his voice. "You're not going to like this, Charlie."

Charlie said nothing.

"You see, I found out something about a car that needed a repair."

Charlie nodded. "That's good, Eddie. Now all you need—"

He did not finish. Again, the finger jabbed against his chest. "I don't need anything, Charlie. You're the one who needs to do something. You need to be very careful."

Charlie took a step back. "You found out who it was?"

"No," said Eddie. "All I did was find somebody who knows somebody. That other somebody is the person who has the car. I don't know who he is, but I do know somebody who knows that."

"Couldn't you—"

Eddie cut him off. "No, I can't. This person who knows this other person won't tell me who he is. But he did tell me something, and that's the bit you're not going to like."

Charlie looked about him nervously. From within the garage,

Fanwell was watching him, but, even so, even here in these familiar surroundings, in broad daylight, he felt afraid.

"What won't I like?" He tried to sound firm, but his voice trembled.

"You won't like this one little bit," Eddie said. "That person—the person with the car—said to the other person—the person I know—that the owner of that car does not want you sniffing around. He said, and I quote him directly; he said: *You tell that guy that if anything happens to me, he's meat for the hyenas.* That's what he said, Charlie—and, in case you haven't got it, I think he means *you.*"

Charlie thought quickly. "But how does he know that I've been asking?"

Eddie replied quickly. "Because I told my friend. He asked me, and I had to tell him. It would be rude not to." This was delivered with a smirk, and Charlie did not respond.

"So," Eddie continued, "if I were you, I'd be very worried."

Charlie looked over his shoulder, as if for support from within. Three pairs of eyes were on him now, in witness of this encounter: Mma Makutsi's, Mma Ramotswe's, and Fanwell's. Only Mr. J.L.B. Matekoni, engaged in a tricky repair of a wheel bearing, failed to observe what was going on.

Eddie turned back towards his car. "Don't follow a regular routine, Charlie," he said. "Be careful of your movements. Okay?"

And with that Eddie left.

"See that?" said Mma Makutsi. "That tall young man has just threatened Charlie."

Mma Ramotswe returned to her desk. "Call him in, Mma. I think Charlie is going to need a bit of advice."

They brought Charlie in. He looked preoccupied, perhaps even shaken, but when Mma Ramotswe asked him what Eddie had said, he replied that he had merely come to report that he had found nothing. They asked him if he was sure, and he gave the same answer.

Then, claiming that he had some chore to perform in the garage, he walked out of the office.

"Charlie's hiding something," said Mma Makutsi. "You can always tell."

Mma Ramotswe did not disagree. "There is something wrong," she said. Life at the moment, she felt, was becoming a bit too complicated. Threats, campaigns, disagreements over hotels—this was not how Botswana should be.

Mma Makutsi looked at her watch. "Tea time," she announced.

Tea, thought Mma Ramotswe—no matter what was happening, no matter how difficult things became, there was always the tea break—that still moment, that unchangeable ritual, that survived everything, made normal the abnormal, renewed one's ability to cope with whatever the world laid before one. Tea.

CHAPTER THIRTEEN

ME? A DETECTIVE? HA!

GOBE MORUTI," muttered Mma Makutsi under her breath. And then repeated, "Gobe Moruti."

Charlie was at the wheel of Mma Ramotswe's tiny white van and Mma Makutsi was in the passenger seat beside him. Mma Makutsi had asked him to drive her to the offices of the Big Fun Hotel developers; although she now had a driving licence, she did not like coping with the traffic and, in particular, with the rudeness of other drivers.

"There are some very rude people on the roads," she had once observed to Mma Ramotswe. And then, developing the theme, had remarked on how strange it was that people should seem to change their personalities once behind the wheel of a car. "Many people are quite polite when on their feet, you know. But then they get into the car and they become very hostile if you make a small mistake."

Mma Ramotswe agreed. She had made a similar observation to Mr. J.L.B. Matekoni after she had incurred the wrath of another driver for simply changing lanes on the Francistown Road. "All I did," she said, "was change my mind. People should be allowed to change their minds, Rra, don't you think?"

Mr. J.L.B. Matekoni was cautious. "Yes, in general, Mma, but . . ." He thought of exceptions. A pilot should not really change his mind about landing once the aircraft wheels were almost on the runway; a surgeon should not change his mind too lightly once he had made the first incision; and a driver . . . well, there were circumstances in which you should be very careful about changing lanes.

"You see," continued Mma Ramotswe, "you may be driving to one place and then you remember that you need to go to another place. That happens all the time, I think. You are driving to one shop and you think, *Oh, my goodness, I need to get to that other shop because I have to buy eggs or potatoes or whatever.*"

"Yes . . . but sometimes it's better, isn't it, to decide in advance where you want to go."

Mma Ramotswe considered this, but only briefly. "You cannot run your life on that basis, Rra," she replied. "The problem is that thoughts don't come into your head in alphabetical order." She paused, and thought of something that made her smile. "That may happen if you're Mma Makutsi and you're filing something. I think that Mma Makutsi may sometimes think alphabetically. It may be deeply ingrained if you have graduated from the Botswana Secretarial College."

Mr. J.L.B. Matekoni grinned. "Possibly, Mma, possibly."

"But as far as the rest of us are concerned," Mma Ramotswe concluded, "we can be thinking of one thing and then another thought comes along because that first thought has made you think it."

Mr. J.L.B. Matekoni returned to the incident. "This other driver, Mma? What did he do?"

"He shouted at me," she said. "He wound down his window and he shouted out something very unkind."

Mr. J.L.B. Matekoni shook his head. "It's very sad when drivers do that. We are all brothers and sisters when we are on the road. There is no excuse for that sort of thing." He was silent for a few moments. The world had changed; even Botswana had changed—a bit. Now everybody was in such a hurry, desperate to get things done in double-quick time, determined to get to their destination as quickly as they possibly could, too busy to allow other people to get there too. But now, in spite of his disapproval, he asked, "What was it that he said, Mma?" Adding, hurriedly, "But don't tell me if he used bad language. I do not want to hear bad language."

Mma Ramotswe shook her head. "He did not use bad language. He shouted, *Even a chicken knows where it's going when it crosses the road!*"

Mr. J.L.B. Matekoni frowned. "What is it they say about chickens crossing the road, Mma? I remember when I was a boy they said something about that. *Why did the chicken cross the road?* Isn't that what they said?"

She remembered too. "We thought it very funny, Rra. We asked our friends, *Why did the chicken cross the road?* And then, when they couldn't answer, we said, *To get to the other side.* And then we laughed a lot."

Mr. J.L.B. Matekoni smiled. "And if you were a boy, and you asked your friend a riddle he couldn't answer, you could punch him on the arm."

"I remember seeing that," said Mma Ramotswe. "I remember seeing boys in the playground punching one another. They did it all the time."

"And kicking too," Mr. J.L.B. Matekoni added. "Boys liked to kick one another—and I think they still do. Do you remember when Charlie put that notice on Fanwell's back? When they were junior apprentices? Remember?"

Mma Ramotswe laughed. "I will not forget that, Rra. Mma Makutsi was so cross because he kicked poor Fanwell when he was looking for something in the office. He'd stuck a piece of paper on his back saying *Kick Me.*"

"They were still small boys inside, weren't they? And they used to make Mma Makutsi so cross . . ."

But now it was different, and Mma Makutsi and Charlie, although occasionally at odds with one another, had a far better understanding. And so, when Mma Makutsi muttered the name of Gobe Moruti to herself, Charlie picked up her anxiety and sought to reassure her.

"You must not worry about this man," he said. "He is just a man, Mma—same as any man."

Mma Makutsi sighed. "I know that, Charlie. But still . . ."

He adopted what he hoped was a cheerful, encouraging tone. "Come on, Mma. You have never been afraid of men."

"I know that," she replied. "But this man is a very rich man. Rich men are different from most men. They are used to getting their own way."

"Not all of them," said Charlie. "I have fixed some cars belonging to rich men. They have been polite—same as anybody."

She was unconvinced. "Maybe, but this one, I think, will not be polite." She based this view on the fact that this was a man who seemed intent on ignoring the wishes of a large number of people, both living and late—if late people could have wishes, which was something she was not sure about. Mma Makutsi was not as sure as some people were about what happened to you at the end of this life. She had had a heated discussion recently with Charlie and Fanwell on this very subject; Fanwell was of the view that there was a simple selection process in which those who had behaved badly were sent to a place of boiling pitch while the meritorious went somewhere higher, probably in the clouds. Charlie laughed at this, saying that nobody believed that sort of thing any longer, and that the modern view was that you went back to where you began and started over again. "That is what they believe in India," he had said. "And now they have scientific proof." He paused. "And so in your case, Mma Makutsi, you'll be going back to Bobonong, to start all over again as a new baby up there."

Mma Makutsi had responded robustly. "There is no proof at all, Charlie. None."

"You'll be back in Bobonong, Mma," he warned. "Don't be surprised when that happens."

She had laughed, but behind her laughter there was a note of anxiety. She was loyal to Bobonong, and always defended her home town when people spoke disparagingly about it, but she was not sure that she could face the prospect of once again going through the first twenty years of her life, particularly if in a fresh incarnation she might not find that golden opportunity to escape from the limitations of her pre–Botswana Secretarial College life.

Now Charlie said, "You'll be fine, Mma. This man will not dare to be rude to you. You are not the sort of lady that men think they can be rude to. That is not the sort of lady you are."

Mma Makutsi was boosted by this, but only slightly. She thought it was still going to be a trial to speak to Mr. Gobe Moruti in his modern office, in a new office building, all glass and concrete, complete with air-conditioning and a man in uniform at the front door. Putting a man in uniform at your front door was a gesture that was unambiguously forbidding, she felt; it was a signal to people like her to keep away and not to bother important and busy people like Mr. Gobe Moruti with idle questions.

Charlie parked under a tree by the side of the road. "I am here if you need me, Mma," he said.

She thanked him, stepped out of the van, and made her way towards the entrance. There was a book for her to sign at reception before she went in—a ledger with *Time In* and *Time Out* columns, along with a space for the name of the visitor's business. Mma Makutsi signed the column labelled *Name,* and then, under *Name of Company,* began to write: *No. 1 Ladies' Detective Ag*— She stopped herself. She had done this automatically, without thinking. She had meant to write *Double Comfort Furniture Store*, but the habit of years had overcome her planned cover, and now the woman behind the desk was peering at her entries, reading them upside down.

Flustered, Mma Makutsi attempted to cross out the offending admission. The woman behind the desk frowned. "Why are you crossing that out, Mma?" she asked, craning her neck for a better view of the entry. "What is this No. 1 Ladies' what? What is that, Mma?"

"I have made a mistake, Mma," said Mma Makutsi. "I meant to write something else."

The receptionist's eyes narrowed with suspicion. "But what is this thing you wrote first? No. 1 Ladies' Detective . . . What is that, Mma? Are you a detective? Is that what you do?"

Mma Makutsi forced herself to laugh. "Me? A detective? Ha!"

"Well, are you?" insisted the receptionist.

Mma Makutsi ignored the question. "What I meant to write was the Double Comfort Furniture Store, Mma. It came out wrong."

"How can that happen?" asked the woman.

Mma Makutsi became suddenly efficient. "Look, Mma," she said briskly. "I have an appointment with Mr. Gobe Moruti. I cannot stand here talking about this and that, much as I would like to. I am a very busy person."

The receptionist drew back, silenced by this display of confidence. Lifting a telephone handset, she dialled a number and announced that Mma Makutsi of the No. 1 Comfort Furniture Store had arrived to see Mr. Moruti.

Mma Makutsi interrupted her. "No, Mma, the Double Comfort Furniture Store, not the No. 1 Comfort Furniture Store."

The receptionist glared at her. "I'm sorry," she said into the handset. "This lady says that she is not from that business but from some other business."

"No, Mma," Mma Makutsi interjected, her voice rising as she

spoke. "It is not some other business. It is the Double Comfort Furniture Store."

The receptionist replaced the handset. "They say you can go up now, Mma." Her tone was polite; the misunderstandings of the last few minutes having been put to one side. "Mr. Moruti is on the second floor. He's waiting for you now."

Mma Makutsi took the stairs, and as she climbed she reflected, with acute embarrassment, on the foolish slip she had made. Of all the incompetent things to do on an undercover mission, surely the most incompetent would be to announce, right at the outset, that you were a detective—and that, in effect, was what she had done. She imagined what Mma Ramotswe would say about that. She would be polite, of course, but she would undoubtedly feel obliged to point out something that Clovis Andersen had written on the subject. She remembered at least one section of *The Principles of Private Detection* where this arose. "If you are using an assumed name," Andersen wrote, "make sure you remember it! I know at least one operative"—the great man liked to use that word, *operative*—"who has been exposed because he has forgotten the false name he was intending to use."

How could she have made such a fundamental mistake—right at the beginning of the mission? If Charlie had done that, it would have been excusable—he was a trainee with very little experience, and also was a young man, with all the impetuosity of the young and the headstrong. She, by contrast, had under her belt years of being a detective, had read *The Principles of Private Detection* at least five times, and of course had achieved ninety-seven per cent in the final examinations of the Botswana Secretarial College; in the light of all that, there was surely no excuse for such a basic error. Of course it was possible that there would be no adverse consequences: the receptionist had not said anything about detectives to the person on the other end of the line. But that did not mean that once she had disappeared up the stairs the woman had not immediately lifted the phone and told Mr. Moruti that there was a suspected detective on her way up to see him.

By the time she reached the glass door labelled *Managing Director,* she had persuaded herself that all was lost. She would be met by a suspicious, possibly even angry Gobe Moruti, who would immediately show her the door amid accusations of making an appointment under false pretences. But that did not happen. When she knocked on the door, it was immediately opened, and she found herself faced with a tall, well-built man dressed in a light grey suit. He greeted her correctly, and warmly, in the Botswana manner.

"Mma Makutsi," he said, "it is very good of you to come and see me."

Completely taken aback, she struggled to find the words. "No, Rra, it is good of you . . . I am here, you see, on business . . ."

He made a reassuring gesture. "Of course you are," he said. "Of course you are."

She said, "It is a very warm day, isn't it?"

Gobe Moruti smiled. It was not a forced smile, but one that seemed to suggest pleasure at a novel observation. "I think you're quite right," he said. "It is warm. Yes, you're right there." He moved a chair and invited her to sit. Then he returned to his seat on the other side of the desk. "We're very lucky to have air-conditioning," he said. "It's a big expense, of course—all that electricity—but there we are, it has to be used for something, I suppose. You can't leave electricity lying around." He laughed at his own joke.

"Electricity is very slippery," said Mma Makutsi. She was not sure whether that was a witty thing to say, but it possibly was.

Gobe Moruti thought so. "Ha! That's a thought, Mma. The slipperiness of electricity. Quite right. You can never get a-hold of it, can you?" He laughed again. Mma Makutsi laughed too.

Then Gobe Moruti asked, "Do you have air-conditioning in your office at the Double Comfort Furniture Agency?"

"Furniture Store, Rra," she corrected.

"Furniture Store—of course. Why would I say *agency*? Careless of me."

"It's a small thing, Rra." And then, frantically, she thought: Do we? Phuti's office always seemed cool enough to her, but that might be because it was under the eaves of the building and had two large windows. Were the windows open? They were, she thought, which meant there would be no air-conditioning.

"We prefer the natural approach, Rra," she answered. "There is a big air conditioner in the sky, I think. It's called the wind."

Gobe Moruti clapped his hands together appreciatively. "Oh, that is very good, Mma! The wind. And the wind is free—or at least it's free at the moment. No doubt the government will find a way of making us pay for it, but they haven't worked that out yet." He reached for a large paper clip on his desk and began to fiddle with it while he spoke. "Now, then, Mma, what can I do for you today?"

Mma Makutsi had mentally rehearsed her opening, and now she used it. "It is about furniture, Rra. I believe that you are the man behind the plan to build a big new hotel."

He held up a hand. "Not just *the man* behind that scheme, Mma. There are many people standing behind me—many people who have a new vision for Gaborone."

She nodded. "Of course, Rra. But you are the main man, I think."

"Possibly. Yes, you might put it that way. But I think of myself as just being the standard-bearer for a whole troop of people, ordinary men and women who support me in what I'm trying to do. I may not even know them—they may be people in the street, but they are with me because they see the benefits of what I'm doing."

For you, thought Mma Makutsi. *The benefits for you.*

"And this new hotel," she continued, "will need furniture, I assume."

Gobe Moruti chuckled. "Hotels usually have furniture, Mma. Imagine if you went to a hotel and there was no bed in the room, and you had to say to the manager, *There's no bed in my room,* and he would say, maybe, *What do you expect for the price you're paying?* Ha! That would be very funny, wouldn't it, Mma?"

Mma Makutsi was about to reply, but he had more to say. "And then perhaps the manager would say, *If you want a bed, you'll have to pay for a deluxe room.* Ha! That would be even funnier—though not so funny for the poor customer."

"It would not," agreed Mma Makutsi. "But you won't want that to happen, will you, Rra? You will need furniture."

Gobe Moruti seemed disappointed to be abandoning the fantasy. "Yes, Mma, we shall need furniture. We'll not only need beds, but we'll need tables and chairs, and desks. And chests of drawers and storage units and . . ." He sighed. "We shall need an awful lot of furniture."

"We sell furniture," said Mma Makutsi.

Gobe Moruti nodded. "So you do," he said. "Or rather, your husband does."

Mma Makutsi caught her breath. She said nothing. Gobe Moruti was looking at her intently. The casual friendliness of the past few minutes seemed to have abruptly evaporated.

He broke the silence. "But of course, Mma, you have many things to do, I suppose. You have your job with that Mma Ramotswe. And your child, of course. And you must be even more busy now that your boss is going into politics. My, you must be busy, Mma." He paused, watching the effect of his words. "I'm surprised you have time to sell furniture as well—I'm very surprised."

Mma Makutsi sat quite still. She felt his eyes upon her, appraising her in an almost amused fashion. He had seen through everything—right from the start—and she had completely failed to spot it.

Gobe Moruti leaned back in his chair with the air of one enjoying the embarrassment of another. He spoke slowly now, measuring the weight of each phrase, each sentence. His tone had become languid.

"I understand, of course," he said. "You see, I am used to these matters, Mma. When you are in my line of business—developing the country—you get used to dealing with politicians and, shall I say, would-be politicians. In fact, the would-be politicians are even easier to understand than the long-serving ones. You know why, Mma?"

He was waiting for her to respond. She shrugged.

"Because they have not yet learned to conceal what they are up to. It's quite amusing, in fact, to see it. They are very obvious in what they do. It's only later, when they've learned the ropes, that they are more discreet. They see one or two people overstep some mark or other and get into trouble, and that is when they learn to be discreet."

He took a handkerchief out of his jacket pocket and wiped his brow. "Please excuse me, Mma, for sweating like this. Even with the air-conditioning, I find it a bit hot at this time of the year."

Mma Makutsi bit her lip. She was unsure whether to rise to her feet and bring this meeting to an end, or to wait and see where it led. In the event, she did nothing.

"So I think I should spare you further embarrassment, Mma. I know very well why you are here."

She made a last attempt. "I am here to sell furniture. That is all that—"

He cut her short. "Come on, Mma, there is no need for us to beat about the bush. You are here on behalf of that Mma Ramotswe of yours. You are here to get my support, in return for which you would like me to help get your candidate elected. And then, if that happens—*if* it happens, Mma, and there is always a big *if* in politics—you will offer to support my planning application for the hotel in return for . . . well, let's say, in return for further support of a practical nature from me."

He stopped. She was staring at him with wide-open eyes.

"Have I surprised you, Mma?" he asked. "Did you not know how these things worked?"

Mma Makutsi found her voice. "That is all wrong, Rra. That is not why I am here. I have not come to ask for anything like that."

She was not ready for his reaction. He was nodding in agreement. "Absolutely right, Mma," he said quietly. "That is exactly what you should say. You are learning very quickly, I think."

"I do not think you heard me, Rra."

"Oh no, I heard you, Mma. And you were saying exactly what you should say in such circumstances. Never say anything that can be quoted back at you. Always deny things. Make sure that any understanding is reached by a nod of the head or even a look in the eyes. Then nobody can come along and accuse you of corruption."

Her voice rose in her refutation. "We are not corrupt, Rra."

"Yes," he said enthusiastically. "That's just the right thing to say, Mma. Just right. And anyway, this corruption nonsense—what are they talking about? Is it corruption to do whatever is necessary to make sure that important economic assets are constructed? Is it corrupt to make sure that jobs are created for people currently without work? Is that corrupt, Mma? If it is, then I would be proud to call myself corrupt. I would go out in the streets and say, *Here is a corrupt man doing his best for the economy of Botswana.* That is what I would say. I would say it openly, and with pride, Mma."

When he had finished, he folded his hands across his stomach in an air of righteous self-satisfaction. Mma Makutsi looked down at the floor. There was nothing for her to say, she decided.

"So," said Gobe Moruti at last, "here is my message for your Mma

Ramotswe. Tell her: *Yes, Mma, we can do business together.* Tell her to talk to me once she has won—*if* she wins. I will certainly make her co-operation worth her while at that stage." He paused. "Of course, she might not win, and I shall be sorry if that happens—for her sake. But I will not be sorry for my own sake, as I have already had very satisfactory conversations with her opponent in this election, and if she wins, instead of Mma Ramotswe, then everything will be fine. So, either outcome will suit me, Mma."

Mma Makutsi struggled to control herself. It should not have surprised her, she told herself, that Violet Sephotho had already teamed up with Mr. Gobe Moruti. They were two peas from the same pod, she thought: two beans from the same row. Peas and beans. Of course they were.

She rose to her feet. "I'm going now, Rra," she said, with as much dignity as she could muster. "And all I would say is this: you have misjudged Mma Ramotswe very badly."

Gobe Moruti smiled as he showed her to the door. "Well done, Mma. A very good denial. You would make a fine politician if you ever chose to stand yourself."

CHAPTER FOURTEEN

DINNER WITH QUEENIE-QUEENIE

THAT EVENING Charlie took Queenie-Queenie to the cinema at the shopping complex on the Lobatse Road. He met her outside, having gone home early to prepare himself for the date. He had been paid that morning—it was the end of the month—and Mma Ramotswe had increased his salary by eight hundred pula, an appreciable increase. His performance, she said, had been more than satisfactory, and she knew how much he struggled for rent and other living expenses. The extra money was in his pocket, right now, ready to cover what he knew would be an expensive evening. Fanwell's disclosure that Queenie-Queenie came from a well-off family had been a cause of concern for Charlie: How could he possibly keep up with somebody whose father had a fleet of trucks? So far, their dates had involved little more than meeting for coffee and, occasionally, for a drink in one of the cheaper bars. But that would hardly be enough to keep a girl like that happy, he thought. Sooner or later the subject of dinner would arise, and that would be the crunch point. Dinner was ridiculously expensive, even at a modest restaurant, and it would be impossible for Charlie to manage more than one dinner date a month—at the most. Even then, it would have to be no more than two courses, with a shared beer, perhaps.

The thought depressed him. And it became worse when he contemplated what would happen if Queenie-Queenie were ever to ask to see his room. It would be impossible for him to take her back to his shared room in that small house in Old Naledi, with its leaky roof, its privy shared with three other families, and its lean-to kitchen. He had not seen her house, but it was, she had told him, not far from Maru-a-Pula School, which meant that it was a comfortable place with a driveway and a garage—at the least—or even one of those substantial properties with a wrought-iron gate and a lawn with built-in sprinklers. How could he possibly ever aspire to court a girl from that sort of background? What if he asked her to marry him and he had to go to her father's people and start negotiating the dowry? How many head of cattle would they expect him to come up with for a girl of that standing? Fifty? Charlie had no cattle—not a single one, and he did not have the funds to buy so much as the smallest heifer.

No, it was impossible. Queenie-Queenie was out of his league, and he would have to acknowledge what should have been obvious from the very outset. And, as he thought about it, it became increasingly clear to him: he would have to bring all this to an end sooner rather than later. If he did nothing about it, it would ultimately become more humiliating; Charlie might be impetuous, he might be headstrong, but he was also sensitive to insult, and he could not bear being laughed at. And people would laugh at him, he thought, if they saw him pursuing the unattainable. That thought, and the sure and certain prospect of rejection, made the decision for him. He would take her to the cinema and then to a meal afterwards. And he would bring everything to an end over the meal. He would tell her the truth—that he could not afford to go out with somebody like her, and that he was sorry if he had misled her. He would leave with his dignity intact.

He arrived in good time and bought himself a cold drink and a packet of peanuts while he was waiting. There were other young men in the same position as he was—waiting for the arrival of a girl; in some cases, any girl—and Charlie glanced furtively at them. They were, without exception, more smartly dressed than he was. They had more money, he thought; of course they did. He thought he was well off with an extra eight hundred pula a month: that was small change to some of these people, with their generous monthly salaries from big firms, perhaps even from some of the diamond firms that had opened up on the airport road. Sorters there were well paid, he had read, and they were training cutters and polishers. It was highly skilled work and it was rewarded accordingly. What girl would decline to go out with a young man in the diamond business? And here was he, Charlie, with his trousers that were beginning to fray at the ends of the legs, with the suede shoes of which he had been so proud showing their bald patches, with his shirt that had the small iron burn at the back—invisible at a distance, he hoped, but quite obvious if you were close up. And you wanted to be close up with a girlfriend, and she would see and say, *But, Charlie, what have you done to this old shirt?* Old shirt; she would say *old shirt.*

It was all very well being a trainee detective, but was it worth it if you had to scrape a living, supplementing it with what you could earn from your greasy hours at Tlokweng Road Speedy Motors, where all the interesting work went to Fanwell now that he was qualified, and you only got the mundane oil changes and such things? That might be bearable for a time as long as there was the prospect of something better at the end of it, but it would be hard to put up with if the future seemed to be composed of nothing but more of the same. Charlie had spent a long time as an apprentice mechanic, and now it seemed that he was destined to spend an equally long period as a trainee detective. Would he ever be a fully fledged *anything*? Not in Mma Makutsi's eyes, he suspected; she was always referring to him as a *junior trainee detective* or even, on one occasion, as a *sub-assistant.* That had been hard to bear. How would she feel if he were to refer to her result at the Botswana Secretarial College as being *sub–one hundred per cent*? That would teach her.

He smiled at the thought, and was smiling when Queenie-Queenie came up behind him and put her hands over his eyes.

"Guess who, Charlie!"

He allowed her to blindfold him for a few seconds more. Then the old gallantry, tried and tested on heaven knew how many girls, came to the fore. "I think it must be the most beautiful girl in Botswana," he said. "Either that, or her sister, the second most beautiful girl in the country."

It was, of course, the right thing to say, perfectly judged, and produced a squeal of delight from Queenie-Queenie as she lowered her hands. Then she said, "Oh, Charlie, somebody's burned your shirt at the back. Did you know that? It must be the woman who does your ironing."

Charlie frowned. There was no woman to do anything for him, but presumably Queenie-Queenie, who lived at home, had several women doing her washing and ironing, and everything else, he imagined.

"You must get a new one," Queenie-Queenie said.

"Woman, or shirt?" asked Charlie.

It was a well-calculated diversion. "Naughty," scolded Queenie-Queenie. "Shirt, of course. Maybe I could help you choose. There are some new shirts in stock at Woolworth's. Very smart. A bit expensive, I think, but fashion, you know . . . fashion's never cheap."

It would be easy, thought Charlie, to say it now. This was a natural point for him to reply, *Well, it's not for me, in that case. Very little money, you see.* But he did not. People were drifting into the cinema as the film was due to start in a few minutes' time. And Queenie-Queenie had taken his arm—this beautiful, desirable young woman had taken *his* arm—the arm of a junior trainee detective, a sub-assistant, a changer of oil in old cars, a man who shared a room with two young cousins now, one of whom, barely ten, still wet the bed. That was the reality of the situation. What possible course of action could he possibly choose but to bring this unsustainable relationship to an end?

They watched the film. A few minutes in, Queenie-Queenie took his hand and clasped it tightly. She turned to him in the darkness and smiled at him. He glanced at her, and then looked away. She stroked his hand and inclined her head so that it was resting on his shoulder. He felt his heart beating. On the screen an expensive car chased another expensive car down a road, somewhere far away, in a world that was so distant from this one. He tasted the salt from the peanuts on his lips—they had been a small treat, which perhaps was the most he could expect from life: small treats, like this, sitting with this girl in a cinema, removed for a short while from the reality of the burned shirt, the shared room, the need to get through life with at least a few shreds of dignity.

He whispered to Queenie-Queenie, "Afterwards, I thought we could have a meal. Would you like that?"

She nodded. "There's a new place. It says it's Italian."

He said nothing.

"Italian," Queenie-Queenie repeated.

"Spaghetti," said Charlie.

"And other things too. They don't just eat spaghetti."

"I know that," he said. "Maybe." It would have to be somewhere else. He had walked past that Italian place and it would be far too expensive for him; he could tell that without even having to go inside. So he now said, "I don't like spaghetti very much."

"There's a Chinese place, then."

He knew that place too. It looked expensive too.

"How about African?" he said.

She laughed. "Fat cakes?"

He saw nothing wrong with fat cakes, but that, he thought, must be a very unsophisticated thing to think. "Only joking," he said.

At the end of the film they went outside into the night. People were getting into cars. Some of the young men had motorbikes and their girlfriends were climbing on the back, hugging their boyfriends round the waist as the motorcycles shot off. Charlie imagined what it would be like to be hugged round the waist by Queenie-Queenie while he guided the machine through the darkness. Bliss; it would be bliss.

It was a short walk to the café he had chosen for their dinner. It was a small place—no more than ten tables—and there were few people in it when they arrived. "People say the chef here is one of the best in Gaborone," he said as they entered.

Queenie-Queenie looked around doubtfully. "I've never heard them say that," she said.

"It's the best-kept secret in town," Charlie insisted. "You'll see."

They sat at a table where a guttering candle, spent by the night, had left a congealed pool of wax on the tablecloth.

"I love candles," said Queenie-Queenie. "I like their light."

"I prefer electricity," said Charlie. His shared room had a candle, and no power, which had been cut off two weeks earlier. Charlie thought his uncle was stealing the electricity anyway, as he had seen a furtive-looking wire snaking out of the back of the house towards a nearby power line.

They ordered, with Charlie carefully calculating how far his money would extend. It would be just enough, but would not allow for a tip. And there was a possibility that he would have to walk home rather than treat himself to a minibus.

He looked at Queenie-Queenie across the table. She smiled back at him. *I have to do it,* he told himself.

"I'm sorry, Queenie," he said. "I really like you, but . . ."

Her mouth opened slightly. She looked away.

"But I haven't got any money, you see. I can't give you the things you expect."

She turned her head. "What do I expect? How do you know what I expect?"

"Things," he said. "Your parents . . . Your father can give you things."

"That's nothing," she said.

"It isn't. How can I . . . ? How can I . . . ?" He could not express himself. Now that he had plucked up the courage to bring up the subject, he could not find the words.

Queenie-Queenie suddenly rose to her feet. "Well, thank you," she spluttered. "Well, thank you, Mr. Big Detective."

He reached out to her over the table, but she drew back from his touch. "Don't bother to follow me," she said. "Good night, Charlie."

WHEN HE ARRIVED HOME that night, there was a light on in the front room of the small house in Old Naledi. Power had been restored—unofficially: his uncle had connected the system to a different mains source. The uncle was standing outside, smoking a cigarette in the darkness. He peered at Charlie as he approached. "Is that you, Charlie?" he asked as the young man emerged from the shadows.

"Only me, Uncle," Charlie called out.

The uncle stepped forward to meet him. "I was worried," he said. "I'm glad you're safe."

Charlie laughed. "I've just been to the cinema," he said, "that's all."

The uncle's tone was grave. "Somebody came round here," he said, reaching out to take hold of Charlie's arm. "Come and see."

He led his nephew round the side of the house, extracting a flashlight from his pocket. This he switched on, directing the beam up towards the high window of Charlie's room. Charlie could see at once that the glass had been smashed; a jagged edge, where the glass still clung to the frame, revealed where a rock, or some other missile, had penetrated.

"Somebody threw a brick," the uncle said, his voice dropping to not much more than a whisper. "Just twenty minutes ago. It just missed your little cousin's head. Neither of the boys was hurt, though; just glass everywhere. Glass. Small pieces, big pieces; glass."

Charlie drew in his breath sharply. "A brick?"

"Yes," said the uncle. "It could have killed somebody inside—if it hadn't missed. That somebody . . ." He paused, and scrutinised Charlie's expression under the beam of the flashlight. "That somebody must have wanted to hurt the person inside the room."

Charlie was incredulous. "Me?"

"Yes," said the uncle. "He wouldn't have wanted to hurt the children. So it must be you, Charlie."

Charlie accompanied his uncle into the house. The shards of glass had been cleared off the bed, but the brick was still on the floor. His two young cousins watched him intently as he picked it up and stared at it. It was a builder's brick, with nothing to distinguish it from a million other bricks. Aware of the eyes of the two boys on him, he said, "An accident. Some careless person . . ."

His uncle opened his mouth to protest, but Charlie glanced at him quickly and then at the frightened children, and he understood.

"People shouldn't throw bricks away like that," said the uncle with brisk jollity. "It is a very careless thing to do."

"Yes," said Charlie. "It is very thoughtless. There are far too many people littering these days."

The children seemed to relax, and the uncle, with a final glance at Charlie, left the room. Charlie lay down on his bed. The air in the room was foetid; the room was too small for three, even if two of its occupants were small. He wanted a wider life, he wanted it so desperately; a life in which there would be room, and fresh air, and a relief from the humiliations of penury. He reached for the candle and snuffed its flame between his fingers. So might hope be extinguished, so quickly and so easily, just like that.

THEY HAD PLANNED a meeting of the committee for the first thing the next morning. The election was only a few days away now, and they had to move quickly on the posters. Pictures of Violet Sephotho had already appeared around the shops at the Riverview Mall. These were arresting—even Mma Makutsi had to concede that—with a flattering colour photograph that vividly displayed the bright red lipstick she was wearing. "You'd think this was all about a beauty contest," said Mma Makutsi, her lip curling in disdain. "Miss Fifty-Two-Per-Cent herself." Underneath the photograph was the campaign promise: *If you want things changed, then change to Violet!*

Mr. Polopetsi, who had a chemist's predilection for accuracy and precision, was particularly scathing about that slogan. "It's meaning-less," he fulminated. "Of course people want change, but change in itself is neither here nor there. People don't think about that, do they? They don't ask themselves what change will lead to. You may change things and then discover you don't like the result. What then?"

"The change you'll get from Violet Sephotho will be change for the worse," observed Mma Makutsi. "And who in their right mind would want that?"

Mr. Polopetsi shook his head sadly. "People are easily taken in by meaningless slogans," he said. "That's why they elect the wrong people. It happens time after time."

The appearance of Violet's posters added an urgency to the final-isation of Mma Ramotswe's own publicity, and this was the main business of that morning's meeting. Mma Potokwane, detained on Orphan Farm business, was unable to be there; in her absence, Mma Makutsi took the chair and announced that the posters would have to be printed that day if they were to have any effect. "I don't think we have time to print a photograph," she said. "Everybody knows what Mma Ramotswe looks like anyway. People have seen her."

"That is very true," said Mr. Polopetsi. "And Mma Ramotswe would never be able to look as glamorous as that Sephotho woman . . ." His voice trailed off; Mma Makutsi was glaring at him. "I mean as *flashy* as her," he added lamely.

"I do not want my photograph all over the place," said Mma Ramotswe. "I don't think how people look should have any effect on an election."

Charlie had been unusually silent. Now he spoke. "It shouldn't," he said. "But it does."

Mma Ramotswe continued. "It's words that count. They are the important things—words. And deeds, of course."

Mr. Polopetsi had an idea. "How about *Deeds Not Words: Vote Mma Ramotswe for Good Deeds?*"

Mma Makutsi mulled over this. "I like the sound of that. I think it's sincere."

Mr. Polopetsi refined his suggestion. "Then how about *Deeds Not Words—Yours Sincerely, Mma Ramotswe?*"

Mma Ramotswe had an objection to this. "No," she said. "You should never claim that you're sincere—that's for other people to do. It's like giving yourself a medal. You should not do it, Rra."

"If I were a general," said Charlie, "I'd give myself lots of medals. Big ones."

"Ha!" Fanwell interjected. "The Botswana Defence Force would have to be really desperate to make you a general, Charlie. Generals have to know what they're doing—like Ian Khama. He did. You'll never be like Ian Khama, Charlie—not in a hundred years." Ian Khama was the son of Seretse Khama, the founder of Botswana. He had been a general before he had been called to the presidency.

Charlie sulked. Mma Ramotswe noticed this. There was something wrong, she was sure of it; Charlie was not himself.

"I think I'll choose the wording myself," Mma Ramotswe suddenly announced. "I would like to say, *I am Mma Ramotswe. I am not much, but I promise you I'll do my best.* Those are the words I want."

This was greeted mutely as they each contemplated this radically different approach. Then Mma Makutsi broke the silence. "I don't think you should be too modest, Mma. Those words . . . well, they don't say what you want to achieve."

"That is because I don't know what that is," said Mma Ramotswe. "I won't know what I want to do until I'm on the council. I should tell people that."

"But you cannot admit it, Mma," countered Mma Makutsi. "If you say that, then people will think: *This Mma Ramotswe is not much good—she admits that herself.*"

"But I can't claim to be anything other than what I am," Mma Ramotswe insisted. "And I can't promise anything other than to do my best."

Mr. Polopetsi raised his hand. "I would like to be recognised by the chair," he said.

Fanwell looked amused. "But everybody recognises you, Mr. Polopetsi. We all know who you are."

"That's an expression, Fanwell," said Mr. Polopetsi reproachfully.

"I recognise Mr. Polopetsi," said Mma Makutsi. "You may speak now, Mr. Polopetsi. You have been recognised."

"A good thing he wasn't in disguise," muttered Charlie. "Then he might not have been recognised."

This brought a warning glance from Mma Makutsi. "Please go ahead, Rra."

Mr. Polopetsi had been perched on a table; now he rose to his feet. "I think that Mma Ramotswe is right," he said. "People don't want false promises. They want honesty. If Mma Ramotswe's posters say what she suggests, then they will think, *This Mma Ramotswe is just like us. We must vote for her, rather than for that lipstick-wearing woman with all her hot air and her Jezebel looks.*" It was strong language for Mr. Polopetsi. *Jezebel looks* . . . he was quite right, Mma Ramotswe thought, but it did not do to throw insults around.

"I think we should get those printed right now," said Fanwell. "Charlie and I can start putting them up by late afternoon."

"Then let's do that, Mma Makutsi," said Mma Ramotswe. She delivered this firmly and Mma Makutsi did not argue—the candidate had spoken.

WHILE THE OTHERS went off to arrange for the printing of the posters, Charlie lingered in the office. From behind her desk, Mma Ramotswe waited until they were alone. "You seem unhappy, Charlie," she said. "Is something wrong?"

Charlie shook his head. "I'm fine, Mma. There's nothing wrong."

She was not that easily put off. "Charlie," she said, "I know you well enough by now. I can tell when something's not right."

He approached her desk.

"You should sit down and tell me," she said.

He told her about the brick through his window. She listened sympathetically, and then asked whether he was sure that it was intended for him.

"It must have been, Mma," he replied. "My room, you see, is round the side of the house. Whoever threw it would have had to walk all the way round. If it were just some random brick, thrown by a passer-by, it would have gone through the front window."

She agreed that this was likely.

"The other day," she said, "when Eddie came to see you, he threatened you, didn't he?" She waited for a few moments, and then continued, "What did he say, Charlie?"

Charlie hesitated before replying. He looked abashed. "He told me that he had found out who was involved in that accident with Dr. Marang. He said that he is a very dangerous man and that he had heard I was looking for him. He warned me to be very careful."

Mma Ramotswe sat quite still. She was the gentlest of people, but every so often it was brought home to her that the job that she did brought her into contact with the bad and the ruthless. She was strong enough for that, of course, and would stand up to such people where necessary, but she did not like that murky world. And the idea that Charlie, who for all his bluster was still really a boy, should be subjected to threats caused her some discomfort. She felt herself responsible for him, and now here he was with a brick through his window—a missile that could well have caused him serious injury had he been in at the time.

Charlie sighed. "It will be that man, Mma. He will want to kill me now."

She tried to reassure him. "Nonsense, Charlie. He will not."

"Then why throw a brick through my window?"

"That is a way of saying something to you. He probably doesn't want to harm you."

Charlie's misery was unassuaged. "I think that if you throw a brick through somebody's window you want to hurt him," he said. And then, his lip quivering as he spoke, "Mma Ramotswe, I am very frightened. I am not very brave, you see. I'm frightened."

She rose from her chair and put an arm around the young man's shoulder. "Oh, Charlie, you mustn't be frightened."

"But I am." His voice was quivering.

"Yes, perhaps you are. But you must remember one thing, Charlie. You are on the right side here. This man—whoever he is—is a criminal. He has knocked over an old man. He has threatened you because you were going to shine a light on his dark deed. Yes, his dark deed, Charlie. And he knows very well that there is only one of him but there are many hundreds of you, thousands, in fact—all the good people of Botswana are lined up behind you, Charlie. The police. The judges. The reverends. The teachers. The President of Botswana himself. They are all on your side, Charlie, and that bad man knows it. He should be the frightened one, I think."

It was a stirring speech, and Charlie felt a bit better after it. But he still asked, "What if he comes again, Mma? What if he waits for me and he has a knife. What then?"

Mma Ramotswe shook her head. She could tell him that one should not run away from bullies, but she knew that such advice, though true at one level, was of little comfort to those who felt at risk. Daylight was one thing, but there would always be the night, when the shadows provided cover for the things that dared not show their face by day but were emboldened by darkness. Who would there be to protect Charlie in the crowded warren that was the back streets of Old Naledi? There were few streetlights there, and the people who occupied the dwellings, the bottom end of the housing market, were famous for not seeing anything. There were often no witnesses to what happened in Old Naledi.

Mma Ramotswe acted on impulse. An hour later, on reflection, she realised that she might have discussed it first with Mr. J.L.B. Matekoni, but now she acted without further thought. It was, she felt, the right thing to do—indeed, it was the only thing to do.

"You must come and stay with us in Zebra Drive," she said. "You will be safe with us, Charlie. Stay with us until this case is closed."

He looked at her in complete astonishment. "With you, Mma?"

"Yes. We have a spare room at the back. It isn't a big room, but you will be comfortable. Then, when it is safe for you to go home, you can do that."

He asked whether anybody else lived in the room. Would he be sharing with Puso, perhaps?

Mma Ramotswe laughed. "No, Puso has his own room. You will be by yourself. Just you."

Charlie looked up at the ceiling. This was almost too good to be true. His own room . . . with nobody else in it. His own room . . . But then he thought: What about the rent? A room in Zebra Drive would be considerably above his means—it would be impossible.

He raised the subject of what payment he would need to make.

"Payment, Charlie?" exclaimed Mma Ramotswe. "No, no: you will be our guest. Guests do not pay to stay in a house."

Charlie swallowed hard. "Oh, Mma, you are so kind to me."

"You can get Fanwell to help you collect your things," she said. "You can take the van."

He thanked her, his voice shaking with emotions of relief and gratitude. She put an arm around his shoulder. "Don't worry, Charlie," she said. "We would never let you be harmed. You know that, don't you?"

"I do, Mma," he said. "I know that well."

"Good," said Mma Ramotswe.

CHAPTER FIFTEEN

AN HONEST WOMAN SPEAKS

OVER THE NEXT FEW DAYS, the election campaign, until then something of a phony war, heated up. For its part, Violet Sephotho's headquarters issued several press statements in which Violet set out her plans. If she were to be elected—and she was confident, she said, that the electorate would make a wise decision—then she would be tireless in improving the lives of the citizens of Gaborone. Not only would the roads become better following her election, but so would standards in schools and hospitals. There would be a marked reduction in crime, too, as she would press for a rise in police pay and the equipping of the police with faster, more powerful cars that would enable them to apprehend lawbreakers "more swiftly and with no nonsense." And added to all these was the suggestion that some of the things that people currently had to pay for—various registration charges and so on—would in future be done for no payment. There would be free tea in libraries, schools, and hospitals. There would be free car wash stations for all motorists, and all bus journeys within the city bounds would be free every first Sunday of the month.

At Mma Ramotswe's headquarters, these claims were met with

hoots of derision. "Who does she think she is?" asked Mma Makutsi. "Miss Can-Do-Anything?"

"She can do none of these things," said Mr. Polopetsi. "Not one. If she wins—and we shall do all we can to make sure she does not—she will not have all those powers. She will just be one member of the council. She will not even be anything to do with the main government. She will be an elected nobody."

But there was one power that she would have if victorious, and that was specifically, and ominously, alluded to in another of her press statements. *We do not have enough first-class hotel accommodation in Gaborone,* it said. *What do visitors think when they come here and find out that there are not enough good hotel rooms? They go right home. This must change: we must make sure that there are plenty of hotels, especially ones that cater for those who want to have a good time.*

Mma Makutsi seized on these last thirteen words. "There," she said knowingly. "There is the evidence to confirm what Mr. Gobe Moruti told me. There it is in print—on the page—for all to see."

The press showed a strong interest in the contest. Violet's press releases were given prominent coverage, as were several lengthy interviews with her. Then, in a development that caused dismay at the No. 1 Ladies' Detective Agency, a newspaper opinion poll revealed that Violet was far ahead of Mma Ramotswe and was expected to take almost seventy per cent of the vote. *Violet Sephotho Expected to Romp Home,* said the headlines. *Major Victory Ahead for Radical Lady.*

Mma Makutsi's reaction was to question the poll. "I just don't believe those figures," she said. "Who did they question? A group of Violet's relatives? People called Sephotho?"

"Or Violet paid them to say that," suggested Fanwell. "Like an advertisement. You have to pay for those things."

"On the other hand," warned Mr. Polopetsi, "it could be true. Perhaps people actually like Violet's promises of free this and free that."

Mma Ramotswe listened carefully. She thought that Mr. Polo-petsi was probably right: people loved presents—of course they did. And if the offer of presents came from a politician, even if that meant that the money used to buy the presents came from the taxpayer, people seemed not to mind too much. But she would not participate in that sort of thing, even if it meant that she lost the election. If you won on the basis of lies and false promises—bribes, really—then your victory would be a hollow one.

At the suggestion of Mma Makutsi, Mma Ramotswe gave an inter-view to the *Botswana Daily News*. The journalist sent to do this was a young man of earnest manner, who wore large, red-framed spectacles of the sort that would appeal to Mma Makutsi. He sat, notebook on knee, pencil in hand, ready to ask Mma Ramotswe a series of search-ing questions, while Mma Makutsi, who had introduced herself as Mma Ramotswe's press officer, made tea in the background.

"Mma Ramotswe," he began, "it says on your poster that there is not much you can do. Is that so, do you think?"

Mma Ramotswe smiled. "If I said it, Rra, then I think it means it is so. We should not say what we do not mean. That is well known, I think."

The young man wrote this down. Then he asked, "But, if there is nothing you can do, then why stand for election?"

Mma Ramotswe thought for a moment. "Because there is not nothing I can do—what I can do is do the things I can do."

"And these things would be what?" he asked.

"You cannot tell," replied Mma Ramotswe. "Nobody knows what you need to do until you need to do it. It is better to be honest about these things."

Now the journalist moved on to Violet Sephotho. "What do you think of your opponent, Mma? She is offering many important reforms."

"That is very kind of her," said Mma Ramotswe.

The journalist wrote that down. Then he asked, "Do you think she's telling the truth?"

Mma Ramotswe smiled again. "What really matters is whether you think you're telling the truth. I think that Violet may think she is telling the truth, but I cannot say: you must ask her yourself. She can then answer. That is my view of the matter."

"And this issue of the Big Fun Hotel, Mma? Where do you stand on that?"

Mma Ramotswe chose her words carefully. "It is not a good thing, Rra. It would be disrespectful of all those late people to put a hotel next to their place. It would make their families sad if they visited the graves of their late relatives and heard lots of drinking and shouting going on just over the fence. That is no way to treat late people."

Finally, the journalist said, "Do you think you will win, Mma?"

Mma Ramotswe thought for a moment, and then answered, "No."

The interview was published the following day. There was a large photograph of Mma Ramotswe followed by her answers, printed verbatim. But then there was the headline and sub-heading, and it was these that counted. *An Honest Woman Speaks,* was the headline, followed by: *Mma Ramotswe says no to drinking and shouting next door to late people.* It was as powerful a statement of principle as one could wish for, and it resonated with the electorate. The electorate listened, and since in the heart of every voter there was a place for a late relative, the message struck home.

CHARLIE HAD SETTLED IN QUICKLY at Zebra Drive. He was popular with the children, particularly with Puso, who gazed at him with unconcealed admiration. And for his part Charlie was happy to reciprocate the attention, spending time with the boy in the construction of an elaborate balsa-wood model of an aeroplane, and wheeling him around the garden in Mma Ramotswe's wheelbarrow, to whoops of delight from both of them. Observing this from the verandah, Mma Ramotswe said to Mr. J.L.B. Matekoni, "Maybe Charlie would make a good father now, Rra. Just look at him."

Mr. J.L.B. Matekoni followed her gaze, and smiled. "He has come a long way." He remembered the earlier days of Charlie's apprenticeship, when he had spent virtually every lunch hour and every tea break sitting on an upturned oil barrel, flirting with any young woman who passed by. The flirtatious behaviour seemed to have gone now, along with the constant glancing into the mirror and preening, and in a curious, unexpected way Mr. J.L.B. Matekoni missed that.

"It's a pity he does not have a girlfriend," mused Mma Ramotswe. "Fanwell told me that there was somebody, but they have recently split up."

"That happens," said Mr. J.L.B. Matekoni. "Young people are always splitting up. It's what they do."

Charlie helped put Puso to bed, telling him a rambling bedtime story that was all about a man who got lost in the Kalahari and was saved by a San tracker. Puso listened wide-eyed, before drifting off to sleep, allowing Charlie to join Mma Ramotswe and Mr. J.L.B. Matekoni for the evening meal. This was stew and pumpkin—the meat being good Botswana beef, the pumpkins having been grown by one of Mma Potokwane's housemothers from the Orphan Farm. Mma Ramotswe watched Charlie tuck in with relish and suddenly thought that for all she knew he was not being properly fed in that overcrowded house in Old Naledi. She gave him a second helping, and a third one after that, and Charlie then wiped his plate clean with a crust of bread.

"You should eat more, Charlie," she said. "You need building up."

After the meal, they moved through to the living room, where

Mma Ramotswe served red bush tea and small, dry biscuits known as Marie biscuits. Charlie dunked these in his milky mug of red bush tea before swallowing them whole.

Then she mentioned the Marang case. "We need to do something," she said. "We can't leave things as they are."

Charlie looked uncomfortable. "I don't know what to do, Mma," he said.

"Would you like me to help you?" asked Mma Ramotswe.

Charlie nodded gratefully. "I would, Mma. I could be your assistant."

She smiled. "Then we shall go to Mochudi, I think. You and I. We shall go on the day of the election, so that I can get away from all the fuss."

Charlie nodded his assent. "You can vote in the morning, Mma—I'll vote in the afternoon, after we get back. If you vote in the morning, you can pick me up at the garage. I will go there early, early, Mma, and work until you are ready to leave."

"And who will you vote for?" asked Mr. J.L.B. Matekoni, smiling.

Mma Ramotswe did not reply straightaway. "I'm not sure," she said. "I don't want to vote for Violet Sephotho, but isn't it a bit boastful to vote for yourself? Are you allowed to do that?"

"Of course you are," said Charlie. "Mma, if you don't vote for yourself, then who will vote for you? Nobody, Mma—nobody."

Mr. J.L.B. Matekoni now asked whether anybody thought Violet Sephotho would vote for herself. "Of course she will," said Charlie. "And that's another reason why you must vote, Mma Ramotswe. Your vote will cancel hers out."

Mma Ramotswe poured herself another cup of red bush tea. As she raised the cup to her lips, she sighed. Politics was definitely not for her; it seemed that you had to boast and brag, make all sorts of misleading statements, deal with intrusive questions from persistent reporters, and then, to top it all, brazenly vote for yourself. She felt comfortable about none of that, and now all she hoped for was a swift end to the whole business—which would come two days later. Violet Sephotho would win, she suspected, but at least she, Mma Ramotswe, would be able to look Mma Potokwane in the eye and tell her that she had stood against her and had done her best. It would be a secret relief, of course, if Violet won, as she herself could then retire gracefully from her political career and concentrate on her real job, which was to help people with the problems in their lives. That was an honourable calling, and she felt that she did not need to justify it: a single good result, even if many other cases were never solved, could make all the difference to somebody's life.

The Dr. Marang affair was a case in point; justice, sheer basic justice, demanded a solution to that case, and, if she managed to find one, then it would somehow balance the scales of justice once again. She had some cause for optimism, even if slight; cases in which there was a complete lack of evidence or clues frequently ended up on the No. 1 Ladies' Detective Agency's list of failures. Eddie's behaviour, however, made this a different matter: at least they now knew *something,* which was that there was one person in Mochudi, apart from the driver himself, who knew who had knocked Dr. Marang down. That person was probably a friend of Eddie's, as it appeared that Eddie had not needed much time to find out who it was. More than that, Eddie was effectively protecting the driver, as he had acted as the intermediary. This suggested that the guilty person was a close-enough friend, as otherwise Eddie would have had no reason to cover up for him. The solution, then, was to find out who Eddie's close friends were, and then find out which one of them had a blue car. That process, Mma Ramotswe thought, would lead them straight to the person for whom they were looking. It would be that simple.

Mma Ramotswe smiled as the pieces of the puzzle seemed to slot into place. Noticing this, Charlie asked, "Do you have a plan then, Mma?"

She replied, "Yes, Charlie. I have a plan."

"A good one, Mma?"

She hesitated, but only briefly. "Yes, Charlie. I think it's a very good one."

Realising that Mma Ramotswe seemed unwilling to say much more about her plan, Charlie looked at his watch, yawned, and announced that he was going to bed. They said good night to him, and he started to leave the room. He stopped at the door and turned around to face his hosts.

"I am very happy," he said. Then, after a short pause, he explained the cause of his happiness. "I am very happy to be going off to my own room in this nice house. I am happy to be safe."

Mma Ramotswe lowered her teacup. "I am glad about that, Charlie."

Charlie hesitated, but he had more to say. "You have been so kind to me, Mma Ramotswe—and you too, Rra."

Mr. J.L.B. Matekoni looked down at the floor. "That's all right, Charlie," he muttered.

"You have been like my mother and father," said Charlie.

Mma Ramotswe smiled at him. "One day you should tell us about your real mother and father, Charlie. You've never spoken about them."

"One day," said Charlie, but with the circumspection of one who has no wish at all to speak about something.

ON THE DAY of the council election, Mma Ramotswe awoke earlier than usual. Her night's sleep had been fitful, punctuated by anxious dreams in which it seemed that everything—and nothing—was happening. Mma Ramotswe normally slept well, and her dreams, when remembered, tended to be uneventful. She often simply dreamed of driving her white van through featureless bush—a strange thing to dream about, she thought—or that she was having tea with Mma Potokwane on the matron's verandah, but not saying very much, just sitting and sipping tea. Other people spoke of vivid things that happened to them in that world of sleep—bizarre meetings, unlikely happenings, magical jumblings-up of people and places—but Mma Ramotswe did not, or, if she did, she did not remember any of it. That was something that Mma Makutsi had pointed out to her: "Everybody dreams the same amount, Mma," she had said. "It's just that we don't remember all our dreams—and that's just as well, if you ask me, Mma!" That last remark had been accompanied by a shake of the head, relieved as much as rueful, which made Mma Ramotswe wonder what sort of dreams Mma Makutsi was talking about, and whether she, Mma Makutsi, suffered from such dreams—*suffer* being the right word there. It must be difficult, she thought, to dream too much about things you would never do, because that suggested, people said, that you really wanted to do those things. So, if you dreamed about cake—and Mma Ramotswe did just that from time to time—then that meant that you secretly wanted to eat more cake, or not so secretly, perhaps. There were some people who very clearly and obviously wanted to eat more cake, it was written all over their faces. One might as well wear a large badge saying *Greedy Person* on it.

But it was not cake that Mma Ramotswe dreamed about on the night before the election, nor was it politics—and heaven knew what politicians dreamed about; meetings, perhaps, endless meetings. Her dreams on that fitful night were, rather, of needing to be somewhere and not being able to get there. And then, when she would emerge into the outskirts of consciousness—that vague state of being awake but not quite awake—she would struggle to work out where she had to be and why, before drifting back into sleep and the recurrence of that sense of unease and anxiety. When she awoke, she saw from the clock beside her bed that it was almost half-past five—too late to go back to sleep, but exactly the right time to go out into her garden and watch the dawn. It was her favourite part of the day, a time when humanity was stirring but had yet to begin to make much noise, and the air was given over to birds, to have their say before their songs were drowned out; it was a time of faint wood-smoke and the smell of acacia leaves unfurling so as to be ready for the first of the sun's warmth, a smell that Mr. J.L.B. Matekoni said was not there, was nothing but imagination, but which she knew existed because she had always picked it up, even as a young child; it was a time when she could call to mind small matters, because the important things that the day brought, the distractions and concerns of life, were not yet elbowing everything else out of the way. *Look at the small creatures on the ground,* her father, the late Obed Ramotswe, had said to her. *Look at those small creatures before the birds wake up and chase them away.* And she had, she remembered; she had watched them going about their minute, generally unnoticed business in their tiny world: engaged in their search for food or for building supplies—blades of dry grass, microscopic fragments of wood, grains of sand—with which they would construct their towns and cities, every bit as elaborate and as impressive as our own human creations.

Now, with her cup of freshly made red bush tea in hand, she made her way out into the garden, still wearing the faded pink housecoat that doubled as a dressing gown, because nobody would see her—except possibly the neighbours, if they were to be up at this hour, and she, anyway, had seen them in their nightwear, taking bowls of food out to the kennel occupied by their ill-tempered yellow dog. Mma Ramotswe was not one to care unduly about fashion or about how she looked, as long as her clothes were clean and in reasonable repair. In this respect

she differed from Mma Makutsi, whose interest in fashionable shoes
was well known, and who tended to prefer bright colours. Mma Ramotswe's own footwear was functional—"Traditionally built shoes are the
right thing for traditionally built people," she would point out—and
she invariably chose shoes that allowed room for her broader foot to
spread out in comfort. She also favoured shoes that would not show
the dust, and so these were almost always brown, the same colour as
the earth. "Dust is a big problem in a dry country like Botswana," she
observed, "and that is why brown shoes are more sensible than white
shoes. Everybody knows that, I suspect, except for those who do not
know it, and whose shoes quickly become scruffy."

In the garden that morning, waiting for the sun to come floating
up over the eastern horizon, she thought about the day ahead. On
occasion, she was able to put thoughts of unpleasant tasks out of her
mind should they come to her while she was enjoying her garden,
but this morning there was no doing that. This was the day of the
election, and the day on which she would have to grit her teeth and
endure attention that she had never sought, was most uncomfortable
with, and really hoped would simply go away. If she could have her
way, she would turn the clock forward, skipping the hours of daylight,
until it was dark once more and she was in her kitchen, the day behind
her, preparing for supper and an early night. That was the thought
that always came to her when she found life trying or unpleasant: the
thought of climbing into her own bed shortly before nine, turning
out the light, and sinking into the arms of blissful sleep. Such a prospect could sustain one through just about anything, just as the imagining of a draught of cold water must sustain some poor soul lost in the
Kalahari, trying to find a path or track that would lead the way home;
or just as the thought of retirement must enable people to do hard and
unpleasant work, knowing that before too long they would say goodbye
to the workplace for the last time, sit themselves down under a tree,

look at the sky, and think of what it was like not to have to do whatever it is that they had had to do, day in, day out, for all those years.

She shook herself out of her reverie. She would face the day as bravely as she could; she would get to the polling station as soon as it opened, slip in and cast her vote, and then absent herself as quickly as possible, seen, she hoped, by nobody. Then she would take Charlie off to Mochudi, as they had planned, and busy herself with what she should be doing—helping her clients—rather than involving herself in the messy and unpleasant world that was politics.

The sun came up, at first a curved slice of golden red, and then a shimmering, glowing ball, lifting itself free of the line of tree-tops, light, effortless, floating. And then the sky opened up, freed of its veils of darkness, a great pale blue bowl above . . . above *me,* thought Mma Ramotswe—and all the other people who were getting up now in Botswana; above people for whom this was their first day on this earth—the tiny, fragile babies—and above those for whom it was their last—the aged people who had seen so much and who knew that the world was slipping between their fingers . . . all—or most of us, at least—trying our best, trying to make something of life, hoping to get through the day without feeling too unhappy, or uncomfortable, or hungry—which was what just about everybody hoped for, whether they were big and important, or small and insignificant. She sighed. If only people could keep that in their minds—if they could remember that the people they met during the day had all the same hopes and fears that they had, then there would be so much less conflict and disagreement in this world. If only people remembered that, then they would be kinder to others—and kindness, Mma Ramotswe believed, was the most important thing there was. She knew that in the depths of her being; she knew it.

The children were aware that the day was a special one and made their preparations for school quickly and co-operatively. Then, once they were out of the house and Mr. J.L.B. Matekoni had driven off to work with Charlie, Mma Ramotswe perfunctorily tidied the kitchen, made a pack of sandwiches to take on the trip to Mochudi, and set off for the polling station that she had been told would be established in the municipal offices on Independence Avenue.

She arrived just as the official opened the door to the room in which the polling booths had been erected. There were three of these—curtained constructions in which the voters could mark their papers in private before placing them in a large box atop a trestle table. This table had been draped in the national flag, reminding voters of the importance of the task they were performing. Although candidates' publicity was forbidden in the immediate vicinity of the polling station, there were several large posters proclaiming civic messages. *It's your democratic duty—cast your vote wisely!* counselled one of these; while another said, perhaps more opaquely, *If you don't vote, then you can't complain!* Mma Ramotswe approached the young man who was sitting at a desk to the side of the booths. She greeted him in the traditional way, and then said, "I would like to vote, Rra."

The young man looked at his watch. "It is too early, Mma. You cannot vote until the polls are open, and that will only be in two minutes."

Mma Ramotswe resisted the temptation to laugh. Rules, she supposed, were rules, but really . . .

"In that case," she said, "could you just check my name on the roll? Then, when you are ready to open, I will be able to go straight in."

The young man shook his head. "I cannot do that, Mma. I must wait for another two minutes before I check your name."

She stared at him. "You cannot . . ."

He shook his head. "No, I cannot do anything until it is the proper time."

There was a note of finality in his voice, and Mma Ramotswe

did not press the matter. After two minutes had elapsed, the young man looked at his watch, adjusted his tie in a self-conscious manner, and eventually paged through a large register on the desk before him. Finding Mma Ramotswe's name, he ticked it off, and handed her a voting paper. "Don't vote for the wrong person, Mma," he said, and then laughed.

Mma Ramotswe smiled tolerantly. "I haven't made up my mind yet," she replied.

The young man's expression changed immediately. "But, Mma, you are a candidate . . ."

Mma Ramotswe assured him that she was only joking. Charlie was the same, she told herself; young men often failed to realise when somebody was not being entirely serious.

The young man now lowered his voice. "I'm not going to vote for that Sephotho woman," he confided. "You don't want a glamorous woman on the council. You don't need that in politics."

Mma Ramotswe raised an eyebrow. "No, Rra?"

"No. You see, a glamorous lady like that will be always thinking *me, me, me*. That's what they're like, Mma. And then . . ."

Mma Ramotswe waited for him to finish.

"So," he continued, "if we must have women on the council . . ."

Mma Ramotswe drew a deep breath. "I'm sorry, Rra," she said, "I didn't quite catch what you said."

The young man shifted in his seat. "I said, if there are going to be women on the council . . ."

Mma Ramotswe raised a finger. "No, Rra, I don't think that's what you said. And you know, we mustn't tell people we said one thing when we actually said another. You know that, don't you?"

Chastened, the young man nodded.

"So, I don't think you would ever say that there shouldn't be women on the council. You wouldn't say that, would you, Rra?"

This brought a miserable shaking of the head. Nothing much had been said, but the sheer authority of Mma Ramotswe had had the desired effect. Now, seeking to explain himself, the young man continued, "What I meant to say, Mma, was that it's better not to have glamorous women, who will not do the job very well, when there are other, not very glamorous women who will be much better. Such as you, Mma—you would be very good, I think."

She inclined her head in acknowledgement of the compliment—if that was what it was. *Not very glamorous . . .* well, she had never pretended to be anything other than what she was. Glamorous people were all very well, but when it came to cooking pumpkin, or repairing children's clothing, or making stew for a hungry husband, or doing any of the other hundreds of things that women had to do every day, every day, then glamour did not get one very far.

She went into the polling booth. Opening the voting paper she saw the two candidates' names: SEPHOTHO, V, and RAMOTSWE, P. The sight brought it home to her that this really was happening: throughout the town, people would be looking at this very slip of paper and seeing her name—her ordinary, mundane name—placed there in print with the authority of no less a personage than the Minister of Local Government. Going back all those years to that school in Mochudi, the old, red-roofed building on the hill with its view of the plains below, who would have dreamed that the small Ramotswe girl would end up with her name on a ballot paper in Gaborone? Who would have thought it? And yet here it was before her, and she now had to make the same decision that everybody else would have to make—she would have to vote.

She felt the back of her neck grow warm, and she knew at once what this was. It was shame; it always happened when she felt ashamed. And her shame on this occasion was entirely to do with her natural modesty. You never congratulated yourself. You never pushed yourself forward in front of others. You never boasted about what you had done or could do. You never did any of these things, she had been taught, because it was wrong, simply wrong, to make much of yourself. She had been taught that by her father, the late Obed Ramotswe, who had been a man of egregious modesty. Everybody knew that his cattle were among the finest in the country; everybody knew that, when it came to judging livestock, to selecting which cow would give birth to the best calves, there was nobody to equal him in Mochudi, nor for miles around, in fact. And people respected him for that, because to be a good cattle man in Botswana, where cattle were so loved and admired, was a mark of the greatest distinction. But he never talked about all this, and would deflect such praise as people gave him, saying that there were many who were every bit as good at judging cattle as he was, and even more who were better—which was not true, of course.

And here she was, the daughter of that great man, about to vote for herself. Wondering what he would have said about that, she reached the conclusion that he would have been astonished that anybody could do such a thing. Yes, she thought, but were he to know what the alternative was, then surely he would understand. She was not sure whether her father had ever met anybody like Violet Sephotho. She imagined that he must have done in the past—he had been a miner, after all, and the women you met in mining camps were often on the fast side—but would they have been as ambitious, as calculating as Violet? Probably not. "Oh, Daddy," she muttered to herself, "don't think harshly of me: this is all Mma Potokwane's doing, it really is. I did not want to find myself in this position. I did not want my name to be plastered all over town. I do not want to be a member of any committee, let alone the Gaborone City Council. I am not that sort of person . . ."

She closed her eyes. The moment of truth had arrived, and she would have to vote. Only half opening her eyes, she stared at the paper momentarily, and then put a cross against Violet's name. She voted for

Violet Sephotho. *It doesn't matter*, she told herself, *one vote won't make the slightest difference. I could not—simply could not—vote for myself.*

SHE HAD PARKED her tiny white van under a tree not far from the entrance to the council offices. As she began to walk towards it, she felt a blanket of shame descend on her. She had voted for Violet Sephotho, and that was the cause of her shame, although she wondered whether she might not have felt even more ashamed if she had voted for herself. Perhaps she should not have voted at all, but then there was ignominy attached to that as well—it was your duty to vote, as Seretse Khama had said, or would have said had anybody ever asked him about it.

When the man came up to her, she did not see where he came from. She was almost at the van when he stopped in front of her and greeted her.

"You are Mma Ramotswe, aren't you?"

There was a note of apology in his voice.

"Yes, Rra," she said. "I am Mma Ramotswe."

She looked at him. He was a middle-aged man, neatly but plainly dressed. He was not wearing office clothes, nor the outfit of one who earned his living with his hands. He was carrying a hat, the rim of which was discoloured through long use. Straitened circumstances lay not far away, she thought. "You do not know me, Mma," he said. "I am just an ordinary person."

She almost said, "But so am I, Rra," but she stopped herself. Everything had changed since the election campaign had begun, and she was no longer just an ordinary person—she was public property.

He gave her his name. He was John Maphephu, he explained, and he was a security guard at one of the banks. "The head security guard," he said. "I have five men working under me, Mma. It is not a big job, but they are good to us. We have good conditions."

Mma Ramotswe smiled encouragingly. "It is good to have a job like that," she said. "You know that you will get paid at the end of the month."

John Maphephu agreed that this was important. He looked down at the ground. Mma Ramotswe waited. Overhead, a large bird, catching an early thermal, circled lazily. Mma Ramotswe glanced up at it, and then looked at the man. She saw that the hand in which he held his hat was shaking slightly; a tremor. She had seen that in her father; his hand had started to shake, and that was the first sign of his illness, she had learned. Was this man ill, or was something making him nervous?

She decided to speak. "What is it, Rra? Is there anything I can do for you?"

People had told her that once you went into politics you could expect people to seek favours. Was this the first occasion of that, she wondered; and would every day be like that if she were to win? Would there be a constant stream of supplicants wanting all sorts of things that she would have no idea how to provide?

John Maphephu was shaking his head. "I'm not asking for anything, Mma. I only wanted to speak to you, to thank you for what you're doing."

It took her a moment or two to respond. "But I've done nothing, Rra."

"Oh, yes, you have, Mma. You've done a great deal."

"I don't think so," she began.

He brushed her objection aside. "Mma, you must remember you are standing for election. This may only be a council election, but every election—even a small one—is important. And now, with you, Mma, we have the chance to vote for somebody who is honest."

She raised a hand to stop him. "But there are many honest politicians in Botswana," she said. "We are very lucky that way. We are not like some other places."

There was no need for her to mention anywhere in particular; everybody knew.

"And there is not a lot of corruption in this country, Rra," she said. "That is another thing we can be grateful for."

John Maphephu accepted all that. "That's true. But this election is different, you see, Mma. This is the first time that somebody has not promised anything. This is the first time that somebody has said: *I cannot work miracles, and I will not promise you this, that, and the next thing.* You said that, Mma. Then you said that you would do your best, even if your best would not be very good."

Mma Ramotswe smiled. "People told me I shouldn't say that, you know."

"Of course they did," said John Maphephu. "But they are wrong, Mma Ramotswe. It is the very best thing that anybody could have said." He paused. "And that is why everybody is going to vote for you."

Mma Ramotswe's mouth opened slightly; she had not expected this.

"Everybody," repeated John Maphephu. "All the people I've spoken to—every single one of them has said, *I'm going to vote for that fat woman who says she can't do anything.* That is what they're saying, Mma."

"Traditionally built," muttered Mma Ramotswe.

"Yes, Mma, that's right—traditionally built. People like to vote for a traditionally built lady who tells the truth."

Mma Ramotswe looked away. She was embarrassed by this display of enthusiasm—and deeply concerned at the implications. If everybody voted for her, then she would win. That seemed to be the logical conclusion of what this man was saying to her, but it was not a conclusion that she in any way wanted.

"And as for that other lady," John Maphephu continued, "nobody is going to vote for her, Mma. Nobody."

Except me, thought Mma Ramotswe.

She looked at her watch. "You have been very kind to tell me all this, Rra," she said.

"It is the truth, Mma. And now I shall go in and vote for you. That is what I'm going to do."

"Then I shall let you do that, Rra," she said. "And thank you." They parted. Mma Ramotswe got into her van and sat lost in thought for a few minutes before briskly starting the engine. There was no point, she told herself, in worrying about the outcome of the election: what was going to happen was going to happen and there was nothing she could do about it now. There was work to be done—the No. 1 Ladies' Detective Agency had things to do, and that day she was planning to go to Mochudi with Charlie. That was something practical that needed to be done, whatever the result of the election, however uncertain her future now looked. *Yes,* she said to herself, *there are things to do, many things* . . . and then, as she drew away in the tiny white van, she looked in the driving mirror and saw that there were more people arriving at the council offices. John Maphephu had gone inside, but there was now a small line of four or five people waiting outside the door. These were the voters; she was sure of it. And with that realisation she gasped and pulled over to the side. These people were going in to vote; they were actually going inside to vote. This was really happening. This was not some scheme dreamed up by Mma Potokwane—this was real.

She let the engine idle as she took a series of deep breaths. She closed her eyes, and then opened them. Botswana was still there. Glancing in the mirror again, hardly daring to do so, but forcing herself, she saw that the voters had begun to enter the door. But more were arriving. She closed her eyes again.

And then something happened that had only happened once or twice before, but when it had done so, it had burned itself into her memory. Her father was there. Somehow, in a way known only to late people, he had slipped into the cab of the van and was seated beside her. Of course, she could not see him—not in the physical sense—but of his presence she had absolutely no doubt.

"So, my Precious," he said. "This is a very important day for you."

He spoke as he always did—it was his voice—but at the same time it was distant, as if it came from a long way away, like the voices of those who spoke to one another in the earlier days of telephones, when it was such a complicated business to call Gaborone from Francistown, all that way down those singing, strung-out telephone wires.

She wanted to say something, but could not find the words. She wanted to say to him that she had never stopped loving him and that she thought of him every day, every day without fail—sometimes in the morning when she went out into her garden to watch the sun rise; sometimes in the kitchen, when she was standing at the sink doing the washing up; or in the office, when she and Mma Makutsi were drinking tea and the sunlight was slanting through the high window, dappling the once-white ceiling boards. She wanted to say that, but she found that she could not speak. He would understand, though, because they had spent many hours together before he became late, when they had said nothing to one another but had nonetheless said everything. Because it was possible, she knew, to say nothing and to say everything at the same time—if you were with somebody whom you understood and loved. It was not necessary to talk in such circumstances; there was no need.

He spoke again, his voice fainter now. "Don't be afraid," he said. "You never were, you know—you were never afraid. Remember this, my Precious; remember this—you have Botswana."

And, with that, he slipped away. Mma Ramotswe held the steering wheel with her shaking hands. She took a further deep breath, and it calmed her. She found herself smiling.

_____

CHAPTER SIXTEEN

THIS IS WHERE I AM HAPPIEST

As THEY DROVE up to Mochudi, Charlie told Mma Ramotswe about Queenie-Queenie. It was an intimate conversation, not one that up until then would have been likely, but now, with new-found maturity, the young man seemed prepared to speak honestly.

"She's a nice girl," Charlie said. "But she's above my pay grade."

"Pay grade?" asked Mma Ramotswe. "What is this to do with pay grades?"

Charlie laughed. "It's a way of speaking, Mma. It means that she's too good for me—not good-good as in going to church and things like that. Not that. No—classy, you see. Too classy."

Mma Ramotswe shook her head. Charlie was driving, and she wanted him to concentrate, as there were large trucks on the road—cattle trucks from the north—and their drivers tended to assume they owned the public highway. But this conversation was too intriguing to cut short. Charlie's love life had been a closed book to everybody in the past; they knew there were girlfriends, but they had never been able to work out who was in favour at any particular time. Mma Makutsi occasionally reported on a sighting she had had of Charlie with a girl somewhere or other, but that was about the extent of the intelligence.

"Cattle," said Charlie.

That made it clearer, and Mma Ramotswe sighed. "Oh, I see." She glanced at Charlie. The *lebola* system, in which the man paid the woman's family a bride price, had hung on in spite of all the changes that the country had seen. People talked about doing away with it; people criticised it for making young women into something that could be bought and sold; but it continued, stubbornly, as these traditions often persisted, and it remained something that a young man contemplating marriage had to face.

"I was reading in the paper," Charlie continued, "that down in Kanye they've been trying to set a limit. They say eight cows, max. People have been greedy, you see. Uncles and so on have been asking for fifteen head of cattle, maybe more."

"That is very bad," said Mma Ramotswe. "You shouldn't make it hard for people to marry, Charlie."

Charlie agreed. "The government should give men cattle in order to marry, Mma. They're always telling us to get married rather than to—" He broke off.

"I know what you mean," said Mma Ramotswe.

"Rather than to have a good time. They should say: *Okay, if you get married then we will give you eight cattle.* They could afford it, Mma. Look at all the money the government has. All that money from the diamonds: Why not give it to men, to encourage them to marry ladies?"

Mma Ramotswe chuckled. "I don't think it works that way, Charlie. The government can't go round giving people lots of cattle. The government hasn't got that many cattle, you know."

Charlie was prepared to compromise. "Well, how about this, Mma? How about the government giving cattle to men to marry those girls who cannot find a husband? How about that? So if there are some girls—and I'm sorry to say there are—if there are some girls that nobody would want to marry because . . . well, Mma, you know there are some girls who haven't got very pretty faces, or who are generally useless: those girls, Mma, they could get a husband if the government paid him enough. There would always be some man who'd say, *Well, give me eight cattle and I'll close my eyes and get on with it.*"

Mma Ramotswe felt it was time to change the subject. "You were telling me about this Queenie-Queenie girl, Charlie. Her father's well off, is he?"

"Very," said Charlie. "So I knew there was no future for me."

"Have you met him?"

Charlie seemed surprised. "Her father? No, Mma. He wouldn't want to meet somebody like me."

"And what does Queenie-Queenie herself say about it?" Mma Ramotswe asked. "Did you discuss it with her?"

Charlie said that he thought there would be no point. "It's not going to happen," he said. "So I didn't bother her with it. I made the decision."

"You? Just you by yourself?"

Charlie nodded. "I ended it, Mma. It was easier that way."

For a few moments, Mma Ramotswe was silent. A large truck, its horn blaring, swayed past them head-on—a truck full of cattle. There was a rush of air and the smell of confined animals, and dust. Cattle, thought Mma Ramotswe. Cattle.

She turned to face Charlie. "Sometimes it's best to talk to people, Charlie. You talk to them, you see, and then whatever problems there are can be sorted out. You should try it."

"There's no point, Mma," he said. "It wouldn't be her decision, you see. It would be her family's, and I know for a fact—for a fact, Mma—that they would think I'm nothing."

"You're not nothing," she said.

"I am, Mma. I'm nothing to people like that."

Mma Ramotswe looked out of the window. They were on the outskirts of Mochudi now—outskirts that seemed to spread further and further into the bush every time she went up there. When she had been a girl, there had been nothing at this point—just virgin bush—and now there were houses, a school, a cluster of small shops.

"Maybe we can talk about it some other time," she said to Charlie. "We have to go to a clinic."

Charlie looked concerned. "Are you not well, Mma?"

"I am very well," said Mma Ramotswe. "But there is a lady there— a nurse—who is an old friend of mine. She is one of these people who knows everything. I want to ask her for some information." She paused. "Remember what I said, Charlie: talk to people. It is the best way of doing things. Talk, talk—you can never have too much talk."

THE CLINIC was at the far end of the town, an outpost of the hospital nestling at the foot of the hill. Its concern was small matters, mostly to do with public health—inoculating children, screening for bilharzia, attending to the minor injuries and complaints that did not merit hospital attention: the cut fingers that had become infected, the bruised ribs, the eye infections that were brought on by the flies that crawled around children's eyes. The human body in a hot climate can go wrong in a hundred different ways, with rashes and bites and infections that luxuriated in the heat, and these were the daily concern of Mma Ramotswe's friend Sister Montsho. The nurse had been a childhood friend of Mma Ramotswe's, having been in her class at school. They had grown up together, and had remained in touch for all but the recent period of two years when Sister Montsho had gone off to Nairobi for specialist training. Now she was back, and the friendship, like so many friendships of early childhood, had proved to be unaltered by the years.

There were people sitting patiently, waiting to be seen, but Sister Montsho, seeing the arrival of Mma Ramotswe's white van, had brought forward the morning tea break.

"I need a break to catch my breath," she said. "This is a busy time of year for some reason. People are treading on thorns, burning their hands on cooking pots, even putting marula pips up their noses, would you believe it? All these things, Mma Ramotswe—every day, every day."

Mma Ramotswe smiled. "If any of those things happened to me, Mma, I would be glad to put myself in your hands."

Sister Montsho clapped her hands. She turned to Charlie. "Hear that, young man? Those are the words of a lady who knows how to make her friends feel good."

"I'm sure it's true, Mma," said Charlie.

The nurse laughed. "Well, if I needed to solve any mysteries in my life I would certainly go to Mma Ramotswe—I can tell you that for sure."

"She is very good at that," said Charlie, a note of pride in his voice. "And I am her apprentice, you see. Mma Ramotswe is teaching me."

"Then you will become a very fine detective, Rra," said Sister Montsho. "But now we must have a cup of tea because I shall have to get back to those poor people out there." She gestured towards the waiting knot of people, seated on benches under a shade awning.

Over tea, Mma Ramotswe explained the reason for her visit. Although Charlie looked a bit uncomfortable, she told the story of Charlie's conversation with Eddie and the subsequent visit of Eddie. Sister Montsho listened intently, sipping at her tea and occasionally looking at Charlie, as if to assess him.

When she had finished, Charlie reminded her that there was something to add. "And I had a brick thrown through my window, Sister," he said. "It could have killed somebody. My little cousins were in the room."

Sister Montsho shook her head. "I know that young man Eddie," she said. "I know exactly who he is." She made a clicking sound with her tongue, an unambiguous sound of disapproval.

Mma Ramotswe looked at Charlie, and then back at the nurse. "If we were able to find out who Eddie's friends are," she said, "then we might be able to work out which one of them is the person who knocked Dr. Marang over."

Charlie had picked up on Mma Ramotswe's plan and now he thought he might explain. "We know it was a blue car, Mma. So if we find one of them who drove a blue car, then that would be him."

"*Could* be him," corrected Mma Ramotswe.

Sister Montsho looked thoughtful. "Why not ask his mother," she suggested. "Mothers usually know everything about their sons, I find. It's just like wives knowing everything about their husbands."

Charlie, who was standing during this conversation, shifted uneasily from foot to foot. "Or husbands," he said. "Husbands will know everything about their wives, remember."

Both Sister Montsho and Mma Ramotswe turned to look at him.

"I don't think so," said the nurse. "Husbands often know very little, Rra. I don't want to sound rude, but that's just the way it is."

Mma Ramotswe was more tactful. "Sometimes," she said. "Sometimes they do, and sometimes they don't. It all depends."

"Well, we could discuss that for a long time," said Sister Montsho. "But I still think you should speak to Eddie's mother. She runs a small store out that way." She pointed vaguely to the north. "It's about five miles outside town—you know, one of those very small rural stores. She comes to the clinic here because she has an albino child." She paused. "That child is the half-brother of that boy Eddie. Same mother, different father."

"Is the albino child not well?" asked Mma Ramotswe.

Sister Montsho sighed. "The child is all right. They can have sight problems, you know, but there is something much more difficult. They cannot be in the sun—because of their skin. They burn very quickly. They can get blisters, sometimes deep burns if the exposure to the sun is too long. They have to use sun-blocking creams all the time. She gets them here from us. The government pays."

Mma Ramotswe exchanged a glance with Charlie. "Now that's a good use of the government's cattle," she said.

Charlie smiled at the reference. "You're entitled to your views, Mma," he muttered.

Mma Ramotswe got the directions from Sister Montsho. "We shouldn't keep you, Mma. You have work to do."

Outside, one of the patients groaned—a long, protesting groan that carried into the nurses' office where they were drinking tea. Mma Ramotswe looked guilty; she did not like the thought that their conversation was holding up the treatment of those in need.

Sister Montsho had heard the groan but was smiling cheerfully. "Oh, that man," she said lightly. "He's here almost every day. He is always groaning, but the doctor can find nothing wrong with him. He was in and out of the hospital, and then they started to send him here. I have something I give him now that is just coloured water. We call it a placebo. He loves it and he comes back a day or two later for more."

"And the government pays for the coloured water?" asked Charlie.

"The government doesn't mind that," said Sister Montsho. "Coloured water is very cheap to make. You just add some of that red colouring they use for icing. Then you put it in a bottle with a pharmacy label and people are very happy. Often it makes them better because they think they are getting a powerful medicine."

Charlie looked up at the shelves lining the office walls with their ordered rows of boxed pills, bottles of medicines, cough syrups, and analgesics. "Perhaps you could give me something," he said. "I would like to be stronger."

Sister Montsho laughed. "You don't need anything, young man," she said. "Just experience. Get experience. That's much better than any placebo."

"*Placebo,*" muttered Charlie, savouring the word. "That's a very good word, Sister."

Sister Montsho nodded. "The human body can be easily tricked, Rra. You have to be careful."

"You hear that, Charlie?" said Mma Ramotswe, rising to leave. "You have to be careful."

They went outside. As Sister Montsho walked to the van with Mma Ramotswe, she raised the subject of the election. She had read about Mma Ramotswe's candidature and was interested to find out how the campaign was going.

"People are voting today," said Mma Ramotswe. "I think the results will be out by nine o'clock tonight."

"I hope you win," said Sister Montsho.

"I don't think I will."

Sister Montsho looked dubious. "Remember my sister?" she said. "The one who lives in Gaborone?" Mma Ramotswe did. "She says that everybody she knows is going to vote for you. That's what she told me."

It was not the news that Mma Ramotswe wanted to hear, but she put a brave face on it. "I don't know what will happen, Mma," she said. "It is in God's hands."

"I know which way he voted," said Charlie.

Mma Ramotswe looked at him disapprovingly, but then both she and Sister Montsho smiled.

"It's not over yet," said Mma Ramotswe. She knew that to be true; it was certainly not over. In fact, it was only just beginning, she told herself, and it would go on, she feared, for a long time yet: meeting after meeting, letter after letter, speech after speech. It was not the life she had planned for herself, but neither was being a private detective. *Life happens,* she thought; *whatever we do, life just happens.*

EDDIE'S MOTHER was Mma Maria Lelotong. Entering the one-room general store, the Good Housewife Shopping Centre, Mma Ramotswe addressed the woman behind the counter, in the correct way of the old Botswana, as *Mma Eddie*—mother of Eddie.

"Yes," said Mma Lelotong. "That is me, Mma." She glanced at Charlie, and recognition slowly dawned. "I think I know who you are. You were a friend of Eddie's a long time ago. I think I have seen you, Rra."

Mma Ramotswe looked at Charlie. He was clearly uncomfortable, but she could not work out why this was.

Charlie inclined his head. "I was his friend, yes."

"Was?" asked Mma Lelotong.

"Am," replied Charlie.

Mma Ramotswe looked about the store. In spite of its grandiose name, there was not much to distinguish it from any number of minute general dealer businesses that dotted the remoter areas of Botswana. It had the characteristic smell of such places too—a combination of the odours of maize meal, paraffin, candle wax, and carbolic soap, all mixed up to create an unmistakable "general store" smell. Exiles from Africa, returning after years away, would know it immediately—the smell of home; comforting as only familiar smells of childhood can be.

Her gaze moved along the shelves. The goods on display told the story of the land and its people. Jars of petroleum jelly were stacked next to tins of baby powder—a reminder of the fact that some people still liked to smear a baby with petroleum jelly to make the infant's skin shine. A brand of well-known cough sweets spoke to the faith that rural people had in such products, even if they were mostly sugar and a token dash of mild antiseptic. Then, in the soap section, a bit further along, there were only two choices: Lux for women, pink, self-indulgent, and Lifebuoy for men—red, bracing, clinical. Then there were tins of baked beans, tubs of margarine, groundnut cooking oil; Tate and Lyle's Golden Syrup, with its lion crest; Lion matches too, a tiny black-maned lion on the box. Batteries. In one corner, against the wall, a religious picture told a different story. Mma Lelotong was a Catholic, Mma Ramotswe saw. That explained her being called Maria.

Mma Ramotswe went straight to the point. "Mma, there is something I need to talk to you about," she began. "It is a very complicated story, and it may be that you cannot help me, but I would like to tell you about it."

Mma Lelotong gave her a guarded look. "Is it something that Eddie has done?"

It was Charlie who answered before Mma Ramotswe could speak. "No, no, not him. One of his friends, Mma. It's one of his friends."

"I think that's right, Mma," said Mma Ramotswe. "We want to know who your son's friends are."

Mma Lelotong looked away. "But why should I speak to you about this, Mma? Why should I tell you about my son's friends?"

Mma Ramotswe spoke quietly. "You know Dr. Marang, Mma?"

Mma Lelotong nodded. "Of course, Mma. He is a good man. We all know him."

"And you know he had an accident?"

The other woman hesitated. "I have heard that."

Mma Ramotswe chose her words carefully. "You are a Catholic, Mma?"

"I am."

Mma Ramostwe waited a moment or two. "Dr. Marang is too, Mma. You'll know that, won't you?" She did not wait for an answer, but continued, "Perhaps I should tell you the full story, Mma."

There was nobody else in the store, and they were invited to sit down on two rickety canvas chairs behind the main counter. Mma

Lelotong herself did not sit down, but leaned against the counter while Mma Ramotswe spoke.

At the end of Mma Ramotswe's explanation, Mma Lelotong sighed. "Eddie is not a bad boy," she said. "He has a kind heart, you know—he has always been like that."

"I'm sure that's so," said Mma Ramotswe.

"But he has some friends who are not so good," went on Mma Lelotong. "Some of them have already been in trouble with the police." She paused, and Mma Ramotswe saw the sadness written across her face. "You said it was a blue car, Mma?"

Charlie answered this. "Yes, that's what the doctor told the police. He saw a blue car—that was all."

Mma Lelotong shrugged. "I can give you the names of his friends. Some of them drive cars, I think, but I do not know what colour those cars are."

Mma Ramotswe became aware that while Mma Lelotong was speaking Charlie had become agitated. Now he touched her briefly on the shoulder, leaning forward to whisper to her.

"Mma, I need to talk to you outside."

Mma Ramotswe glanced at Mma Lelotong. "Would you excuse us for a moment, Mma?"

They went outside, into the sun. The sky was high and empty, the heat pressing down upon them.

"What is it, Charlie? Why have you—?"

He cut her short. "It's Eddie, Mma. He is the one."

She stared at him. "Eddie?"

"He's the one with the blue car. It is him, Mma. I know because . . ."

She waited for him to finish. He lowered his head, as if ashamed.

"I know because when he came to see me he was driving a red car. But I looked closely at the paintwork and I could tell that it had been repainted."

She said nothing.

"I knew," said Charlie. His expression—and his tone of voice— were ones of misery. "I was frightened, you see, Mma. I was too frightened to tell you, but now I realise that was wrong. I should have told you before." He paused. "I am very sorry, Mma."

She looked at him. "Charlie," she said, "you may have been frightened, but now you are brave."

"I should have told you, Mma. I should have—"

She silenced him with a gesture. "It doesn't matter," she whispered. "And now we should go back in."

Mma Ramotswe did not have to confront Mma Lelotong. When they went back in, they found her with her head sunk in her hands. Gently, Mma Ramotswe asked if she was all right.

"I am all right, Mma," replied the other woman. "But I am very sad—that is all."

Mma Ramotswe waited a few moments before she asked, "Does Eddie drive a blue car, Mma?"

Mma Lelotong dropped her hands. "Oh, I am very sad, Mma— very sad. He did. Then his car became red. It is now a red car."

Charlie glanced at Mma Ramotswe. "When, Mma? When did this happen?"

Her voice was shaky. "It was just after I went to the dentist, so that would make it . . ." She struggled to remember, and then gave them the date. It was, as Mma Ramotswe expected, a day or two after Charlie's earlier visit to Mochudi, when he had informed Eddie that the car they were looking for, the car that had hit Dr. Marang, was known to be blue.

Mma Ramotswe reached out to touch Mma Lelotong on the forearm. "I am so sorry, Mma. I really am."

"Will he be arrested?" asked Mma Lelotong.

"Yes," said Charlie quickly. "The police will take him."

Mma Ramotswe raised a hand. "It's not that simple, Charlie."

And then, to Mma Lelotong, "There are many ways of dealing with a problem, Mma. Going to the police is not the only way."

Charlie disagreed. "We have to, Mma. And what about that brick through my window? What about that?"

Mma Lelotong lowered her eyes. "I am ashamed. I am very ashamed that it is my own son who does these things. But—"

Mma Ramotswe interrupted her. "But you are his mother, Mma. That is something that does not change. You will always be his mother."

They lapsed into silence. Charlie was staring at the shelves, his eyes fixed on a row of cans. Mma Lelotong was twisting the hem of her skirt with her right hand, worrying away at the fabric in her distress. Mma Ramotswe sat quite still.

"So," Mma Ramotswe said at last, "I'm going to suggest something to you, Mma. You may not want to do it, but I think you should at least give some thought to it."

Mma Lelotong looked at her with gratitude. "I am listening, Mma. I will listen to every word you say."

CHAPTER SEVENTEEN

THIS RIFF-RAFF PERSON

WHEN MMA RAMOTSWE ARRIVED at the office the following morning, Mma Potokwane was already there, sitting in the client's chair and drinking a cup of tea brewed for her by Mma Makutsi. They both rose to their feet on Mma Ramotswe's entry, putting aside their teacups and both giving voice to the traditional ululation that greeted any special achievement in Botswana. "Here she is!" cried Mma Potokwane. "Here she is! The winner of the election!"

"Here she is!" echoed Mma Makutsi. "The famous councillor!"

Mma Ramotswe's embarrassment was obvious, causing Mma Potokwane to signal restraint to Mma Makutsi. "Well, Mma," she said. "We are maybe a bit too excited, but we are very, very pleased with the result. We just want you to know that."

Mma Ramotswe accepted the congratulations. "I didn't think I'd win," she said. "I was very surprised when they phoned me last night."

"Well, there you are," said Mma Potokwane. "Now that you're on the council, we can put a stop to that hotel."

"And sort other things out as well," contributed Mma Makutsi. "That intersection near my house needs traffic lights. Perhaps you could—"

Mma Potokwane shook her head vigorously. "No, Mma Makutsi, you must not ask Mma Ramotswe to do anything like that."

Mma Makutsi glared at Mma Potokwane. "It's a legitimate request," she said, pouting in displeasure. "That's what councillors are for, isn't it? They have to do things for the people who voted for them."

"I could try," said Mma Ramotswe, reaching her desk and sitting down. "I don't know how these things work, but I suppose I could try."

"Traffic lights would be very helpful," said Mma Makutsi, staring defiantly at Mma Potokwane.

The matron did not argue; she had larger fish to fry.

"Do you know when the first meeting will be?" she asked. "They will probably discuss the hotel then."

Mma Ramotswe explained that the official who had telephoned her with the result the previous evening had mentioned that there was to be a meeting in two days' time. "He told me that I would get the papers for the meeting later today," she said. "I will know then what's going to be discussed." She paused. "I shall do my best, Mma Potokwane, but I can't guarantee anything."

"Of course you can't," said her friend. "Nobody can guarantee that anything will happen—ever—but as long as we do our best to stop that thing, that's all we can do."

Mma Ramotswe was about to express her agreement with this, but the telephone now rang, to be answered by Mma Makutsi. Mma Ramotswe and Mma Potokwane listened as Mma Makutsi engaged with the caller.

"I don't think it will be possible for you to speak to Mma Ramotswe this morning," she said. "She is very busy now."

There was a brief pause.

"No," Mma Makutsi continued. "I do not think that she will be able to help you, Rra. I'm very sorry."

The call was ended. Mma Ramotswe frowned. "Who was that, Mma?" she asked. "Was that for me?"

Mma Makutsi was businesslike. "Just a cold call, Mma. Nothing more than that." She looked to Mma Potokwane for support. "We cannot have all sorts of riff-raff calling every ten minutes asking for Mma Ramotswe to do things. Where would it end?"

Mma Ramotswe wanted to know who the riff-raff had been, but there was something in Mma Makutsi's manner that suggested the subject was closed. Mma Potokwane, though, felt that she should know. "You should tell Mma Ramotswe who that was," she insisted. "This riff-raff person—Mma Ramotswe might need to know about him."

Mma Makutsi shrugged. "It was somebody calling himself Maphephu. He was wanting Mma Ramotswe to speak to somebody about a job. I told him it was impossible."

Mma Ramotswe caught her breath. John Maphephu—the man who had been so complimentary when she had met him outside the polling station. He had sung her praises because she had not promised anything very much, and yet here he was asking her for a favour on the very first day of her membership of the council. Was this what being a politician was going to be like?

"Riff-raff," said Mma Makutsi.

MMA RAMOTSWE attended her first council meeting two days later. She had, as promised, received the papers for the meeting in advance, and had been able to go over them with Mr. J.L.B. Matekoni and Mma Potokwane, on the understanding that they respected the *HIGHLY CONFIDENTIAL* stamp that appeared at the top of the agenda. "We have a proper interest in seeing these papers," reasoned Mma Potokwane. "We are your private office, so to speak, Mma. People in a private office have to see these confidential things in order to give advice. Everybody knows that." As expected, the main item on the agenda was the planning application for the Big Fun Hotel. This matter took up thirty of the forty-five pages that made up the meeting's papers. It included several internal memos, a business consultant's report, letters from a variety of government bodies, and a slew of submissions from objectors to the proposal. The issue was finely balanced; the council's own planning officers had recommended in favour of the proposal and, according to the records included of past council meetings, the project had been enthusiastically supported by a number of councillors.

"It's going to be a difficult business," observed Mma Potokwane, shaking her head. "Your vote is going to be very important, Mma."

Mma Ramotswe did not relish the prospect of an acrimonious argument. "I hope it doesn't go on too long," she said.

"The public is admitted to these meetings," said Mma Potokwane. "We shall be there, won't we, Mr. J.L.B. Matekoni?" Then she added, "And Mma Makutsi too. She will want to come."

This did not make it any easier for Mma Ramotswe. The thought of speaking in public was bad enough, but the prospect of doing so in the presence of family and friends seemed considerably worse. Mma Makutsi would be on the lookout for mistakes—she was sure of that—and these would be brought up later. And if she failed to impress the other councillors and the vote was lost as a result, then she would have to live with the thought that it was her fault—or partly her fault.

In the event, Mr. J.L.B. Matekoni was unable to make the meeting as he had to attend to the breakdown of a client's car. Mma Potokwane was there, though, and brought Mr. Polopetsi with her. He was wearing an ill-cut brown suit, several sizes too large for him, and a small pork-pie hat. Mma Potokwane had on a blouse and skirt in the colours of the national flag. They were conspicuous, but Mma Ramotswe tried not to catch their eyes as she took her place at the council table. She knew she was being watched—not only by her supporters, but by the existing members of the council, whom she had first met only a few minutes earlier.

The chairman introduced the main item on the agenda. It was, he said, the most important issue that the council had been obliged to deal with for many years. He acknowledged that the proposal was a controversial one, but he believed, as many of the other councillors did, that the matter was of immense significance for the well-being of the city. "We must have hotels," he said. "Hotels provide a place for visitors to stay, and visitors are the life-blood of the tourism industry."

This brought nods of approval from a number of councillors, but solemn disapproval from what appeared to be an equal number of others. Sensing this division, the chairman dropped his bombshell.

"I feel very strongly about this," he declared. "As do many of my colleagues. In fact, we feel so strongly that, if this proposal is rejected, we have decided to tender our resignations."

There were gasps of astonishment from the public benches. Mma Potokwane exchanged glances with Mr. Polopetsi, who whispered something in her ear. In the front row, only recently spotted by Mma Ramotswe, sat Mr. Gobe Moruti. He smiled when the chairman made his threat, nodding in grave agreement. His body language was clear: good commercial sense would prevail; this was not some tin-pot country up north, this was Botswana.

The debate started. There was a great deal of invective. Dire predictions were made by the opponents—the next step, they warned, would be to dig up the graves of the late people in the cemetery so that more hotels could be built. Nonsense, replied the supporters of the Big Fun Hotel—there were no plans to do anything else in the vicinity. And the Big Fun Hotel, they claimed, would be perfectly respectable.

After two hours of intense discussion and argument the chairman announced that it was time to put the matter to a vote. On the public benches, Mr. Polopetsi fingered the band of his pork-pie hat; Mma Potokwane narrowed her eyes in anticipation.

There was a show of hands. A nervous council official, standing behind the chairman, began to count. The vote was evenly split.

But then Mma Ramotswe remembered to vote. She had been watching the other councillors and had momentarily forgotten that she was a councillor herself—and that she had a vote. She caught the chairman's eye. "Excuse me, Rra," she said. "I haven't cast my vote yet."

The chairman looked aghast. "But Mma . . ."

There was a chorus of shouts from some of the other councillors. "You must let her vote, Rra. She is entitled."

The chairman looked about him. Mma Potokwane was later to say that she thought she had seen him look for guidance from Mr. Gobe Moruti, but she could not be absolutely sure.

"Very well," the chairman conceded. "I suppose you are entitled to vote, Mma. Which way is it?"

"I vote against the proposal," said Mma Ramotswe. She spoke clearly, as it was her maiden speech and she did not want there to be any mistaking her views. And, bearing in mind what had happened last time she had voted, she felt that clarity was of the essence.

In the uproar that followed, Mma Ramotswe lost track of what was actually being said. The chairman tried to speak, but was shouted down by people on the public benches. Mr. Gobe Moruti rose to his feet and stalked out of the room. Then, when things died down, the chairman stood up and announced that he, and six other councillors, were now resigning. "And that means that the entire council is inquorate and out of office. There will have to be fresh elections for every seat."

Mma Ramotswe stared at the papers on the table in front of her. Hers had been a brief political career, but she had done what Mma

Potokwane and others had asked of her. The Big Fun Hotel would not be, and she imagined that the late people might be grateful to her for that. And it was better, she thought, to be held in high regard by late people than to incur their wrath.

Mma Potokwane and Mr. Polopetsi were waiting for her outside.

"Well done, Mma," enthused Mma Potokwane. "You did it."

"Yes," said Mr. Polopetsi. "That was masterly."

"I don't know about that," said Mma Ramotswe modestly. "I didn't say very much."

"Five words," said Mr. Polopetsi. "I counted them. But they were five words that meant everything, Mma."

"And now I'm out of office," said Mma Ramotswe. "I am an ordinary citizen again."

"You are an ex-councillor," Mma Potokwane pointed out. "That counts for something."

"I feel very relieved," said Mma Ramotswe. "All my cares are over, I think."

"Then you should take the day off," said Mma Potokwane, looking at her watch. "It will be lunch time soon, and I think we should have a picnic."

The suggestion was a spontaneous one, but it met with the approval of both Mma Ramotswe and Mr. Polopetsi. Mma Ramotswe was too overcome to work, and for his part Mr. Polopetsi was too excited by what he had seen. A picnic would allow everybody to relax and reflect on what had happened.

"I shall go back and collect a few of the children," said Mma Potokwane. "They'll enjoy running around." And then, as an afterthought, "And I'll pick up some cake too. I've been baking."

In her state of elation—and relief—Mma Ramotswe would have agreed to anything. But a picnic was just right, she thought; there was no better way of celebrating a deliverance—and that was what had happened—than with old friends, and particularly with old friends who liked cake as much as Mma Potokwane did.

MMA RAMOTSWE drove back to the office in an almost dazed state. She had not imagined that this first day of her political career would be anything like this—this first and last day, in fact. She felt freed of more than one burden. Her obligation to Mma Potokwane had been discharged; by remaining in office until the dissolution of the council—even if that was only for a period of a few hours—she had done her duty by the voters; and she had helped to save the town from the indignity of that noisy and unwelcome hotel. Now she could get back to work, and to the affairs of her friends and family.

Mma Makutsi had opted to stay and look after the office while Mma Ramotswe was at the meeting. She had already heard, though, of the result of that morning's deliberations, as Mma Potokwane had called her almost immediately after the vote had been taken. She had also mentioned the picnic, which had given Mma Makutsi time to slip out to the stores to buy food, leaving Charlie in sole charge of the office. He had set himself up at Mma Ramotswe's desk and had occupied himself drafting a memo on the Marang case.

But then, a few minutes after Mma Ramotswe returned to the office, Dr. Marang himself arrived, accompanied by his daughter, Constance. Mma Ramotswe had been expecting to hear from him, but she had not thought he would call on her quite so quickly. The visitors were offered chairs and, while Mma Makutsi made tea, Mma Ramotswe enquired after Dr. Marang's health.

"I am very much better," he replied.

Constance looked disgruntled. "He is still weak," she muttered.

"I am feeling better now that everything is settled," he continued. "Knowing what happened has made it possible for me to—"

"—move on," interjected Mma Makutsi.

Dr. Marang turned to her and smiled. "Exactly, Mma. I never wanted revenge, you know."

Constance pursed her lips. "That young man should go to prison," she said.

Her father reached out and placed his hand on hers. "No, Constance, sending people to prison helps nobody. It generally just makes people worse."

"That's a matter of opinion," snapped Constance.

Mma Ramotswe guided the conversation away from this disagreement. "I take it that Mma Lelotong came to see you."

Dr. Marang inclined his head. "She did, Mma. I have known that lady for many years. She is a good woman."

"With a bad son," said Constance.

"Nobody is entirely bad," soothed Dr. Marang.

"He is," answered Constance.

Dr. Marang sighed. "That is a matter of opinion, I think. And anyway, he is selling his car. There will be compensation for us from the proceeds of that."

Mma Ramotswe was pleased to hear this. "His mother has made him do that?"

"Yes," said Constance. "He would never have done that without her. It's only because of her that he has apologised to my father and will be making that payment. He would never do that himself."

"And was anything said about the brick through Charlie's window?" asked Mma Ramotswe.

"The mother is going to make sure that that is properly dealt with," said Dr. Marang. "And I have found some work for that young man to do—supervised work that will help him to become a better person."

"Fat chance of that," said Constance.

Dr. Marang glanced at her briefly. He was patient, with the

understanding that came from years of looking after others. "There is a youth project. They were looking for somebody to teach young people basketball. That young man is very tall—that's what you need for basketball."

Giraffe, thought Mma Ramotswe. She made a gesture that indicated that she, at least, was satisfied. "I think everybody deserves a second chance," she said. "Even somebody like Eddie."

"Third chance?" asked Constance, her voice rising. "Fourth chance? Fifth chance?"

"However many chances are necessary," said Mma Ramotswe evenly.

Constance said nothing.

"So," said Mma Makutsi. "That is another successful outcome for the No. 1 Ladies' Detective Agency."

"Bah!" said Constance.

THEY HAD THEIR PICNIC out at the dam, finding a suitable spot under a cluster of acacia trees. Charlie made a fire between some stones, and on this they fried sausages and sliced potatoes. A blackened range kettle, perched on the edge of the fire, was soon hissing from the fire beneath it. Mma Potokwane had brought several cakes, and there was enough to provide three slices each, if the appetite were there. She had also brought three children with her from the Orphan Farm. Mma Ramotswe recognised one of these, the small boy, Mpilo, who had stolen the bird's eggs. He had seemed sullen and withdrawn then, but now he was bright and communicative. She beckoned him over, and he stood politely before her, his eyes fixed on the ground at her feet. She asked him if he was enjoying himself, and he replied that he was. He looked up, and he smiled. She put her hand on his shoulder and then, on impulse, took him into her arms and hugged him. He did not resist. She felt him against her, a sliver of humanity called a small boy, with the smell of boy and cake and the dust in which he had been playing with the other children. Then she released him, as we release children into their own lives, and he ran off.

Mma Potokwane, witnessing this, said simply, "Some things work out, Mma."

"Yes," said Mma Ramotswe. "Some things work out." But she was puzzled. "How did you do it, Mma?"

Mpilo had run over to join his friends. Mma Potokwane pointed to his shoes. "The new shoes," she said.

Mma Ramotswe waited.

"Sometimes," said Mma Potokwane, "small things can lead to big things."

"But . . ." Mma Ramotswe was thinking of the lightning.

"He had never been given anything like that," said Mma Poto-kwane. "Never. Not once in his short life had he been given anything that was special to him. He loved his shoes. He loved them, Mma, and they . . . well, they made him feel very much better."

"I suppose it's sometimes that simple," said Mma Ramotswe.

"Often," said Mma Potokwane. "Not just sometimes, Mma—often."

Mma Ramotswe lay back on one of the rugs they had brought with them. A small platoon of tiny black ants had ventured onto this rug, but she did not disturb their reconnaissance—the rug was big enough for all of them, and for others too, if they should wish to join her. As she lay there, waiting for the sausages to cook and the kettle to boil, she listened with half an ear to a conversation that Charlie was hav-ing with Mma Makutsi on the other side of the fire. He was planning on seeing Queenie-Queenie that evening, he said. He had contacted her and she seemed keen to see him again. "You never know," said Charlie. "It may work." And then she heard Charlie say, "She has a brother, you know. Hercules. Apparently he told her that he liked me—we arm-wrestled, you see. And she thought that was a big point in my favour. So there might be a chance after all."

Of course there is, thought Mma Ramotswe. *Of course there is— there always is a chance.* And she wanted Charlie to have a chance; she wanted that a great deal.

"She has invited me to her parents' place," said Charlie. "I have said yes. But I am a bit worried, Mma. Her father is a big man, you see."

Mma Makutsi shook a finger at him. "You're a big man too, Charlie."

"Me?"

"Yes, you, Charlie. You are. And I don't want to hear you ever saying you aren't. You are."

Mma Ramotswe let her mind wander, which was what it always wanted to do when she was out in the bush—her beloved Botswana bush. She thought, *This is where I am happiest—here on the earth of the land that I love so much, and always will, always.* And she thought of her father, and of where she imagined he might be. She was not entirely sure—who could ever be completely certain about such a thing?—but she thought that he would be in the place to which late people went, just above this Botswana, that other Botswana which is the place of those who are late, where there would be green grass, rich and abundant, and water, and all the other things that people need. And because he was who he was, Obed Ramotswe, fine judge of cattle, he would be helping to look after the cattle in heaven, which were special cattle, broad of back and shoulder, with sweet-smelling breath, and wide brown eyes. And the late children would be riding on the backs of those cattle, those white cattle, and the other cattle too, as there were cattle of all colours in that place, gentle cattle, who knew that they were loved and who loved their keepers in return. For that was a very special sort of love, she realised—love given back to one who loved you; that love was like the first rain, the longed-for rain, which washed away the pain and sadness of the world so that you forgot that those things had ever been there.

afrika
afrika afrika
afrika afrika afrika
afrika afrika
afrika

ABOUT THE AUTHOR

Alexander McCall Smith is the author of the No. 1 Ladies' Detective Agency novels and of a number of other series and stand-alone books. His works have been translated into more than forty languages and have been best sellers throughout the world. He lives in Scotland.

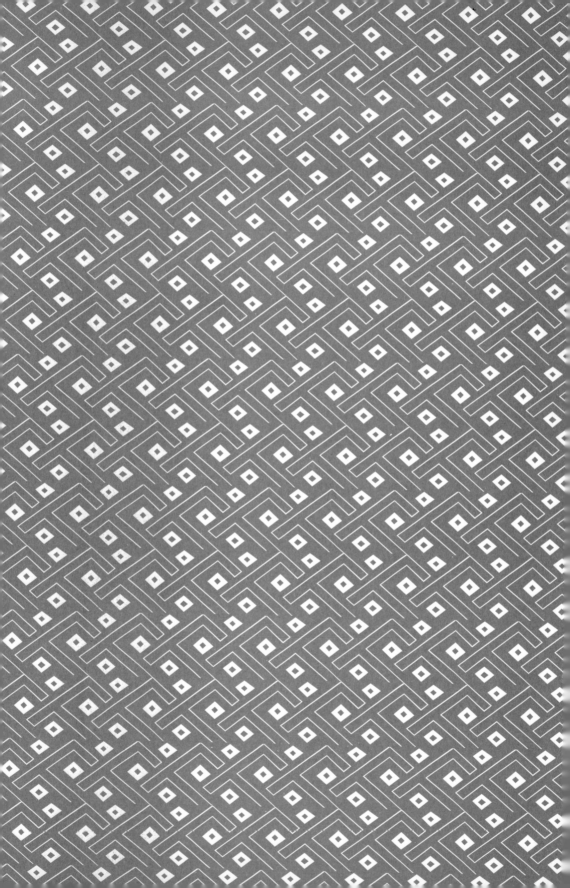